The vampires want it.

The demons want it too.

And someone is willing to kill Val for it.

Val and Fang have to find the powerful Encyclopedia Magicka before either of San Antonio's warring underworld factions locate it, or the consequences will be deadly for the entire city.

As usual, Val's vampire enemies (they still call her The Slayer), want her dead, and even some of her fellow demons may be less than trustworthy, since they'd like to grab the legendary book of spells before she does. Val has a personal claim to the Encyclopedia—her demon father left it to her when he died—but someone stole it recently. Where did the thief hide it?

Battling vamps and dodging demons, Val struggles to unravel the mystery. At the same time, she's fighting her attraction to sweet, sexy Shade, her favorite shadow demon. Rumor has it that Val will lose her part-demon, vampire-fighting powers if she gives herself to him.

With a crowd of vamps and demons out to trick her or kill her, it's not a good time for her to risk her job as the city's best vampire hunter by falling in love. The stakes are high—and aimed right at her heart. But Lola, Val's hungry little lust demon, doesn't like being denied. Will Lola finally get her way?

Fang

Me

Parker Blue

Bell Bridge Books

Bell Bridge Books
PO BOX 300921
Memphis, TN 38130
ISBN: 978-1-61194-012-1

Bell Bridge Books is an Imprint of BelleBooks, Inc.

We at BelleBooks enjoy hearing from readers.
Visit our websites – www.BelleBooks.com and www.BellBridgeBooks.com.

10 9 8 7 6 5 4 3 2

Cover design: Debra Dixon
Interior design: Hank Smith
Photo credits:
Room scene - © Unholyvault | Dreamstime.com
Girl - © Konstantin Yuganov | Dreamstime.com

:Lmf:01:

THE DEMON UNDERGROUND SERIES

Parker Blue

BITE ME
TRY ME
FANG ME

DEDICATION

For the wonderful furry creatures who fill my life with love and companionship—Mo, a terrier-poodle mix (the model for Fang) rescued through Dreampower Animal Rescue; Daisy, a sweet Maltese rescued from a puppy mill by National Mill Dog Rescue; and Spooky, a long-haired white cat inherited from my mother, who adopted him from the local humane society.

Pets fill your life with joy and laughter and love you unconditionally—what's not to like? Adopt one today and practice responsible pet ownership!

WHAT HAS GONE BEFORE

My name is Val Shapiro, and I'm a succubus lust demon. Well, partially anyway. I'm only one-eighth demon, but that's the part that dominates my life. It's a bitch to keep the lust under control—I almost drained a guy dry of his sexual energy when I was sixteen—but I do a good job of keeping it in check by channeling the lust and the extra strength and speed that comes with it into slaying vampires on the dark streets of San Antonio. Hence my nickname, the Slayer.

My dumb younger half-sister, Jen, wants to be just like me, even though she's totally normal. If you can call a perky blonde cheerleader type normal . . . . Anyway, when Jen sneaked out to join me on one of my hunts, my mom and stepfather panicked and figured I was a bad influence on her, so they fired me from their New Age bookstore and kicked me out of the house—on my eighteenth birthday no less. Happy birthday to me.

It turned out okay, though, 'cause I gained an awesome new telepathic canine friend, Fang—part hellhound, part scruffy terrier, and all snark. He was sent to me by Micah Blackburn, leader of the Demon Underground. I hadn't even known it existed until then, probably because their main goal in life is to keep themselves hidden and help each other find jobs and live ordinary lives where so-called "normals" won't freak out at the sight of them or what they can do.

Oh, yeah, I also lucked out and found a job with the city's Special Crimes Unit, so I actually got *paid* to kill vampires. When they paired me up with mortal Dan Sullivan to shut down a vein of bloodsuckers who were terrorizing the city, we learned they were actually an organization of "good" vamps called the New Blood Movement who set up blood banks so they could snack on stupid volunteers. I thought Dan and I had kind of a romantic thing going, but when I lopped off the head of the real bloodsucker responsible for the vampire problem, Dan's ex-fiancée Lily Armstrong, it kinda ruined that. Not to mention that he was totally weirded out when the succubus inside me—I call her Lola—tried to sink her hooks into him and slurp up all his yummy goodness.

So, he dumped me and found someone human to snog with. No biggie. I got over him when I got to know Shade. Part shadow demon, he has interdimensional energies whirling through his body. All you can see of him is that swirl, unless he's touching someone else to ground himself in this reality. Then he's totally hot. And he touches me a *lot*. Just to help me keep Lola under control, you understand. Not that it's a hardship. Did I mention he's totally hot?

Anyway, someone stole the *Encyclopedia Magicka* that my demon father had given me, and used it to poison the blood banks and turn the vamps insane. Not that I was totally opposed to that, but it meant they were hurting innocents, so I helped the vamps catch the phase demon, Josh, who'd poisoned them, and Andrew, the fire demon who tried to burn down their home.

Turns out the books have some kind of dark magick inside them that make the demons go nutso. But to make it up to the Movement, I agreed to take some time off from the force and help them find the books before the dark magicks make someone else do something stupid.

How? I have no clue.

CHAPTER ONE

Weird. Definitely weird. I stood outside the wrought-iron gates of the Alamo Heights mansion at a quarter to midnight and gawked. Sure, the dark spooky brick mansion housed the biggest vein of vampires in San Antonio—I knew that. But the fact that said creepy mansion was lit up by cheery red and green Christmas lights? Too surreal.

Okay, it was the season, with Thanksgiving over and done with a week ago, but after all the mayhem and violence that had happened here, it seemed totally bizarre.

Fang snorted. YOU WERE PART OF MOST OF THAT MAYHEM AND VIOLENCE, he said on a private channel in my mind.

Here I am, Val Shapiro, the mighty Slayer, feared by vampires, demons and humans…yet somehow totally *dis*respected by my own dog.

SOMEONE HAS TO KEEP YOU FROM GETTING A FAT HEAD, Fang retorted. AND WHO BETTER THAN YOUR BEST FRIEND?

It was my turn to snort. Fat head, me? Fat chance.

Shade bumped my shoulder with his. "You okay?"

Ah, Shade, my new boyfriend. How did I get so lucky? The shadow demon and I tried to date like a normal couple, but our relationship wasn't exactly ordinary. I kept the shadow demon within Shade grounded in this reality so he didn't let the big bad demons through into our world, and he fed the lust demon within me.

Not like *that*. I was still untouched, cherry, a total "V". I'd just found out recently that giving that up would be a way bigger choice than I'd ever dreamed. Lose my virginity, lose my powers. Yep, those very things that made me the Slayer—enhanced senses, fast reflexes, and rapid healing—would be forever lost to me if I ever did the deed. So, I remained a frustrated slayer.

As Fang put it, sucks to be me.

Oh well, circumstances had forced me to be the Slayer for a while longer. Once this job was over, I'd have to make the big decision.

I bumped Shade back. "I'm fine."

3

"You don't really have to do this, Val," he said.

I sighed. It was what I wanted to hear, but it wasn't true. "Yeah, I do. I not only gave my word, I signed a contract." Though it had taken a week for the demon lawyer and the vampire lawyer to hammer out a contract we could all agree on.

Fang spoke to both of us this time. DEMON LAWYER . . . BLOODSUCKING LAWYER. REDUNDANT MUCH?

Shade chuckled and I gave Fang a wry grin. "I really don't have a choice. Besides, I took leave from Special Crimes and if I don't do this, there's no pizza in your future." Hellhound or not, Fang liked the creature comforts of urban living.

THEN GET IN THERE. GO TO WORK. WORK, WORK, WORK.

I didn't mind working. I just wished I could bring home the bacon by slaying evil vampires on the dark streets of San Antonio. That was a whole lot more appealing than playing assistant to Alejandro, leader of the New Blood Movement, one of the "good" vampires . . . who apparently had strung up twinkling Christmas lights as a sign of the Movement's sweetness and light.

I glanced at the lights again and sighed.

"I'm sure Lieutenant Ramirez would take you back in the SCU in a heartbeat," Shade said.

I COULD EAT CHEAP, Fang offered. THIS ISN'T WHAT I SIGNED ON FOR.

Too bad I had. "It's only midnight to dawn, five days a week," I reminded them. The lawyer had gotten me that much. That was about seven hours a day this time of year, but hey, it was better than fourteen.

Shade hugged me with one arm. "I worry about you."

My legs went all limp and rubbery. Sheesh. Here I was, eighteen years old—an adult who faced down bloodsuckers—and feeling all gooey and dopey like a kid, just because a guy said he cared about me.

GAG ME.

I glared at Fang. *Shut up. You're no better when you're around Princess.* Fang had a thing for Shade's dog. Her royal highness claimed to be a pure-bred Cavalier King Charles Spaniel, but there was definitely a lot of hellhound in her, too.

Ignoring Fang's eye roll, I hugged Shade back, loving the way it felt to touch a guy without worrying about Lola ripping his energy out of him. "I'll be fine. And you can always call me if you get too worried."

"Okay." Then, a little tentative and awkward, he placed his hands on either side of my face, so that the swirling mess that was his face disappeared and revealed the sight of Shade I couldn't get enough of. He kissed me gently, and I melted.

Lola stirred. She liked Shade a *lot*, and was obviously up for any lust energy he cared to send our way. But I didn't like to take advantage too often. Nothing wrong with going in to a dangerous situation feeling a little edgy. Kept me on my toes.

But turning down all that sexy energy didn't mean I couldn't enjoy the heck out of his kiss. I met his with a hungry one of my own, and it was just me . . . and Shade. I loved this kind of kiss, where I knew he was kissing me because he liked *me* and not just because Lola made him feel really good.

Fang butted in between us. ENOUGH WITH THE LOVEY DOVEY STUFF. YOU PROMISED TO MEET ALEJANDRO AT MIDNIGHT.

Reluctantly, I pulled away and checked my cell. Yeah, I had five minutes. "I'd better go," I told Shade.

He nodded. "Okay, but call me as soon as you get home."

"I will." After one last brief kiss, I let go of him and grabbed my Valkyrie motorcycle.

Shade punched in the combination to open the gates and Fang trotted along beside me as I walked the bike up the long driveway. It seemed a bit out of place next to the limo and shiny black luxury cars, but who cared? I wasn't here to impress anyone.

I heard Shade's motorcycle roar off and I steeled myself. Alone now except for Fang, I might as well get it over with. There were no guards at the door this time. I hesitated for a moment, wondering why I had no problem battling a brace of vampires, but felt a twinge of fear at the thought of playing nice and being assistant to the one vamp I actually considered *good*.

BECAUSE YOU'RE NOT STUPID, Fang said. AND HE PRETTY MUCH OWNS YOU UNTIL YOU FIND THE MISSING *ENCYCLOPEDIA MAGICKA*.

I grimaced. Too true. But before I could knock on the door, it was opened from the other side.

Austin, a tall, lean cowboy, and one of Alejandro's lieutenants, stood there grinning at me. "Hello, darlin'. You plannin' on coming in sometime tonight?"

Though Austin was always nice and polite, he also usually managed to make me feel foolish.

"Sure, why not?" As a comeback, it was pretty lame, but a few hours from now, I'd think of a real zinger.

Austin bowed me through with a flourish and I tried to act nonchalant as I sauntered in the door. I followed him into the great room—a huge space with soaring ceilings, immaculate dark hardwood floors and lots of heavy wood and wrought iron furniture. Very Spanish Mediterranean.

Not that I could see much of it today—the entire place was filled with bloodsuckers. What the heck . . . ? Vampires, wearing black leather, black silk, black you-name-it, filled the room to overflowing, spilling down the hall and into the next room like an inkblot. Conversations came to a halt and I saw nostrils flare as if they scented my humanity and the blood that lay beating just beneath the fragile layer of my skin.

Fang's hackles rose and he took a step back, growling.

Fear spiked through me, making my blood sizzle and my eyes flash purple. Lola leapt up, ready and willing for action. I checked to make sure the stakes were still hidden under my vest in the back waistband of my jeans. Yep, but three wasn't gonna do it with this crowd.

When the vamps didn't move, I realized maybe attack wasn't what was on their bloody minds. Instead, they all stared at us, unmoving, some with amusement or boredom on their faces, some disgusted, but most with no expression at all.

"What's going on?" I asked Austin.

Alejandro swept forward, all Latin grace and sophisticated host. "My apologies," he said, smiling at me with his typical charm. And he had a lot of it. With his long, dark hair, smoking hot bod, and a natural charisma, he oozed sex appeal . . . and he knew it. Luckily, I'd never been sucked in under his spell. A little matter of his drinking blood . . .

He seemed embarrassed. "I should have warned you I invited all of the members of the Movement to meet you."

No kidding. But now that I'd relaxed, I noticed something else—pine garlands with red bows topped the windows, holiday do-dads seemed to perch on every surface I could see, and there was even a Christmas tree in the corner . . . with twinkling fairy lights on it, fergawdsakes. Baffled, I asked, "What's with the holiday cheer?"

Alejandro laughed. "Only Valentine Shapiro would notice such a thing in a roomful of vampires."

Luis, another of Alejandro's lieutenants and a snooty Spanish aristocrat type, sniffed with disdain. "There is more than one reason for the season. Some of us like to celebrate the holidays just like humans." But from the sneer on his face and in his voice, I gathered he wasn't one of them.

WHY NOT? Fang asked. THEY WERE HUMAN . . . ONCE.

I guess . . . . It was just hard to picture Luis and some of the others knocking back a bit of egg nog or hanging stockings by the chimney. Of course, there were no nativity scenes or crosses. There was a limit to how completely the vamps could co-opt Christmas.

Rosa, a gorgeous Latina with long flowing hair and the third of Alejandro's lieutenants, gestured impatiently. "Why not? Besides, it makes us seem more . . . likeable . . . when we come out, yes?"

Now that made more sense. The vampires of the New Blood Movement wanted to come out into the mainstream, wanted to be accepted for what they were, not what the lurid literature and entertainment industry had made them out to be.

OH, YEAH, ALL THIS CRAP IS GONNA *REALLY* MAKE THEM LOOK HARMLESS.

I agreed, but tried to be more diplomatic. "Uh, maybe. But do you think you might be trying a little too hard?"

"Told you so," someone muttered from the crowd.

Alejandro sighed. "Perhaps you are right. But we want to put people at ease, let them see there is nothing to fear."

WHAT THEY WANT IS MORE DONORS FOR THEIR BLOOD BANKS, Fang added cynically.

That was true, too, but who could blame them? And, much as I disliked the blood banks, they were a whole lot better than the huge amounts of random fangings—and bloody deaths—we'd had in town before Alejandro started his Movement.

"There, you see?" Alejandro exclaimed. "Already you have helped us. You are just what we need." He made a beckoning gesture. "Now come, I wish to introduce you to the rest of my family."

I went to stand in front of the Christmas tree next to Alejandro, feeling strangely self-conscious with all eyes on me. Vampires of all shapes and sizes stared back at me. You'd think from seeing Alejandro and his lieutenants that all vamps were totally hot. Not so much. The ones staring . . . hungrily? . . . at me pretty much ran the gamut of human society.

"Furthermore," Alejandro said, "I wish to use this occasion to have all of you reaffirm your oath to the Movement in the Slayer's presence."

Whoa. Tension suddenly filled the room at the mention of the "S" word. Why? Surely they'd all known what I was before this. Then the light dawned. He wanted me to read their minds while they swore undying allegiance.

Fang chuckled humorlessly. YEAH. HE WANTS YOU TO FIND OUT IF HE HAS ANY MORE TRAITORS TO WORRY ABOUT.

Oh, crap. No wonder they were upset. I mean, who liked to have their mind read? They had no way of knowing it wasn't my thing, that I didn't really enjoy mucking about in the dregs of a vampire's mind. Besides, I could only do it when one tried to control me, and I only did it then to confirm the bloodsucker's guilt or to protect myself and others . . . or apparently, when I was working for Alejandro.

Protests burst out around the room. Alejandro tried to calm them, but I tuned him out as a familiar sensation crept through me. Someone was trying to control me, someone named Jasper. Worse, he wanted both Alejandro and me dead . . . this very moment.

You two behind her—get her! someone yelled mentally.

I whipped two stakes out of my back waistband and whirled around, looking for the assailants. No one there. Were they in front?

I spun again to face the crowd, stakes at the ready. No one moved. What the hell?

The air took on a real tinge of unleashed danger as all those expressions sharpened and turned wary . . . and Jasper's thoughts turned to triumph.

Oh, crap. He'd played me, and I'd gone and done the stupid thing he'd hoped for. I'd just threatened an entire vein of vampires with only my trusty hellhound for back-up.

We're toast.

CHAPTER TWO

"She's attacking Alejandro," someone yelled.

Three of them rushed me, moving inhumanly fast. Well, guess what? I was that fast, too. I jerked aside so the leading bloodsucker flew past and crashed into the Christmas tree. It fell, bulbs popping and glass icicles shattering. Fang jumped on him, snarling and biting.

The other two grabbed my arms to immobilize me. They yanked the stakes out of my hands, and I would have been cool if they'd stopped at disarming me. But when one of them bent and tried to fang me, I lost my temper. I jerked backward and brought my wrists together as hard as I could. They didn't expect me to be as strong as they were, so their hold wasn't as tight as it should have been. Their heads banged together and their surprise made them let go.

I whirled, looking for weapons, and saw that Austin had hold of the tree hugger. The tree! I grabbed an unbroken icicle decoration as the fanger rushed me and I lunged for his heart with my makeshift stake.

DON'T KILL HIM, Fang shouted in my mind.

It was almost too late, but I was able to deflect my aim and stab him in the shoulder instead. The rest of the crowd surged forward. Alejandro yelled, "Stop," but some were too ticked off to listen.

Time to let Lola loose. My blood was already sizzling with lust for the hunt, so it was easy to call on my inner succubus. I reached down deep inside and yanked off the lid on the part of me I kept bottled up. Lola burst free, spilling out of me in a wave of lust to instantly enslave every male in the house. "Stop," I yelled, echoing Alejandro.

TOOK YOU LONG ENOUGH, Fang muttered.

Maybe, but using Lola was like using a grenade to squash a fly, and I hated pulling out all the stops unless it was absolutely necessary. Besides, I'd tried for so long to avoid using her that it wasn't usually the first weapon that came to mind.

The men all obeyed immediately, seeing me as the ultimate woman, their goddess, their reason for being. Using the line of force that connected me to each man's chakras like a puppet string, I pulled, they responded. I could make them dance any way I wanted them to. Kind of sickening, really.

Lola wanted to hoover up that bounty of overflowing energy to fill up our chakras, but I stopped her. For one, it seemed like bad manners from an invited guest. For another, I couldn't afford to be distracted. I still had the female vamps to contend with. After all, *they* weren't affected by Lola.

The women had hesitated for a moment, but now a few of them shoved toward the front, my murder in their eyes. I wasn't stupid enough to think they were less of a threat simply because they were female. I readied myself for action again, wondering if I could control all those strings while I fought. Probably not. Crap.

One of them lunged for me, but Rosa darted in front of me and shoved her back. Planting her hands on her hips, she said, "You heard Alejandro. He does not wish her harmed."

Oh, yeah, I still had her boss under control. I took a couple of moments to isolate the strings holding Alejandro and Austin and released them. They staggered for a moment then joined Rosa as a living shield.

Alejandro held up his hand, palm out. "Anyone who harms Ms. Shapiro will answer to me."

The women immediately froze in place.

"If you would release Luis . . . ?" he added.

I knew Alejandro trusted his lieutenants, which is why I'd released Austin, but Luis irritated me. I sighed inwardly and released the last of Alejandro's lieutenants from Lola's control. But I kept the rest. It would do them good to let them know what it felt like to be enthralled for a change.

Luis seemed royally ticked off, but just folded his arms and glared at me, then shifted his gaze to Alejandro, waiting for orders.

The women all waited, too, so Alejandro stepped aside to let them see me. "Perhaps you would explain why you drew weapons in my home?" He said it softly, but his steely gaze let me know the answer better be damned good.

"Someone tried to control me, made me think they were rushing me to kill both of us. But what he really wanted was for me to start a riot so I'd be torn to bloody bits."

A small smile flitted across Alejandro's face. "So you did exactly as he wished?"

I squirmed and glanced away. "Hey, the guy on the floor tried to bite me." Which, come to think of it, was pretty stupid on his part. Didn't he get the memo that drinking demon blood could make him crazy?

Unfortunately, I could tell from everyone's expressions that my reasoning sounded totally lame.

Fang hooted in my mind. DAMN SKIPPY.

I glared at him. *You're supposed to be on my side.*

I AM ON YOUR SIDE, BUT WHEN HE'S RIGHT, HE'S RIGHT. APOLOGIZE TO THE NICE MAN.

I sighed and decided to man up. Or was that woman up? Demon up? Whatever. "I'm sorry. It was kind of an instinctive reaction." After all, I'd been killing the nonaffiliated bloodsuckers—the ones not in the New Blood Movement—for years. I'd only started deliberately letting Lola loose as a weapon for about a month, so that skill didn't come as naturally. Muscle memory took over and had me pulling stake, which had been my go-to weapon as long as I could remember.

Alejandro gave me a slight bow, accepting my apology far more graciously than I'd given it. "And who tried to control you?"

"I don't know . . . only that his name was Jasper." It wasn't exactly a common name. Maybe there'd be only one.

Everyone turned to stare at the guy who'd led the rush and landed in the tree. He didn't look so threatening now, with cuts on his face, bits of broken glass on his bad-ass leather clothing, and tinsel draping his shoulders. Not to mention that he was standing stock still, gazing at me as if I were Angelina Jolie and he desperately wanted to be Brad Pitt.

I glanced at Alejandro for direction, wondering what he wanted me to do about it.

"Please, ask him to answer my questions truthfully."

I nodded. With Lola's hooks into him, Jasper had to do anything I told him to. I ordered the guy to answer his leader's questions honestly.

The vamp leader strolled over to his enthralled minion. "Why did you goad the Slayer, a guest in our home, deliberately?"

"Because she kills our kind. She killed Lily and you let her live." He appeared confused, his true beliefs warring with how Lola now forced him to feel about me.

Rosa stepped forward, frowning and looking as though she was about to open a can of whup ass on his butt. Apparently she didn't like anyone dissing her boss.

Alejandro stopped her with a raised hand. "Let him continue." Turning back to Jasper, he asked, "What did you hope to gain?"

"The Slayer's death."

"Did you arrive at this plan on your own or did someone put you up to it?"

Jasper thought for a moment. "The three of us discussed it, but I wasn't the one who came up with the idea. That was Neil."

Rosa kicked the guy lying on the floor, who still adored me even with an icicle stuck in his shoulder.

Fang snickered. THREE GUESSES WHO NEIL IS.

"I'll get to him in a moment," Alejandro said. "Jasper, do you harbor evil thoughts in your heart? Do you seek to injure me or thwart the aims of the New Blood Movement?"

"No. I support you fully."

Alejandro nodded. Turning to me, he said, "He is merely misguided. I suspect the real culprit lies elsewhere." He glared down at Neil. "Get up."

Neil didn't move, so I ordered him through our link, "Do as he says."

The enthralled vamp got to his feet, and Alejandro yanked the icicle out of his shoulder, tossing it aside. Neil gasped and swayed but Alejandro ignored his pain and nodded at me.

I loosened Lola's hold on Neil a little so he wouldn't seem so robotic. Let him dig his own grave. "Tell us everything you plotted and why," I told him.

Freed of inhibitions, Neil sneered at Alejandro. "You and your pansy ass Movement. We are superior to mere humans. United, we could take over the entire world. Yet you, you hold undreamed-of power and what do you do with it? You try to make *friends* with our food."

Whoa, harsh.

"Lily was the only one with guts enough to say the truth," Neil continued with a sneer, "but you let the Slayer kill her. She must die for that."

I thought we'd rooted out all of the members of her cabal, but we must have missed one.

Alejandro let him spew his venom for awhile, but when Neil changed to berating Alejandro for trying to partner with the Demon Underground and letting the spawn of Satan—that would be me—poison his mind and heart, Alejandro finally interrupted him. "Enough.

What did you hope to accomplish?"

Forced to tell the truth in my thrall, Neil admitted, "That you and the Slayer would kill each other. That your loss would leave a vacuum of power."

Luis snorted in derision. "And you thought you could step in?"

"Why not? Austin doesn't want to lead, Rosa is nothing but a hanger-on, and no one in their right mind would follow *you*." He was almost panting now, though I wasn't sure if it was from the pain in his shoulder, or his rage. Probably both.

They all seemed taken aback at Neil's assessment. "You did ask for the truth," I reminded them. Oops. Maybe I shouldn't be agreeing with the raving vampire. Not a good idea to piss off the guys on your side. "At least, the truth as he sees it."

Fang chuckled. GOOD CATCH.

Alejandro shook his head, his expression sad. "You took an oath. An oath to honor the Movement, an oath to forego harming the humans who live alongside us." He sighed heavily. "With your actions and your attempt to bite a guest in my house, you are foresworn. And what is the punishment for that?"

"Death," Luis said, sounding overly pleased.

Alejandro nodded, looking as if a huge weight had just settled on his shoulders. He glanced at me. "Since the offense was to you, would you like to do the honors?"

Whoa. Act as his executioner? True, I was the Slayer and I'd killed a lot of evil bloodsuckers, but not like this.

When I hesitated, Alejandro pushed. "Your choice of weapon . . . stake, sword, or succubus?"

"He's injured and unarmed," I protested. Not to mention helpless in Lola's clutches. He had to do anything I told him, so where was the fun in that? And while Lola leapt with excitement at the thought of sucking him dry, I'd never killed anyone that way and never would. If I went that far, I was afraid I'd lose the bigger, human part of myself.

"You tried to stake him earlier," Austin reminded me. "We know you could have hit his heart. Why did you stab him in the shoulder instead?"

Now I was confused. Was Austin testing me? Not wanting to admit the dog made me do it, I said, "I didn't think Alejandro would appreciate it."

Austin nodded and smiled slightly as if I'd given the right answer.

"Then you refuse to execute him for me?" Alejandro asked.

He didn't seem ticked off, so I tried to slide around it. "I'd rather not. Hey, if he rushes me again, no problem. But I don't like staking the defenseless. And his offense was intended more for you than me."

Alejandro smiled this time. Oh, good. Another right answer. Why didn't they just pat me on the head and feed me my lines?

BECAUSE HE KNEW YOU'D DO FINE WITHOUT THEM, Fang said smugly.

Know it all.

The vamp leader bowed to me. "An excellent point. It is I who sentenced him. It is I who should mete out the punishment."

Fang nodded approvingly. AS ALL GOOD LEADERS SHOULD.

With one swift movement, the vamp leader scooped up one of my stakes from the floor and slammed it into Neil's chest. The traitor fell with a thud, and I felt the cord between us snap as he died—permanently this time. No one else made a sound. Alejandro turned to the crowd. "Is there anyone else who harbors evil intent, anyone who seeks to harm the Movement?"

"If so, uh, raise your hand," I ordered. It wasn't exactly how I'd planned to question them all, but it sure saved time.

No one moved.

Alejandro continued. "Do you reaffirm your oath to leave innocents unharmed, to take only the lifeblood that is freely offered, to abide by the tenets of the New Blood Movement, upon pain of death?"

"We do," they chorused.

They'd pretty much already proved that, but people—even undead people—like the ceremonial stuff.

With a sigh, Alejandro said, "Release them, please, all but the other two who attacked you."

I nodded. "Give me a minute." It wasn't as easy as he made it out to be. Kind of like trying to remove a hook from a trout's mouth, with the added problem of trying not to draw blood. Or, in this case, not drawing out any lust that Lola could feed on.

I got a firm hold on Lola and released each invisible tentacle, one by one, holding on only to the two who'd rushed me. As the lines of force loosened and lay slack, I drew the invisible energy conduits back in to myself.

Alejandro spoke to his people from over the body of the dead traitor. "I thank you all for your confidence in me and your belief in the tenets of this Movement. For those who question why I invited the

Slayer into our home, the answer is clear. She does not kill indiscriminately, nor does she take undue advantage of her great gifts, as she has demonstrated. Like us, she has honor." He glared out into the audience, daring anyone to contradict him. No one did. "Ms. Shapiro is contracted to me and will be in this house a great deal. I expect you all to treat her with the same respect you give me. Is that understood?"

They nodded and Alejandro inclined his head. "Thank you. Gentlemen, you may leave and go about your business. Ladies, please remain."

As they dispersed, I said awkwardly, "Uh, what about the other two who attacked me?" Lola still had them in her clutches.

Alejandro gave my attackers a dirty look. "They were led astray by lies. They do not deserve to die, but neither do they deserve to get off scot-free. If you wish, you may feed upon them."

Lola practically stood up and boogied, but I wasn't so sure.

When I hesitated too long, Austin drawled, "Please do. It'll make them think twice before doing something so darned bullheaded again."

Well, if Austin thought it was all right . . . I drew on the strings that connected me to the two of them, and let all that lustful energy flow into the deep wells of my body, filling them with the essence I craved so much yet tried to deny myself. I slurped up enough to keep Lola happy without draining them completely, then released them.

Once they regained their senses, they apologized profusely.

Alejandro, his expression cold, ordered, "Leave us. And take this mess with you." He gestured at the staked vamp on the floor.

Rosa stalked forward and swept her long dark hair out of her face. "They must clean up the rest of the mess, too." She flung out a hand toward the downed pine. "And redecorate the tree. Do you know how long it took me to get it just right?"

Alejandro suppressed a smile and nodded. "As she said. Rosa will supervise until you have it exactly to her liking."

The two vamps looked appalled, seeming more upset by this punishment than by Lola's caress or taking out dead bodies.

IT'S A GUY THING, Val, Fang said. YOU WOULDN'T UNDERSTAND.

You got that right. Men. Can't live with 'em; can't kill 'em. Mostly.

Rosa nodded in satisfaction as the men hauled Neil's body away.

Alejandro had me read the minds of all the women in the room, and I cleared them all. They were all worried about me learning their secrets, but who could keep them all straight? They all kind of blurred together after awhile, and I really didn't like wallowing in the muck of the vampire psyche anyway.

When we were done, I felt suddenly tired and hungry. Since the vamps didn't eat, they let me order in pizza, which I shared with Fang in the empty kitchen. That, plus the energy Lola had dragged out of the two who attacked me, helped to restore me fairly quickly.

After we ate, we rejoined Alejandro in his study, just the three of us. I slumped into one of the fancy wing-backed chairs in his very masculine study, all done up in earth tones, tile, and dark wood. The only thing I liked about this place was the mural on the wall opposite Alejandro's desk, depicting a sun-drenched landscape—a view from a villa on the Mediterranean.

"Okay," I said bluntly, "they might buy that stuff about how noble I am and all that, but I don't. After all, I've killed many vamps and I could be lulling you into a false sense of security. Why *do* you trust me?"

Alejandro smiled from behind his mahogany desk. "You have a great deal of integrity."

"You don't know that." Heck, I wasn't even sure if I knew that or not. I was still learning things about myself all the time.

"Oh, but I do. You've proven it several times over. Also, do you remember the night I spoke to the Demon Underground, the night the *Encyclopedia Magicka* was stolen?"

"Of course."

"I happened to brush up against a soothsayer demon that night."

A what?

TESSA, Fang explained.

Prophecy girl?

YEAH, WELL, THE PREFERRED TERM IS SOOTHSAYER DEMON.

When the elfin-looking Tessa touched someone, she sometimes involuntarily spouted fortune cookie-type prophecies about their future. "Tessa gave you a prophecy?" At his nod, I asked, "What was it?"

"She said, 'Lead with an honest heart by your side and you will achieve all that you desire.'"

Ooookay. "'An honest heart' could refer to anyone, like Austin or Rosa."

"Perhaps, but a soothsayer's prediction is never that straightforward. It is often couched with double meanings."

I knew that. "Yeah, so?"

"So what is another word for heart?"

"I don't know." And why did it matter?

"Isn't your full name *Valentine* Shapiro?"

Oh, crap. Had Tessa really told him I was the salvation of a vein of vampires? And why hadn't she told *me*?

I gaped at Alejandro as he sat in the throne-like chair behind his massive wooden desk. No, I didn't buy that I was the Movement's savior. I couldn't. "How can I possibly help the New Blood Movement?"

"You already have," Alejandro pointed out, "by exposing traitors within our ranks."

"Oh, good. Can I go now?"

I started to rise, but Alejandro halted me with a disappointed glance. "You know better than that. We have a contract."

NICE TRY, Fang said.

I sighed. "Look, I know the contract said I'm supposed to assist you with your coming out plans, but I don't get how I can do that. I have no political influence. I'm no party planner."

"I have other people to do those things. All I really expect is to have you by my side for now, a talisman if you would."

A freakin' lucky charm? Did I *look* like a leprechaun?

Alejandro continued, "But it would help greatly if you could assist me in convincing the Demon Underground to reveal themselves to the general public at the same time we do."

Shaking my head, I said, "You know I can't do that. For one thing, I'm not sure any of them would listen to me. And, for another, that's Micah's decision. He's the one you have to convince." Thank goodness that wasn't part of the contract.

"With your help, perhaps?" Alejandro suggested, raising one eyebrow.

I shook my head. "I don't even know if I agree. I don't get how it would help the demons. After all, the whole point of the Demon Underground is to help them pass as normal in human society."

YEAH, Fang agreed. WE DON'T WANT ANY WITCH HUNTS HERE.

"But wouldn't they rather be accepted as they are?" Alejandro persisted.

"That would be nice, but do you really think that's gonna happen? 'Cause I sure don't see it."

"Not even if we announce our existence to the world during Christmas, the season of good will?"

AND THE SEASON WITH THE MOST SUICIDES . . . .

I nodded at Fang—he had a point. "What's your hurry, anyway? After all, you can potentially live forever."

"Yes, but the Movement cannot support new members without a continuous stream of donors at our blood banks to provide the sustenance we need. With the backing of some key political leaders we have *now*, we must use this time before another election occurs. And with the legislation we plan to put in place, vampires belonging to the Movement will be protected while those who don't will be outcast. It will be far more difficult for the unaffiliated to get away with their attacks on humans."

Okay, saving the human race was a good reason, but—

The door opened and Rosa stuck her head in the study. "Micah Blackburn is here to see you."

Alejandro nodded. "Send him in, please."

My cousin—by demon powers though not by blood—came in, and Alejandro waved him to a seat. Micah came right to the point. "As we agreed, I have Josh and Andrew here to start their punishment. They're waiting in the car."

Lucky for them, Alejandro had recognized the demons had been influenced by their grief and the dark magicks in the *Encyclopedia Magicka* when they attacked the Movement. So instead of calling for their blood, he'd agreed to let them work off their debt to his organization.

Alejandro nodded. "Have you made any progress in learning where the fire demon hid the books?"

Micah sighed heavily. "Not yet. We've tried everything we can think of to get the information. The books somehow erased or magically protected his memory of where he hid them." Micah shook his head. "All we really know is that they're in San Antonio somewhere. Andrew didn't have time to take them anywhere else, and he definitely remembers putting them somewhere safe, not mailing them."

Apparently, when the books didn't want to be found, they made sure of it. The question was, why didn't they want to be found? I'd had them for years. Why hide now?

I couldn't answer those questions, so I asked Alejandro, "What are you going to have Josh and Andrew do?"

"I thought I'd put them under the supervision of one of my lieutenants. Luis."

Now that was true punishment. How diabolical.

"That takes care of the boys," he continued, "but I am wondering about the books. They are too dangerous to leave lying around for anyone to find. You had them for a long time, did you not, Ms. Shapiro?"

I nodded.

"And you had no problem with them trying to control you. Why is that?"

"I don't know," I admitted. "I don't think anyone does."

"Maybe there's one who does," Micah corrected me.

News to me. "Who?"

"Someone showed up a few hours ago from the Demon Underground in Los Angeles. He felt the books wake up and came to warn us about them."

JUST A TAD TOO LATE, Fang snarked.

My thoughts exactly.

Micah continued, "He claims to be an expert on them. I thought we might all want to speak to him, so he's waiting in the other room."

"Then let us bring him in," Alejandro said. He stuck his head out the wooden door that could have belonged to some ancient castle and asked Rosa to fetch the so-called expert.

Rosa had an amused smile on her face as she showed the guy in. Slim with nicely defined muscles, he was styled to the nth degree with a casually chic fitted jacket over a tight white T-shirt and jeans. With his carefully moussed and highlighted hair, tasteful earring, and just the right amount of sexy beard stubble, he appeared as if he'd just stepped out of a Calvin Klein ad. He even made Alejandro seem slightly shabby in comparison.

So that's what metrosexual looked like . . . .

Fang snorted.

Alejandro told Rosa she could go, and the pretty boy smoothed his hair back. He gave her a smoldering glance as she left, as if rewarding her with a prize. Strange. I'd never seen a non-vamp so . . . comfortable around the undead.

Fang laid down and put his head on his paws, sighing in disgust. CAN YOU SAY NARCISSIST?

True, but I had to admit the guy was great eye candy.

"This is Trevor Jackson," Micah said, then introduced the rest of us and gestured Trevor to one of the leather wing-backed chairs.

The guy sat gracefully, appearing oh-so-casual as he adjusted his jacket just so. "Call me Trevor." He smiled lazily but his voice had an edge to it. "I'm the keeper of the *Encyclopedia Magick* and I've come to take it back where it belongs."

CHAPTER THREE

I choked back a laugh. Pretty boy was trying to tell the leader of the two most powerful organizations in San Antonio what to do? Either the guy was stupid or he had more guts than I gave him credit for. What was he, anyway? Some kind of fashion demon?

Fang chuckled in my mind. NO SUCH THING, BABE.

Then what is he?

Fang tensed beside me. I DON'T KNOW. I CAN'T READ HIS MIND.

Whoa. That was a first. If Fang couldn't read his mind, then . . . "Are you human, Trevor?" I blurted out.

Trevor appeared miffed at having his big announcement interrupted. "No, or Micah wouldn't have brought me here."

"Tessa checked his credentials," Micah confirmed.

I wanted to ask Trevor point-blank what kind of demon he was, but that wasn't considered good manners in the Demon Underground. There was no rule about asking other rude questions, though. So far as I knew.

"So why can't my hellhound read you?" I asked bluntly.

Trevor shrugged. "Part of my training is to learn how to protect my mind from intrusion." His dismissive gaze skimmed Alejandro and Fang, the two who might have been able to worm some secrets out of him.

"Really? Do you have something to hide?" I asked.

LIKE WHAT? THE SECRET OF WHAT'S GOING TO BE SHOWING ON THE RUNWAY NEXT SEASON? Fang drawled.

"The training is so I can keep the books out of my mind," Trevor explained. "So they can't control me. That is why I am their proper keeper. Trust me, you don't *want* them on the loose in your city."

Something didn't ring true. I turned to Micah. "I had them for thirteen years, and your father had them before that. How long?"

"I'm not sure," he said, glancing speculatively at Trevor. "Ever since I can remember."

Alejandro raised an eyebrow and voiced what the rest of us were thinking. "You do not appear old enough to have had custody of such important magickal artifacts before they came to Micah's father."

Something flickered in Trevor's eyes, but I wasn't sure what. Annoyance? Embarrassment? He shrugged, trying to look sheepish but not quite pulling it off. "My father was keeper before me," he admitted. "He lost them and trained me to take his place in case they ever appeared again."

"So you've never actually been a keeper?" I persisted.

"I am fully trained, I assure you. I've been studying them all my life. That's how I knew when they woke here in San Antonio."

"Does that mean you can sense them now?"

"Afraid not. They're hiding." His smile was lazy, his eyes hooded. Unexpectedly sexy. I bet he got a lot of mileage out of that calculated smile.

Fang poked me with his nose. DON'T LET IT WORK ON YOU.

Not a problem. He's not my type. He liked himself too much. But I had to admit watching him was entertaining.

Alejandro raised an imperious finger from behind his desk to gain Trevor's attention. "Earlier, you stated that we would not want them loose in San Antonio. Why is that?"

He shrugged. "I suspect you figured that out for yourselves when they woke."

Micah and Alejandro exchanged a look I couldn't interpret.

"Do they always try to control people?" Micah asked.

"Usually. It's why they need a keeper."

Micah glanced at me. I took the hint. "But I had them for many years and they didn't try to control me," I told Trevor.

He raised an eyebrow. "Didn't they?"

That took me aback for a moment. Had they controlled my actions without my knowledge? What a disturbing thought.

No, wait. Josh and Andrew said the books had spoken to them. I didn't remember anything like that. More confident, I said, "No, they didn't. They never spoke to me, never tried to get me to do anything at all."

His brow furrowed in puzzlement and he asked, "Did you read them? Did you try any of the spells?"

"Uh, I just read the first volume that explained about all the different kinds of supernatural creatures. I didn't try any spells." They must have been in the last two volumes. I'd glanced through them, but wasn't interested in the mumbo jumbo stuff.

He nodded as if his suspicions were confirmed. "That explains it."

"Can you prove you're the keeper?" Micah asked. He obviously wanted to keep the books and didn't want to think his father had anything to do with stealing them.

"Absolutely," Trevor confirmed. "When we find the encyclopedia."

"Can you track them?" I asked eagerly. The sooner we found the books—no matter who kept them—the sooner I could get out of my contract with Alejandro.

"Only when they're actively trying to control someone. When they're not, I can't sense them at all."

"Then how do you expect to find them?" Alejandro asked. I'd expected him to be impatient by now, but he merely seemed curious.

Trevor shrugged, looking rueful. "I can only hope they reveal themselves by trying to manipulate someone else. And if I get within five hundred feet of them, I'll be able to sense them even if they're hiding."

That would be handy.

"And once you find them?" Alejandro persisted.

"I'll be able to control them," Trevor said with confidence.

"How?" Micah asked.

A corner of Trevor's mouth quirked up. "I'm afraid that's a trade secret. Too many people want to possess the *Encyclopedia Magicka* for, er, nefarious purposes. You understand."

Clearly, Micah didn't. "And how do we know your purposes aren't nefarious?"

"Because I'm a keeper," Trevor said, as if that explained everything. "You know where they were last, and some of you had contact with them. I'm hoping I can learn something that will help me find them." Trevor paused. "And since you so obviously want to find the books yourselves, can you tell *me* why?"

Alejandro scowled. "They were used against members of the New Blood Movement. I do not wish this to ever happen again."

"Ah, yes, Micah explained your Movement to me. I would be happy to remove them from San Antonio for you. And you?" Trevor asked Micah.

"They have a lot of knowledge about the abilities of our own people that the Demon Underground can use. It's an invaluable resource for understanding ourselves."

Before he could ask me, I said, "I just want to help Micah and Alejandro." Not to mention complete that contract so I'd be free.

Trevor nodded. "I think we can work something out with the Underground here. With your knowledge of their recent whereabouts and my ability to find them, we'd be better off pooling our efforts to find the books." He glanced between the two leaders who still looked uncertain. "Why don't I leave you to talk about it?" He took a business card out of his pocket and slid it across the scarred surface of the old wooden desk to Alejandro. "You can reach me at this number." He paused, giving us a charming smile. "If you wouldn't mind providing me a ride back to where I'm staying?"

Alejandro nodded. "One of my people will drive you."

Cocking his head with a slight grin, Trevor murmured, "Would it be possible to have the charming Rosa?"

"Of course," Alejandro said smoothly and left to get his lieutenant.

While he waited, Trevor shook Micah's hand and murmured some pleasantries, then crossed the room to shake mine. Lola didn't seem at all interested in him, but I urged her to enthrall him . . . just a little. Maybe if he was feeling a little happy, he'd be more willing to share what he knew.

Nothing. *Nada.* Zilch. It was like trying to get lust from a stone.

His eyes widened and he placed his other hand on top of mine. "Oh my, a little succubus. I would never have guessed."

What the hell did that mean? I yanked my hand out of his, wishing I could come up with a great line that would skewer him and his amusement, but my mind went blank. *Help me here,* I begged Fang.

SORRY, BABE. I GOT NOTHIN'.

Too late anyway as Alejandro came back in with Rosa. Trevor's eyes gleamed in appreciation as he looked her over. For some reason, it annoyed me.

Fang huffed. WHY DO YOU CARE WHAT HE THINKS, ANYWAY?

I don't, personally. But he should have responded to Lola and thought *she* was all that. Why hadn't he?

Alejandro closed the door and the three of us looked at each other. Micah spoke first. "I don't trust him."

"Nor do I," Alejandro said. "But I think we must work with him in order to locate the encyclopedia. I would like it found before we announce our existence to the world, if at all possible." He glanced at me. "I would like you to assist him, Ms. Shapiro. Accompany him on his search."

Somehow I knew that was coming. I grimaced, but nodded.

Micah added, "I noticed you used your gift on him, Val. How did it work?"

"It didn't. I guess the same shield that kept Fang out of his mind kept Lola out of his chakras. He could feel Lola, but Lola couldn't feel him."

"I was not able to penetrate it either," Alejandro said. "That shield would be a very useful thing to have. If it would keep humans from being enthralled by my kind, they would feel safer, more likely to respond positively to our coming out. Perhaps you could persuade him to give you the secret of it."

I shrugged. "I doubt it. Rosa is more likely to get something from him."

"Perhaps," Alejandro conceded. "She will call when she drops him off. Let's see what happens then."

While we waited, they discussed the Movement's coming out, Alejandro politely pressing Micah to join them, and Micah just as politely refusing. Way too civilized for me.

When Rosa called, Alejandro talked to her then hung up and said, "She didn't learn any more from him, except that he has rented a condo nearby."

Not a hotel? Dang. "That probably means he thinks it'll take a long time to find the books," I said. More time to spend with the self-absorbed demon. Great.

Micah frowned. "You're right. Val, I'm not sure it's safe for you. If your powers don't work on him . . . "

"No problem, cuz. As long as I have my strength and power, I'm good."

SO LONG AS YOU AND SHADE DON'T HOOK UP, THAT IS. Strangely, that thought from Fang didn't come out snarky. Instead, his furry little brow wrinkled in concern.

And he must have broadcast it to the other two also, because Micah said, "Fang's right. Until this guy leaves, maybe you and Shade—"

I cut him off with a gesture. I soooo did not want to discuss my love life here. Not only was it embarrassing, it was none of their business. "Don't worry about me," I snapped. "I can control myself . . . and Lola."

Alejandro glanced back and forth between us, looking curious. "What is it that you and Shade should not do?"

Crap. I'd forgotten he didn't know. Apparently, so had Fang

because he licked my hand in apology. As I hid my face behind my hand and stared at the plush blood-red rug, Micah explained the whole lose-your-virginity-lose-your-strength bit to the vampire leader.

Could this possibly get any more embarrassing?

Apparently, it could. Alejandro cleared his throat and said, "Ms. Shapiro, I find myself in the regrettable position of having to echo Mr. Blackburn's sentiments. If you would kindly refrain from—"

"I already said I would," I bit out. "Sheesh, it's not like we're horn dogs or anything." Jeez, even if I did do the deed, it wasn't like I'd be helpless—I'd still have the powers of your normal, average non-virgin succubus—no strength or accelerating healing, but plenty of ability to cloud men's minds. "Can we change the subject, please?"

Alejandro looked concerned, but nodded. "Let me call Mr. Jackson to confirm we would like to work with him." He dialed and held a brief conversation, then handed the phone to me. "Mr. Jackson would like to set up a time for you two to meet."

I took the phone and asked Trevor, "Where?"

"I don't know San Antonio very well, but I do know where Alejandro and Rosa live. Why don't I get some sleep to get rid of the jet lag, then meet you back there first thing in the morning?"

"I usually work midnight to dawn, but I can meet you outside the mansion after I get off." I didn't really need that much sleep.

Trevor hesitated, then said, "Okay. Dawn it is."

"You got it."

We hung up and I handed Alejandro his phone back, saying, "We meet here at dawn tomorrow."

"Good," Micah said and stood. "If you don't mind, I'll send Josh and Andrew in, then take off. I'm needed at the club."

I didn't doubt it. Micah ran the popular Club Purgatory down on the River Walk. Not only was it a great place to employ the more obvious demons in the Purgatory theme of the club, it brought in quite a bit of money. It should be hopping at this time of night.

After Micah scratched Fang behind his ears and left, Alejandro gave me an approving nod. "An excellent arrangement with Mr. Jackson. Though this is not how I planned to use your services, it will do almost as well."

"How *did* you plan to use me?" I asked, curious.

He played with a pen on his desk for a moment, then said, "We strive for acceptance, not fear. Therefore, before we announce our existence to the world, I would like to . . . deter . . . the unaffiliated of my kind from causing any trouble that would put us in a bad light."

HE MEANS HE WANTS YOU TO HELP HIM KILL THEM, Fang said.

Yeah, I got that. He wanted to make it too miserable for them to continue attacking humans. I definitely approved. "Okay, I'll do that, whenever Trevor and I aren't searching for the books. In fact, we have the rest of the night left, so why don't we go kick some bad vamp butt?"

Fang scrambled to his feet and yipped to show his approval. I'M IN!

CHAPTER FOUR

Before we could go hunt fangbangers, the doorbell rang—Josh and Andrew, no doubt. When Alejandro didn't move from the throne-like chair behind his desk, I said, "Uh, are your people gonna be cool with having the two demons here who hurt—"

Before I could finish, he was up and out of his chair, and down the hall with his lightning-fast speed. I hoofed it after him, glad to see that most of the bloodsuckers had left. Only the three lieutenants and a few others remained in the great room, cleaning up the mess. Luis had his hand on the door handle but Alejandro stopped him with a word. They whispered for a little bit, then Alejandro opened the ancient-looking wooden door.

Sure enough, Josh and Andrew stood there, looking more than a little apprehensive. Ludwig, the massive water demon, loomed behind them. Since Ludwig had saved the mansion when the redheaded fire demon tried to burn it down, and was humongous enough to make anyone think twice about attacking him, he was a good choice to escort them. Good—Micah had been thinking.

Alejandro stared sternly at the two.

Andrew looked sullen, but Josh had turned white under his wavy blond hair. I feared he'd phase out right there, but Ludwig had a firm grip on him so he couldn't.

Luis, of course, wore a sneer, though whatever his boss had told him must have him in check.

"Has it been explained what we require of you?" Alejandro asked the demons.

They nodded.

"Good. You will be under Luis's direction. Tonight, you will accompany him and Ms. Shapiro to assess the vulnerability of the blood banks. You must do exactly as he says, do you understand?"

They both jumped as if they'd received an electric shock and stared at Luis as if he were evil incarnate. What was that all about?

Fang chuckled. LUIS JUST ENTHRALLED THEM AND SHOWED THEM WHAT HE COULD DO IF THEY SCREWED UP.

I hid a grin. Luis had his uses. But I wasn't thrilled about going hunting with him and two newbies. I'd have to watch out for them as well as myself.

Ludwig frowned and glanced between the demons and the vamps, not letting go of Josh. He didn't have a hellhound explaining what was going on, so he must be confused.

"I'll take care of them," I told him.

Apparently reassured, the man mountain nodded and left.

Andrew stuck his hands in his pockets and hunched his shoulders. "Now what?"

Luis's lips spread into a smile . . . and it wasn't a pleasant one. With his dark goatee, long hair clubbed back into a ponytail, and slashing eyebrows, he appeared really sinister. "Now you do exactly as you are told." He gestured toward the string of dark luxury automobiles Alejandro kept lined up on the long driveway. "We shall take one of the cars."

We followed him to the last one. "Whoa, what's this?" Andrew asked, running his hand over the gleaming black finish. Apparently, he liked shiny things.

"A Lincoln town car," Luis said with pride. "Top of the line, of course." He opened the door and the two miscreants piled in the back seat as I got in the front.

Fang jumped up to curl in my lap. I'M GONNA TAKE A NAP. WAKE ME WHEN WE GET THERE.

The warm weight of him was nice, comforting. As the guys talked cars, I zoned out and stroked Fang's wiry fur. The hellhound pretended to be gruff and macho, but he enjoyed the petting as much as I did. He just wouldn't admit it.

Fang opened one eye. CAN YOU STOP THINKING SO LOUD? I'M TRYING TO SLEEP HERE.

Then stop listening.

He pointedly put a paw over his ear. Okay, I got the message. Unfortunately, being left alone with my own thoughts meant returning to the one thing that had been spinning through my brain ever since I'd learned what losing my virginity would really mean.

It wasn't an easy decision. I mean, sure, it was a huge deal for anyone, but in my case, doing the deed meant the Slayer would no longer have the ability to slay. My reflexes would slow and so would my speed and healing.

All my life, I had longed to be normal like my half-sister Jen . . .

not to have to worry about accidentally turning men on by getting too close, not to be treated like a freak by the full human side of my family. But now that I faced being normal, I still kind of wanted that, but I kind of didn't, too. It was part of me, what I'd always known.

Things had changed. The Demon Underground proved there were others like me, others who understood what I was going through or at least valued me for my abilities. Plus, those same abilities gave me respect from the humans in the Special Crimes Unit. My demon side made me special . . . maybe I wasn't as big a freak as I thought after all.

But how special would I be if I all I could do was make men lust over me, once I lost the slaying ability that had defined me for so long? Women all over the world could make men lust—not like it was that hard. And how about when the vamps learned I was no longer as powerful? Would they come after me? Would I have to leave San Antonio, the city I loved?

It was a depressing thought, but the alternative wasn't much better. To keep my slaying ability, I had to keep my virginity. That hadn't been an issue so far, but with Shade letting Lola feed on him whenever she needed it, I was afraid it would only be a matter of time before something irreversible happened. Especially since Shade was so totally hot.

Sure, he had a dark side. Shadow demons acted as conduits between our world and other dimensions. If Shade got too angry or lost control of his demon side, all hell could break loose. Literally. Demons on the other side could seize control and pour through into our world.

But Shade was such a white hat he'd rather kill himself than let that happen. Luckily, I seemed to be able to keep his demon under control while he kept Lola happy. It's as if we were meant for each other.

Cue sappy music here.

Yeah, it was pretty inevitable that we'd hook up eventually, but I wanted to be able to choose *when*. While I still worked for Alejandro, not such a good idea. And if I lost my powers, I'd have to find a new job, too. I wouldn't be much use to the Special Crimes Unit then. I'd still be able to enthrall men, but I'd never really liked using my succubus powers. And if I let Lola have her way too much, she might take over completely.

If I did lose my strength, what would life be like? Though Micah was an incubus, he got along fine without the extras, but being a guy, he'd lost his cherry way early and never knew what powers he'd lost along with his virginity.

Also, if I did the deed, would it be worth it? Would Shade even stick around? Look what had happened with Dan and me. Would it all be for nothing?

Lots of questions. No answers. Not good ones, anyway.

I sighed. For now, it would be best to stay away from Shade as much as I could. Fighting vamps seemed to satisfy my demon's lust. With any luck, we'd find some to whale on tonight.

We arrived at the old brick hotel that had been converted into a blood bank, and Luis parked in the back. I'd been here before, but not through the back way. Luis got us in easily past the security cameras and fancy intrusion detection system and headed for the elevator.

"Why are we going upstairs?" I asked. The bad guys would be downstairs or outside.

He pressed the elevator button. "To give these pups some way of defending themselves," he said, raking them with a look that said he considered them pond scum. Or worse—a greasy layer below pond scum.

He used a key card to take us to the fourth floor, to the penthouse executive suite. I'd never thought about it before, but I wondered what was on the second and third floors. Probably where the other members of the Movement slept during the day, since they obviously didn't all stay at the mansion.

Made sense. No wonder most of the blood banks were converted hotels.

Focus, Val, focus, Fang reminded me.

Yeah, I needed to do that. But when Luis led us into the "living room," it was hard to focus on anything but the décor. It wasn't something I'd ever choose. Brilliant white contrasted with dead black. Add splashes of blood red and hard angles, and the room screamed modern design.

Strange—it was so different from Alejandro's warm, comfortable home. This was where the vamp leader had brought me the first time we met, so I gathered it was how he chose to show his public face. What message was he trying to portray? It was as if he'd taken the Hollywood vamp stereotype and aggressively brought it into the twenty-first century.

I felt uneasy here—which could be the point—but Josh and Andrew seemed impressed by it all. Or maybe they were wowed by the state-of-the-art electronics everywhere. Luis seemed really comfortable here, which was strange. It didn't appear to be the kind of place a Spanish aristocrat would like. At least, that's what I'd always assumed he'd been when he was alive. He sure had the attitude.

IT SUITS HIS PERSONALITY, Fang muttered. COLD AND LIFELESS.

"Stay here," Luis ordered. "I'll be right back."

He returned quickly, carrying a couple of crossbows and some stakes.

"Whoa, dude," I exclaimed. "What are you doing with vampire-slaying equipment?"

His lips stretched in a thin smile. "We took them off some would-be slayers who couldn't tell the difference between the people of the Movement and the filth who prey on the weak."

Josh and Andrew seemed impressed by his passion, so I didn't ask him how long he'd been one of the filth before he joined Alejandro.

Luis added, "Lately, it has become necessary to arm our volunteers and customers occasionally when the dregs come calling."

That seemed dangerous, but I guess he could compel them not to use those weapons on his own undead body.

TOO BAD, Fang muttered.

Yeah, Luis didn't exactly endear himself to anyone. Except maybe Alejandro.

Luis led us to an area in the back that resembled a gym or training room, with padded blue mats lining the walls and floors. He showed the guys how to use the crossbows and let them practice a few times. They did surprisingly well. I gave them a few pointers on how to use the stakes and avoid a fanging, but they were nowhere near ready to go *mano-a-mano* with angry fangbangers.

Luis knew it, too. "These are a last resort only," he told them. "If a rogue vampire or gang attacks the blood bank tonight, you are to observe only. Use these weapons only to protect humans. Do you understand?"

Josh and Andrew nodded soberly, but I didn't trust the gleam in their eyes.

"Use it only if one of them attacks you first," I added. Didn't want them going off half-cocked and shooting one of the good guys. "Oh, and one more thing. Micah still wants to keep the Underground secret, so don't even think about using your powers in public or you'll have a whole boatload of pissed-off demons to deal with. Got it?"

Andrew scowled, but I didn't relax my glare until they both

nodded.

"So what do we do now?" Josh asked. "Patrol?"

Luis shook his head. "Too obvious. We don't want to scare them away. We want them to feel safe enough to strike, so we can try to reason with them." But from the way he hefted the stake in his hand, I wasn't sure he thought mere talking would be enough.

"You expect them here tonight?" I asked.

Luis nodded. "It fits their pattern. We have warned most of our regular customers away, but will need someone to lure them in. Many of them know the Slayer, so . . . " He turned a speculative gaze on Josh and Andrew.

"You want to use us as bait?" Andrew asked in disbelief.

"One of you," Luis said. "Him." He pointed at Josh.

It made a lot of sense. If Josh knew they were coming, he could phase out before they grabbed him. And he was slighter, looking less likely to fight back than the stocky redheaded fire demon.

Josh gulped visibly. "But what if one of them grabs me before I can phase? I can't phase when someone is holding onto me." He sounded on the edge of panic.

"Don't worry," I assured him. "We'll be watching you and won't let you get hurt."

Not much, anyway.

When Josh paled even more, I realized Fang must have shared his thought with the demon. I glared at the hellhound who acted as if he had nothing on his innocent little mind except for scratching his ear. *You're not helping.* Aloud, I added to Josh, "You know better than anyone that if one tries to bite you, they'll regret it. Remember, vamp drink demon blood, vamp go crazy." That's what had gotten Josh into trouble in the first place.

"That's settled then," Luis said, though Josh didn't look as though he thought it was settled at all. "Their normal method of operation is to have two or three band together to attack someone alone on the street outside, then drain them almost completely and dump them at the door before anyone can raise an alarm." He shook his head. "We've been able to get some of the victims to the hospital in time or replenished their blood with our own supply, but it's not enough."

From the grit in his tone, I figured he wasn't happy that the unaffiliated ones thumbed their noses at the Movement in this way.

Luis glared at Josh and Andrew. "And thanks to you, our supplies are way down."

Andrew backed off, holding his hands up. "Whoa, not me, dude. All I did was try to burn your house down."

Stupid to remind us. Luis's eyes narrowed, but before he could ream the fire demon a new one, I said, "So what's the plan? Throw Josh out as bait and watch in the shadows to see if we can reel in some bottom feeders?"

"Indeed," Luis agreed. "Though they will suspect something if they sense anyone else on the street. We shall wait in the lobby."

Josh's brow furrowed. "Then how will you know if I'm in trouble?"

"I shall enthrall you lightly and remain in your mind the whole time," Luis said.

"Huh? No way, dude." Josh backed off, holding his hands out as if to ward off the vampire.

"Then what do you suggest?" Luis bit out. "Would you rather the succubus enslave you?"

Whoa—I so didn't want to go there. I stepped in. "How about if Fang keeps tabs on you, Josh? He's read you before and can alert me right away if you're in danger. Fang, you can do that, right?"

YOU KNOW I CAN.

Yeah, but I want you to reassure Josh.

As Josh hesitated, Fang broadcast, YOU KNOW I'LL TAKE CARE OF YOU, OR SHADE WON'T LET ME SEE PRINCESS ANYMORE. IT'S ME OR HIM, BUDDY. WHO'S IT GONNA BE?

"Okay, okay," Josh said. "Fang can watch out for me."

And Fang did as Josh wandered the streets for a couple of hours without a nibble, careful not to go beyond Fang's range. The rest of us hung out in the lobby, watching customers come and go. Most who did arrived in a group or were escorted by a member of the Movement and wore large silver crosses until they got inside.

Though the Movement gave the option of donating blood in a sterile location downstairs, the vast majority of these nighttime visitors chose the other—far more personal—method of donating. It made sense. The other kind of donation could be given during the day. Since the up close and personal kind required fang to neck, the sun had to be down. Unfortunately, that meant the bad vamps were out and about as well. But since the "customers" got a thrill along with the donation, a lot of them were willing to risk it. I bet some of them were becoming addicts. Would we soon see Fangees Anonymous forming here in town?

My musings were cut short as Fang alerted us that Josh had spotted someone tailing him. I didn't get too excited since we'd already had a couple of false alarms. One was a stray dog and the other some blood bank customers. But we moved toward the door just in case. Not too fast—we didn't want to spook the customers—but to be there in case Josh needed us.

IT'S THEM, Fang confirmed, and we all charged out into the street.

Lust for the hunt sizzled in my blood. As we burst outside, I saw four vamps chasing Josh toward the blood bank. One reached for him and Andrew yelled, "Phase, now!"

Josh went transparent for a moment and the vamp's hand went right through him.

"Here," Andrew shouted again, "I have your weapon."

Josh continued his rush through a parked car. Two of his pursuers crashed into it. The other two swerved in time and came around it— smack into Luis and me. I was ready with a stake and plunged it into one's heart. He fell like a rock. Luis scuffled with the other one so I looked back to check on Josh and Andrew.

They had their backs against the brick wall and were scrambling to arm their crossbows. Fang had jumped protectively in front of them, bared his fangs and growled, his eyes flashing purple. He was actually holding the two bloodsuckers at bay. I took a running leap and tackled one of them. He slammed into his buddy, taking them both down. Bowling for vampires, anyone?

I fumbled for a stake as the two unwashed dead fought to get out from under me. Sheesh, it smelled like they hadn't bathed for a month. Phew!

Uh oh. All that writhing woke Lola up, and they were inside my energy field, which meant I didn't even have to try to make them want me. The male vamps suddenly seemed far more interested in holding on to me than in fighting me off. Ick. Was one of them seriously trying to hump my leg?

Forget using Lola to tame them. I didn't want their smelly energy anywhere near me. I jumped off of them, feeling as though I'd been slimed. Now I was able to grab another stake from my back waistband. I slammed it toward the one who'd been humping my leg. He rolled to the side. Missed. I hit his buddy in the thigh instead. He screamed and Fang lunged for his crotch. The stabbed vamp's scream took on a higher pitch and he curled up into a ball. That ought to keep him out of action for a bit.

His friend scrambled to his feet, looking royally pissed, and flashed his fangs at me. Something slugged me on my left side, making me stagger forward a step. Searing pain followed shortly after, but I couldn't deal with that right now. The standing vamp rushed me and I stepped aside. He missed me, slamming into the parked car. I heard something whoosh past me—a fireball! It hit the vamp right in the chest and he went up in flames, screaming. Luckily, he fell on the sidewalk instead of against the gas tank, and thrashed in agony until he died.

Barbecued vamp . . . not a nice smell. And a sucky way to die.

I turned to see a pale and horrified Josh and Andrew staring at the three undead who were definitely *dead* dead now. Not a pretty sight since Luis had twisted the head off of his opponent. He now held the last one standing—the one I'd bowled over—pinned to the wall by his throat. The stake was still in the vamp's thigh and his crotch probably hurt like hell, judging by his whimpering.

Luis whispered fiercely into his ear. "The Movement and the Slayer will no longer tolerate your harassment and killing of humans for sustenance. From now on, we cry war against all of the unaffiliated. Join us or die."

The vamp, who seemed to be no more than twenty years old, gaped at me in horror. Though my side was hurting like a son of a gun, I tried to come across as all mean and slayerish.

"I didn't know," the vamp sobbed. "I didn't know."

Luis flung him away in disgust and yanked the stake out of his thigh. "Go, tell the others. As for you, if we hear of you attacking anyone again, we will hunt you down, and your ending will make these deaths look like a walk in the park. Got it?"

The vamp gave a jerky nod. "Okay. I-I'll join tomorrow. Right after I tell everyone else."

"You do that," I said sternly as he hobbled away on his injured leg as fast as he could.

Fang came to stand beside me, his tongue lolling in amusement. *YOU DO THAT?* WOW, GREAT LINE.

Oh, shut up. It was the best I'd been able to come up with, considering the pain in my side. Speaking of pain, I glanced down and saw that a crossbow bolt had pierced the outer edge of the skin above my hip and was sticking out both in the back and the front. Crap.

I turned to glare at the two demons. The first time I'd been really injured . . . and I'd been shot by my *own side*?

"It was an accident, I swear," Josh said, his crossbow on the ground and his hands held out as if to ward me off. "I was aiming at the vampire."

Luis's reply almost sounded like a growl. "Didn't we tell you two to use those weapons only as a last resort?"

"Yes, but there were two of them and Val—"

"Val had them under control," I said. "And see what you did? You shot me!"

Luis glared at Andrew. "And *you* were told not to use your powers."

Andrew lifted his chin defiantly. "I killed him, didn't I?"

"You do as you're told!" Luis slapped Andrew, hard, and for some reason, that shocked me more than anything else that had happened this evening.

But it reminded me that he could have done much worse if he wanted to. And, it apparently did the same thing for the two demons, because their eyes widened and they paled even more.

Bet they were really sorry they hadn't listened.

YEAH, Fang snickered. LUIS PUT THEM IN DEMON TIME-OUT.

"Stay here," Luis ordered. "I will do damage control, to clear the minds of any who witnessed this."

Sure enough, there were horrified lookie-loos staring out of the blood bank and cruising down the street.

"I'm so sorry," Josh said. "It won't happen again, I swear." He seemed to be genuinely apologetic.

HE IS, Fang confirmed. YOU'RE HIS NEW HERO.

Huh?

Fang chuckled. HE'S GOT THIS IMAGE OF YOU IN HIS MIND, STANDING LIKE A FEARLESS GUNSLINGER WITH AN ARROW IN YOUR SIDE, HALOED BY THE STREETLIGHT, FACING DOWN THE EVIL BLOODSUCKERS. ANDREW, TOO.

Oh, great. Groupies. "So, what are we going to do about getting this thing out of me?" I took off my vest and carefully peeled away the shirt around the wound, wincing as the cloth brushed against the short bolt. It had caught only about an inch of my skin so nothing vital was hit, but it hurt like hell, especially now that the adrenaline was wearing off. Luckily, it didn't have any barbs on the pointy end, or it would have done a lot more damage.

"Sorry," Andrew muttered. "Does it hurt?"

Duh. "Oh, no, I'm good," I said, not bothering to hide my

sarcasm. "I think I'll start a trend with the latest rage in body piercings." When his eyes went wide with surprise, I snapped, "Of course it hurts, you moron." More and more with each moment that passed.

Luis, his mind-bending apparently complete, returned to our side and bent to inspect the bolt. "You need to remove that."

"Yeah," Josh said. "And call Shade."

"No, not Shade," I protested, struggling to keep the pain from showing on my face.

"Why not? He can heal you."

YEAH, Fang echoed. WHY NOT?

I'll explain later, I told the hellhound. Aloud, I said, "This is trivial. Call Gwen. She's a trauma nurse—she'll know what to do." Besides, she knew what I was and wouldn't make a fuss. "She's on duty at the ER tonight." I handed Josh my phone and pulled a Special Crimes Unit locator out of another pocket. I activated the beacon to send our GPS coordinates. Soon, the SCU ambulance would be here to cart away the remains.

Andrew and Luis stared down at the bolt in my side. "It's silver," Luis said, "or I'd remove it."

"I don't have a problem with silver," Andrew said. And before I realized what he planned, he grabbed the back of it and yanked it out.

Agony burned through my side, radiating through my entire body, and I barely kept from screaming. But no amount of will could keep me conscious. My brain fuzzed out and I crumpled to the ground.

CHAPTER FIVE

I woke to a throbbing ache in my side, with the occasional piercing pain. Where was I? I lay curled on my right side on a comfortable surface that appeared to be made of soft, supple leather. Wherever I was, it was moving. I opened my eyes and stared straight into concerned brown eyes framed by wispy reddish blond hair. Fang.

He licked my nose. YOU'RE IN THE BACK SEAT OF LUIS'S CAR, Fang said from the floorboard. WE'RE TAKING YOU TO GWEN'S ER.

Good. There were closer hospitals, but Gwen would be discreet. I shifted to a more comfortable position and pain lanced through my side. I winced. Note to self—don't do that again. *Where are Josh and Andrew?* If Luis had done something to them—

HE DIDN'T, BUT I DID. I CHEWED ANDREW'S BUTT FOR THAT STUPID STUNT.

Literally?

NAW, THOUGH I WANTED TO. THEY'RE SHARING THE FRONT SEAT. NOT HAPPY ABOUT IT EITHER.

I glanced up to see Josh peering around the seat at me. "Her eyes are open! Val, are you okay?"

Okay? How could I be okay? He'd shot me in the side, fergawdsakes. "Yeah," I managed to say.

"You sure you don't want us to take you to Shade?"

"I'm sure," I croaked. "I want Gwen."

Fang poked me with his nose. AND ARE YOU GOING TO TELL ME NOW WHY YOU WON'T DO THE SENSIBLE THING AND HAVE SHADE HEAL YOU?

I gave him a reason he'd understand. *Remember what happened when Shade healed Josh?* Opening the healing conduits to the other world made Shade more vulnerable to the demons waiting there. Since exchanging healing energies took a lot out of him, he was less able to keep the demons at bay. He'd almost lost control then and would have killed himself to keep the demons out of our world if I hadn't stopped him.

BUT YOU WERE ABLE TO GROUND HIM THEN, Fang reminded me.

YOU CAN DO IT AGAIN.

I did it then with Lola's help. Her seduction had proved more powerful than the demon's pull. But seducing him right now . . . no. Neither of us needed that kind of temptation. And while I was all gung-ho to have Shade as a boyfriend, keeping us dependent on each other couldn't be a good idea.

Besides, I wasn't sure I'd have any oomph left to control him immediately after he healed me. If I remembered right, the others he'd healed had been pretty much exhausted afterward. Plus there was another reason, but I didn't want to go into it right now.

I could feel Fang's attention sharpen on me. YOU *WANT* TO FEEL THIS PAIN. MASOCHIST MUCH?

I should have known he'd sniff it out anyway. *I'm not a masochist. It's just that* . . . Heck, I didn't know how to say this. As the Slayer, I didn't get injured often. What would happen if Shade and I made love, then I got hurt and couldn't heal as fast? I needed to know what it was like to feel pain as full humans did. I needed to know if I could handle it. I needed to know if it was worth it.

The hellhound poked me in the stomach with his nose. HOW'S THAT WORKING FOR YOU, VAL?

I'll let you know. Luis hit a pothole and agony seared my side. But I wasn't about to let a little pain stop me. I was determined to not be a wuss. After all, I had to live up to that heroic image in my groupies' eyes.

Fang snorted then raised his nose, sniffing as the car slowed and turned. WE MUST BE AT THE HOSPITAL.

Luis stopped the car and took charge. "Andrew, go get a wheelchair. Joshua, you get the trauma nurse." The vamp came around to open the door by my head.

I struggled to sit up. "I don't need a wheelchair."

"Don't be stubborn," Luis snapped. "We don't want to attract undue attention."

"Yeah, right. Like being pierced by a crossbow bolt is an everyday occurrence."

"They don't have to know what wounded you." Luis gave Andrew a passing glare as he returned with the chair. "Tell them some children were playing with bows and arrows and got out of hand."

Andrew's face turned as red as his hair, but he didn't respond to the taunt. "Do you need help?" he asked me.

Gwen came running up, her bouncing red curls not quite as brassy as Andrew's. My normally cheerful, upbeat roomie was all business as she pushed her way into the car beside me. "What happened?"

We explained and I said, "I don't want Shade for this. Can you take care of it . . . discreetly?"

She frowned. "I have to use the resources here at the hospital, which means you'll have to be seen by a doctor. Is there anything . . . unusual about your blood or anything?"

"I don't know. Probably."

Andrew nodded. "Definitely."

Crap. "And you'd better make sure it's a female doctor. If a guy gets too close . . . "

Gwen's mouth rounded in an "o" of realization.

"Don't worry," Luis said dismissively. "I shall ensure no one remembers anything unusual tonight."

Gwen glanced at him curiously but didn't ask how or why. That was only one of the many things I loved about her.

"Okay," Gwen said decisively. "I'll make sure she gets help." She eased me gently into the chair and glanced at Fang. "I'm sorry, but he can't come in."

My best friend couldn't be by my side? Then I wasn't sure I wanted to go.

YOU CAN STILL REACH ME MENTALLY, EVEN IF I STAY OUTSIDE.

He was right. I hated hospitals, so I was just trying to delay the inevitable. Sighing, I thought back at him, *Okay.* I nodded at Gwen and she turned to Luis. "Can you deal with the paperwork?"

He frowned, but obviously didn't want to admit there was something he couldn't do.

"I'll get the info from Micah," Josh said. "Do you want me to call anyone else? Your family?"

Lord, no. "Anyone calls my mother and they're dead meat. Got me?" I did *not* want her hovering over me, trying to act all maternal and caring when it probably wasn't serious.

Josh looked surprised, but everyone nodded, so Gwen whisked me inside. I had an impression of light tiled floors, white walls, ugly harsh white lighting . . . and the distinctive hospital smell that had the blood draining from my head. If I wasn't sick before, that smell would do it every time.

IT'S PSYCHOSOMATIC, Fang told me.

How do you even know those kinds of words?

BEFORE I MET YOU, I DID A LOT OF PEOPLE-WATCHING AND SAW

A LOT OF TV THROUGH WINDOWS. HAD TO ENTERTAIN MYSELF SOMEHOW. AMAZING WHAT YOU LEARN.

I guess. But psychosomatic or not, being here made me feel worse. I liked it even less when the doctor came in to work on me.

A couple of hours later, I was bandaged up and woozy from the medication they'd given me. The doctor must have noticed something odd because she wanted to run some tests, but Luis, who pretended he was my brother so he could be by my side, used his mind-control mojo to persuade her otherwise.

When she left, I turned to Gwen. "Did she talk to anyone about my strangeness? Is there anything written down?"

"She only mentioned it to me," Gwen assured me. "And your . . . brother," she glanced askance at Luis, "took care of the lab techs who tested your blood. Josh helped me find all your records. There's nothing weird in them."

"Good."

I fell asleep on my way home. When I woke, I was in my own bed, Fang curled up beside me, and practically everyone I knew was standing around—Luis and his two troublemakers had been joined by Shade, Alejandro and Micah. They were all chatting quietly at the foot of my bed. Gwen must have gone off-shift, because she was standing over me, checking my pulse. Made me feel a bit like Dorothy, with Gwen playing Auntie Em and Fang as Toto. Guess who the two brainless scarecrows were?

SHE'S AWAKE, Fang announced. BUT I THINK SHE'S DELIRIOUS.

No, just feeling a little goofy. "What's going on?" I said aloud. I lifted myself up onto my elbows, wincing. Note to self: movement causes pain. "Am I about to die or something?"

"You're fine," Gwen soothed. "You'll just need some peace and quiet to heal from your injury." She glanced at the guys who had come to surround my bed, but none of them took the hint.

"Then why the death bed scene?" I persisted.

Micah grinned. "We wanted to see you for ourselves."

Alejandro nodded. "But this will not get you out of your contract, you know." He smiled, and I realized he was making a joke. Would wonders never cease?

"Well, I don't know about you, but I'm hungry," Gwen said in her brisk nurse tone. "Who wants to help me make something to eat?"

She collected Josh and Andrew with her gaze and they went willingly—Gwen's cooking was legendary in the Demon Underground.

She was one of the few humans who knew about us, and because of her cooking and nursing, everyone had sort of adopted her as one of us. Luis followed, too.

When they left, I noticed Shade hadn't approached the bed. He just stood there and, because of the swirls where his face should be, I couldn't tell what he was thinking.

HE'S NOT SURE YOU WANT HIM HERE, Fang told me.

Why not?

BECAUSE YOU REFUSED TO LET HIM HEAL YOU. DUH.

Sheesh. I wondered how to reassure Shade without letting him know Fang was picking his brain for me.

"Why didn't you want Shade to heal you?" Micah asked, sitting on the end of my queen-sized bed.

What a great coincidence. I glanced at Fang. Or maybe not.

From the smug look on his face, definitely not. The furry telepath had struck again.

I answered Micah's question but looked at Shade. "Because I know how much it takes out of you . . . and what happens afterward. I didn't want that for you."

I held out my hand and Shade took it. His features blipped into focus then, and he looked both pained and relieved at the same time. He sat gingerly next to me on the bed. "I would've healed you, gladly."

"I know, and that's why I couldn't let you do it."

AWW, HOW SWEET, Fang cooed, projecting his thoughts to all who could hear him.

Micah chuckled.

"Don't encourage him," I warned. "Or you might be his next target."

"Oh, I've been used for target practice many times," Micah said with a laugh. "Remember, he was with me before he came to you."

"And now I see why you foisted him on me." I rubbed Fang's fuzzy head to let him know I didn't mean it. I didn't have to, though—he knew it. And if Fang ever lost his snark, I'd probably think he was possessed or sick or something.

"So," Alejandro said. "No more vampire hunting for you until you are well. Besides, Luis tells me that the message was delivered."

"Yes, but the other vamps aren't really organized, so I don't know how the word will spread. Or how much good it'll do if you're not willing to back up Luis's threats . . . ."

"That will not be a problem. We will indeed take the war to the streets. We cannot jeopardize our big announcement. He spoke for me in this matter."

I shrugged then winced when the movement hurt my side. "Okay, boss. I won't purposefully hunt down any vampires. But I'm scheduled to meet Trevor at dawn." Which was probably coming up really soon.

Alejandro nodded. "I called him and let him know you will not be able to make that appointment, so he plans to canvass the city on his own. He asked if you could meet him at midnight tonight." He looked at Micah. "Will she be well enough then?"

My cuz nodded and said, "She'll still be in pain, but her accelerated healing will help. So long as you weren't planning on her doing anything strenuous, she should be fine."

I hated the way they talked about me as if I wasn't there. Strengthened by Fang and Shade's nearness, I said, "*She* is right here and can decide that for herself."

Micah lifted an eyebrow. "And what does *she* decide?"

"That I can meet Trevor, because it shouldn't involve anything more strenuous than driving around in a car looking for some sign of the books."

"Very good," Alejandro said. "I shall see you then. And now, if you will excuse me? It's approaching dawn."

He bowed and left. "I'd better go, too," Micah said, and gave me a kiss on the forehead. "Take care of yourself."

"I will," I promised.

After he was gone, only Shade, Fang and I were left in the room. And with all the other distractions gone, I was a hundred times more aware of Shade. So was Lola, and, pain or not, she was kind of interested in coaxing him down to lie beside us.

I CAN LEAVE IF YOU WANT, Fang offered.

No, don't. The plan was to stay away from Shade as much as possible until my contract was over. He was just too much temptation.

Shade looked concerned. "Are you really okay?"

"I'll be fine. I heal fast and this wasn't enough of a wound to call out the big guns." I yawned. "I don't know if it's the meds or what, but I'm suddenly very tired."

"Should I leave you alone then?" Shade asked, looking reluctant.

"If you don't mind. You'd better go and get some of Gwen's cooking before those others scarf it all down."

"Don't you want some?"

"Not now. The meds are making my stomach a little queasy. I'll eat later." Then, to punctuate my decision, I let out another huge yawn.

"Okay," he said and leaned over to give me a peck on the lips. "Get well soon."

I watched Shade leave with regret. It would have been nice to snuggle up with him, but not the best choice when I was so weak. As Shade closed the door softly behind him, Fang cuddled even closer. YOU'RE NOT GOING TO MAKE ME LEAVE, TOO, ARE YOU?

Not a chance. Pets are therapeutic, haven't you heard?

YOU GOT THAT STRAIGHT.

Chuckling, I stroked his soft ears and closed my eyes, letting the medication fog my brain. With any luck, I'd soon be fast asleep.

I was partway there when a faint, urgent thought pierced through the fog.

Help me. Find me.

Huh? Who the hell was that?

CHAPTER SIX

When I woke the next day, I felt really groggy. It was dark again, so I must have slept a long time. Better for healing, I guess. Something niggled at the edge of my brain, something I wanted to remember. It took a moment, but I recalled the voice I'd heard right before I drifted off to sleep. Was it real, or the product of a drugged mind?

I listened, but didn't hear anything now, not even Fang. I hadn't recognized the voice, and doubted anyone could send a thought from a distance into the head of someone they'd never met. Sheesh, I'd probably dreamed the weird incident. No more of those drugs for me.

Fang was nowhere around and the townhouse was quiet. I sat up and turned on the bedside light. Feeling a twinge of pain, I reminded myself to take it easy. I would have liked to stay and snuggle longer, but my bladder and stomach were both protesting.

I used the bathroom and showered, checking my wound. It was healing nicely. I still had some pain, but nowhere near yesterday's level. Gwen had left some bandages and instructions, so I was able to replace the dressing. Feeling better now that I was up and around, I wandered into the kitchen to find something to eat.

Shade was there, reading a book. It looked kind of weird given the general swirliness of his hands and face, but I was getting used to it.

Now that we were dating, should I kiss him each time I saw him? I wasn't sure about the protocol between boyfriend and girlfriend. On TV, they seemed to suck face all the time, but it didn't seem like people did that in real life. And with us, kissing could lead to other things left better unthought-of.

"Hey there," he said softly. "How do you feel?"

I hesitated but when he didn't make a move toward me, I wasn't sure if I should be offended or happy. Lola was disappointed, of course. But, like a two-year-old, she needed to learn that she didn't always get everything she wanted. Besides, she'd gotten pretty stoked at Alejandro's house and should be good for awhile. "Better, thanks. Where's Fang?"

"I brought Princess over, and they took off together out the

46

doggie door. He said he'd be back in time to go to work."

"Good." I opened the refrigerator and looked inside, hoping I'd find something I wouldn't have to cook.

"Gwen left you some lasagna," Shade said. "She wouldn't let anyone else touch it. Some garlic bread, too."

"She's a goddess," I said with relief. Too bad garlic didn't really deter vampires. I found the covered plate and put it in the microwave, careful not to stretch my injured side too much.

"You're not really going in to work for Alejandro today, are you?"

"Sure. Why wouldn't I?" Shade might be my boyfriend, but he didn't dictate what I could and couldn't do. I'd had enough of that from my mother to last me a lifetime.

"Oh, I don't know. Because you're stiff and still hurting, maybe?"

Shade, sarcastic? That was a new one. I turned to look at him to gauge his expression. It didn't do any good, of course. The swirls seemed more agitated, if that meant anything. "It's that accelerated healing of mine. I really do feel better. Besides, I'm not doing the Slayer thing tonight. Just going to look for the books."

"With Trevor Jackson?"

I didn't quite understand the tone of his voice. "Yes, and whoever else Alejandro sends along." The microwave beeped and I took the food out. Maybe he didn't trust Trevor either. "Did you meet him when he came to see Micah?"

As I joined him at the small round table, Shade said, "No, but I heard about him."

Again, the tone of his voice was sarcastic. Wanting to see his expression, I casually placed my hand on his arm. Because people rarely saw his face, Shade had never learned to hide his feelings. He was getting better at it with exposure to the Demon Underground, but it was still incredibly easy to read him. Right now, he looked hurt . . . and defensive.

Whoa. Was he jealous? He had absolutely no reason to be. I took a bite of Gwen's fabulous lasagna then said casually, "So you heard he really likes himself . . . and Rosa?"

I left my hand on his arm so I could gauge his emotions.

He looked surprised then frowned. "I heard he likes you, too."

"He flirts with everyone. He has a very high opinion of himself and thinks everyone else should, too."

Shade relaxed, moving his arm so his hand covered mine. "And do you?"

I shrugged. "He hasn't shown me anything yet but a nice exterior." I grinned. "But yours is prettier." I leaned over to kiss him. It seemed like the right time. More natural. Gee, maybe I'd get the hang of this dating thing soon after all. Lola's interest spiked, but I pulled away before she could do anything about it.

Shade grimaced but it wasn't because of the kiss. He stroked my arm possessively, like he wasn't even aware he was doing it. Kinda nice. "Guys aren't pretty," he protested.

"Devastatingly handsome then," I teased. When he twisted his lips in protest, I added, "Oh, come on, you have to know you're gorgeous. I'm glad you're a shadow demon so other girls don't see the real you. Otherwise, I'd have to beat them off with a stake." I took a bite and grinned at him, wondering how he'd respond.

He gave me a slow smile that had my blood sizzling and Lola wanting to play. He leaned forward and caressed my cheek. "I thought you loved me for my mind . . . and my ability to please Lola."

I swallowed and the lasagna went down hard. Oh, my. The "L" word. Love, not Lola. Had we really progressed that far . . . or was it just a figure of speech? Better assume the latter.

Trying to act casual, I speared another bite and waved my fork airily. "That, too," I said, trying to keep it light. But in reality, what I loved about Shade was his willingness to accept me totally as I was, without trying to change me. The eye candy was just a great bonus.

His expression softened, looking almost sappy. It was nice to see how much he cared about me, but embarrassing, too. I felt my face warm and didn't know how to react, where to look. Plus, I didn't want him to see how much I cared about him. That would just make it harder to stay away from him. So, I pretended to be really interested in the food for awhile.

I owed him the truth, though. I stared down at my plate, unwilling to raise my eyes yet. "Shade, I just want you to know that if I seem a little distant lately, it's not you."

"It's not?"

He sounded doubtful so I looked up and gazed into his fabulous blue eyes. "No. It's this whole . . . thing," I said, for lack of a better word. Or rather, lack of any words I wanted to use in front of him.

Luckily, he seemed to get what I was trying to say. "You mean making love?"

"Yeah, that thing." I avoided his gaze again.

His voice softened. "I told you I wouldn't push you. I understand what a huge deal it is for you, and we won't do anything unless you're absolutely ready."

That's how he felt now, but what if I put the decision off for months, even years? Would he be so understanding then? He was a guy, after all. A guy with needs that Lola stirred up every time we touched.

I was afraid to ask that question, so I said, "It's just that I want to make that decision myself, not lose control accidentally and be coerced into it by the demon inside me." Sheesh, this was getting intense. To lighten it up, I added, "You're just too tempting, you know?"

He laughed. "So are you. But don't worry, I totally get it. We'll tone it down a notch."

Relieved, I said, "Why don't you come along with us tonight . . . unless Micah has something else for you?" I didn't want him to think there was any reason to be jealous of Trevor, and meeting the keeper for himself should do that nicely.

Another smile spread across his face. "Sounds good. Micah let me off work to look after you as long as you're still not a hundred percent. I picked up your bike from Alejandro's."

That annoyed me a little—I could look after myself. But there was no use quibbling about it. I glanced at the clock. Wow—I'd slept for a long time. It was almost ten o'clock.

We watched television for awhile then took off when Fang and Princess came in. Though Shade had installed a sidecar on his Ducati for Princess, we didn't take her with us. Her bluntness and willingness to speak whatever she heard in someone's mind often made her a real pain in the butt and had caused problems in the past. She was just as willing to stay at my place and chill.

I didn't realize how painful the ride over would be. But every time I cornered or changed balance, my side screamed at me. Thankfully, the mansion wasn't too far away. Rosa answered the door this time and Trevor was waiting for us in Alejandro's Christmassy great room, chatting with Andrew. He was so crisp and fashionably put together that he looked radically out of place in Alejandro's old-world style home. Rosa excused herself, leaving only non-vamps in the room.

Trevor rose from the dark, heavy couch with a wide smile. "Please, introduce me to your friend," he said to me, not taking his eyes off Shade.

I did, and Trevor looked delighted when he shook Shade's hand and his features appeared. "You're a shadow demon?"

Shade nodded. "Yes. And you?"

SMOOTH, Fang said approvingly.

Yeah, the Demon Underground might consider it rude to ask about a person's demon origins, but Shade managed to make it sound natural.

"The keeper of the *Encyclopedia Magicka*," Trevor said, not letting go of Shade's hand.

Which didn't answer the question about what kind of demon he was, darn it.

"Are you joining us?" Trevor continued.

It didn't seem to bother Shade that the guy was still holding his hand and gazing into his face, especially since Trevor seemed so genuinely glad to meet him. "Yes, if you don't mind." He even smiled.

What was up with that? He met Trevor and suddenly all his jealousy vanished?

HE CAN SEE NOW THAT TREVOR IS NO THREAT TO HIM.

Humph. He could have taken my word for it . . . .

"I don't mind at all." Trevor turned to glance at Andrew, who seemed less sullen in Trevor's presence. "Andrew tells me that he doesn't remember where he hid the books, but I thought we could retrace his steps, see if I can sense them."

"Works for me," I agreed, wondering why if the reason he still hadn't let go of Shade's hand was because the swirls made him uncomfortable.

I DON'T KNOW, Fang said. MAYBE THE DUDE SWINGS BOTH WAYS.

I hadn't even thought about that. Or maybe his kind of demon learned more about people by shaking their hand? Naw, a bit far-fetched.

Rosa returned with a set of keys. Handing them to me, she said, "Alejandro is loaning you one of his cars tonight, to make it easier to search. Please, do not damage it. The cars are his pride and joy."

I appreciated the offer. It would be possible to search together on our motorcycles, but difficult. Besides, I didn't want either Trevor or Andrew riding behind me on my bike, with their arms around me. The thought made me squirm, and not in a good way. And I really wanted to give my injury a break. "I'll try not to," I said. Best not to make promises when I never knew what we'd encounter. "Thanks."

I'M SURE ALEJANDRO HAS INSURANCE, Fang said with a doggie grin. YOU MIGHT NEED IT.

Gee, thanks for the vote of confidence.

Andrew got into the front with me so he could give directions, and Shade and Trevor rode in the back, Fang riding on Shade's lap so the shadow demon would look normal to anyone we passed.

"So, where do we start?" I asked, fumbling with the unfamiliar controls.

Andrew shrugged. "The last place I remember having the books was at Mood's house." He turned around to speak to Trevor. "She locked me in her basement because I was planning on burning down the mansion, but I broke out."

"Okay, let's start there," I said.

Andrew gave me the address and I drove toward the west side of town, near Lackland Air Force Base, following his directions. Trevor and Shade were chatting in the back seat, having a good old time. "Uh, Trevor, the books may be hidden anywhere along this route. Shouldn't you pay attention?"

"No need," he said airily. "I'll feel them if I get within five hundred feet, no matter how much I'm enjoying myself."

And he continued to enjoy himself while I played chauffer. By the time we reached Mood's house, he'd learned more about Shade than I'd ever thought to ask, like the fact that his parents were both dead, Micah's father had taken him in as a kid, and his favorite hobbies were learning about demonkind and competing in online games against other players. It annoyed me that I felt embarrassed for not knowing these things.

"Okay, we're here," I said, sounding more snappish than I'd intended as I turned off the engine. "Now what?"

Trevor shook his head. "They're not here."

"Can you tell that they've been here?" Shade asked. "Can you track them?"

"I'm afraid it doesn't work that way." Trevor tapped Andrew on the shoulder. "What do you remember after leaving here that night?"

Andrew thought for a moment. "I remember the books encouraging me to use my powers to get back at the vampires, so I was all about burning their house down. But the books were afraid they'd burn, too, so they told me to hide them." He paused, then added slowly, "That's the last time I remember seeing them."

HE'S TELLING THE TRUTH, Fang confirmed.

"Think harder," Trevor urged. "What do you remember immediately after you left here? Do you remember arriving at the mansion? What direction did you come from?"

Andrew shook his head. "I'm sorry, but all I remember is the books badgering me to hide, hide, hide. I've been trying to remember for days, but all I recall is leaving here to find a hiding place. Then the next thing I knew, I was splashing gasoline on the side of the house, more powerful and more pissed off than I've ever been in my life."

Trevor clenched his fists on his thighs and persisted. "Do you have any idea how much time passed between the two memories?"

Again, Andrew paused. "I'm not sure 'cause Mood used her mojo on me to make me stupid happy. It was about noon when she put me in the basement. She put me to sleep and took away my cell so I don't know what time it was when I woke up." He shook his head. "I don't know how long I slept. All I know is that it was still daylight when I left."

"Andrew arrived at the mansion right before the sun went down," I added. "So he could have had plenty of time to hide them anywhere inside or outside the city."

"I was afraid of that," Trevor muttered. He sighed. "I didn't get very far trying to find them yesterday. I guess we'll just have to start at the center and spiral out from there."

That sounded really tedious. "I know San Antonio looks like it's circular on the map, but that's gonna be more difficult than it sounds."

"It's worth a shot," Shade said.

Yeah, fine for him. He was having a fun time with his buddy in the back while I had to drive. But I wasn't planning on going anywhere until I got some answers. I twisted around in my seat to look at Trevor. Pain stabbed through me. Damn, I'd forgotten about my wound. This being more human stuff wasn't such a good idea. "Maybe if you told us more about the books, it would help us figure out where to look."

He grimaced. "I doubt it."

"Makes sense to me," Shade said.

Now that Shade had suggested it, Trevor was all over it. He shrugged and said, "The encyclopedia was created a long time ago—I don't know when—by a group of demons who wanted their part-human descendants to understand their heritage. Unfortunately, it's patchy in spots. Partially because they assumed people would know more than they do, and partially because some demons were more reluctant to put their strengths and vulnerabilities down in writing than others."

So that's why the succubus and incubus entries were so incomplete, Fang said.

Yeah, I'd wondered about that. "That explains the first volume," I said, "but what about the rest? The two with the dark magicks?"

I sensed Trevor really didn't want to answer me but he finally said, "They were both created by one particular kind of demon who wanted to pass his magickal knowledge on to his descendants."

"What kind of demon?" I persisted.

Trevor paused, and Shade snapped his fingers. "The two books are about magickal spells, right? Was it a mage demon?"

Trevor looked annoyed, so I guess Shade hit it on the head. "What's a mage demon?" I asked.

"One of the most dangerous demons to enter our world," Shade explained. "They can tap into emotions and use them to power magickal spells . . . and most of them are pretty evil. Those are the dark magicks people sensed." He turned to Trevor. "Right?"

"For the most part," Trevor conceded. "But the demon's descendants can't create new spells—only full-blooded mage demons are able to do that. Their descendants are only able to use the ones set down in the books."

"Whoa," I said. "That's a dangerous thing to leave lying around."

Trevor nodded. "Exactly. When the Demon Underground was formed and they tried to keep demonkind on the down low, some of the demons became keepers—the ones who could sense the dark magick and keep it contained."

"Why didn't they just destroy the books?" I asked.

"Let's just say that destroying them would release dark magicks in an explosion far more catastrophic than any nuclear warhead. At worst, it would destroy this world. At best, it could severely warp our reality."

Fang laid his head down with a sigh. LET'S NOT DO THAT, THEN.

Andrew looked horrified at the thought that he'd had these things in his possession.

"So why not just let them stay hidden?" I suggested.

"Because keepers aren't the only ones who can sense the magicks in the books," Trevor said.

Shade petted Fang absently. "I imagine the mage demons can, too." At Trevor's nod, Shade asked, "Are there any in San Antonio?"

Trevor shrugged. "It's the same as with the books. I can sense one if I come within five hundred feet, but otherwise, I have no idea unless they use some of the dark magicks. But they probably sensed the books waking at the same time I did. There may be some of them searching here as well."

Oh, crap. Better find them fast, then. Driving in spirals it was. I started the car and headed toward the center of the city, while Trevor pulled up a map on his Smartphone.

"Your knowledge of mage demons is impressive," Trevor told Shade.

"As I said before, it's a hobby. I've been trying to learn as much about demons as I can."

Yeah, with his ability to bring them through from the other side, I guess he wanted to know what he was dealing with.

"How did you become a keeper?" Shade asked.

"My father was a keeper before me. He taught me everything I know."

"I thought you said your father lost them," I said, wanting to taunt him a bit.

"Not exactly."

I turned onto US 90. "What do you mean, not exactly?" I distinctly remembered that's what he said.

"Actually, it's my father who's lost."

Crap. Now I felt guilty for trying to poke at him. "I'm sorry. What happened to him?"

"The books happened to him," Trevor said bitterly. "They ate him."

CHAPTER SEVEN

I glanced at Trevor in the rear view mirror. "They what? They *ate* him? How is that possible?"

"Not literally. He's trapped inside them."

"How can he *fit?*" Andrew asked in bewilderment.

"It's magick," Trevor said in an irritated tone. "He's stuck in some kind of . . . pocket universe or something."

I had this strange image of the books hoovering up Trevor's father like a swish of smoke, like in *I Dream of Jeannie*.

WOW, THOSE BOOKS MUST REALLY SUCK, Fang snarked.

I stifled a laugh. It really wasn't funny. "Are you sure about that?" I asked. "I mean, do you know for certain he's still alive?"

"Yes. I-I know he's still in there."

"How did it happen?" Shade asked.

Trevor looked out into the night, hiding his expression from everyone, so I turned my attention back to the road.

"If you don't want to talk about it, that's okay," Shade said.

Like hell. I pulled over into an empty parking lot under a light and parked so I could make my point. Turning around to glare at them, I said, "No, it's not okay. If those things are likely to eat someone else, we need to know about it right now."

"They won't," Trevor bit out. He got out of the car and slammed the door, running his hand through his gelled hair as he turned his back on us.

I grabbed the keys to keep Andrew from doing anything stupid and followed him. "How do you know that?"

He whirled around. "I just do, okay?"

"Not good enough. Those books are loose in San Antonio somewhere, and we need to know as much as we can so we can figure out what to do when we find them."

Shade and Fang had jumped out of the car as well, though Andrew chose to stay out of the fray. Shade drew his hoodie up over his face then made calming motions with his hands. "We're all friends here, right?"

How could I be friends with someone I didn't trust?

Trevor glanced at Shade then took a deep breath and breathed it out before saying, "That's why we're out here, together, to find them. And when we do, I know how to handle them."

I crossed my arms, and tried to sound reasonable. "If your father couldn't handle them, why do you think you can?"

He glared at me but didn't let his pissiness show in his carefully deliberate voice. "Because I've had more training than he had. I did a lot of research to figure out exactly what happened. I know what he did wrong and I won't make the same mistake."

"What did he do wrong?"

He looked about ready to explode, but kept it together. "It's confidential—for keepers only."

"What if someone else does the same thing 'by mistake' and gets sucked up into the book as well? Shouldn't we try to keep that from happening?"

He waved that argument away impatiently. "It's something only a keeper would attempt."

"Then what *can* you tell us?"

Trevor paused for a moment. "Look, knowledge is passed from one keeper to another, teacher to apprentice. It's too risky to write it down, too dangerous to share. Don't you get it? These books are *not safe.*"

I shrugged. "They were safe with me for many years."

"Until you gave them up. Now that you know what they can do, they won't be safe with you anymore either. Only with keepers."

"So, why isn't *your* apprentice here?" If these things were that dangerous, he really ought to train someone else how to handle them, too.

"I don't have one. Yet. I was waiting until I found the books before I chose one." He paused, then added, "In case you're wondering, you wouldn't qualify."

"I wasn't." Like I'd *want* to work with him. "But what I *was* wondering is how you got training when your father, the former keeper, got sucked into the book. You had to be like an infant when that happened."

He shrugged. "I'm older than I look. And my father's mentor was still alive—he helped me a lot."

There were still a lot of unanswered questions. "What happened to the books after your father got sucked in?" I asked. "How did you lose them?"

"I didn't lose them—I was only a kid at the time. The Underground in LA took them. They told me someone was careless and they were stolen."

BOY, HE HAS AN ANSWER FOR EVERYTHING, DOESN'T HE? Fang said.

Yeah, he was a bit too glib for my tastes. Maybe that's because it was all true?

Then again . . . maybe not.

I SURE WISH I COULD READ HIS MIND RIGHT NOW, Fang said.

Ditto.

"Do you know how to release your father once you find the books?" Shade asked.

Trevor smiled at him, seeming relieved for a question he was willing to answer. "Yes, I do. And I have everything I need to do just that."

The way these two got along set my teeth on edge. "What if something happens to you?" I persisted. "What if you die before the books are found?"

Trevor smirked. "You'll just have to make sure that doesn't happen, won't you?"

I wasn't about to play bodyguard to some idiot demon with delusions of grandeur. Unfortunately, my brain didn't catch up with my mouth in time to stop me from saying, "The hell I will. How do we know you're not lying?"

Shade tried to step in. "Val, really—"

"That's it," Trevor said, throwing his hands up in the air. "I'm not gonna take this crap from a baby succubus who can't even cut it in the real world." He looked me up and down. "I have no idea what anyone sees in you."

Fang growled and the hairs along his spine stood up on end. WATCH IT, BUDDY.

The so-called keeper turned and walked off. "I'll find the encyclopedia by myself," he tossed over his shoulder.

"Aren't you going to stop him?" Shade asked.

"No, why should I? He can take care of himself. He's the *keeper*, you know."

"Val, really. You're sounding childish now."

"I'm *what?*"

Ignoring my indignation, Shade added, "He doesn't know the city. He could get lost."

"Not with that Smartphone of his."

"He's on foot, without a car, and this isn't exactly the best neighborhood."

I folded my arms and tapped my foot. "So? He can call a taxi or rent a car. And if he can handle dark magicks, surely he can handle a mugger or two."

What was wrong with everyone? Had Trevor enthralled everyone but me into believing he was the best thing since submachine guns?

Fang scratched his ear with his hind leg. NOPE. NO SIGN OF THAT IN SHADE OR ANDREW. I WOULD HAVE NOTICED.

Then what has them so snowed?

IT'S CHARM, BABE. CHARM. YOU MIGHT WANT TO GET SOME OF IT.

"What's gotten into you?" Shade asked incredulously. "You really seem to have it in for this guy."

"I don't believe him, that's what. Ask Fang. He'll tell you—he doesn't believe Trevor either."

Fang backed off. OH, NO. I'M NOT GETTING INVOLVED IN THIS. YOU TWO DUKE IT OUT AAAAAALL BY YOURSELVES. He trotted back to the car to join Andrew who had scrunched down in his seat, both apparently trying to stay out of the line of fire.

"Why don't you believe Trevor?" Shade persisted.

"He's just too good to be true. I don't trust him."

Shade paced in a circle, and I could read tension in his body and in the agitated whirling of his face. "That's ridiculous. He's just trying to find his father and save the world. What's wrong with that?"

"Nothing. If it's true."

"And what do you base your suspicion on?"

"My gut," I shot back. "It's helped me survive quite a few vampire attacks. What do you base your *trust* on?"

He halted suddenly and turned his swirly hooded face toward me. He let out an incredulous laugh and came over to grasp my hands. "Is that it? Are you *jealous* of him?" He looked stupidly delighted by the thought.

"Don't be ridiculous. I know you like what Lola does for you too much to give it up for some pretty guy."

WHOA, BABE, Fang said from the car, to me alone. THAT'S HARSH. YOU MIGHT WANT TO DIAL BACK THE TONE A BIT.

I thought you were staying out of this? I snapped at him.

OKAY. THIS IS ME STAYING OUT. DIG YOUR OWN GRAVE.

Shade looked hurt, then let go of me so I couldn't see his features anymore. "I didn't mean jealous of *me*," he said slowly. "I meant jealous of Trevor."

"What the hell does that mean?"

Shade stuck his hands in his pockets and his shoulders went up and down in a shrug. "You know . . . he's good-looking, he makes friends easily with all of *your* friends, *and* he's the only one who can save the world. That's usually your job, isn't it?"

That was so unfair I didn't know what to say. What made it worse is that he said it in such a matter-of-fact way. Was it true? I spluttered for a moment, then demanded, "Do you really believe that?"

"Can you honestly say it's not true?" he asked softly.

Oh, no. He was *not* going to try to use calm reason on me to get me to agree with him. "Yes, I can. I don't trust him because . . . because . . . " My thoughts were whirling too fast to make sense of them. "I just don't, that's why."

"Maybe if you thought about it for a moment—"

"No." I held up a hand. "I am *not* talking about this anymore. We're going to go back to the mansion and we're going to start over, okay?"

"Okay, but I'll drive. You're too upset."

And that ticked me off even more. "Fine," I yelled and threw the keys at him. "You drive and go get your new friend. I'm walking."

I turned on my heel and proceeded to do just that.

"C'mon, Val . . . " Shade protested.

I ignored him, too mad to even talk to him right now. Instead, I put my head down and quickened my stride. I needed to walk this off.

He started the car and pulled out of the parking lot—away from me. Figured. Perversely, it ticked me off that he didn't even try to ask me to stop.

BECAUSE I TOLD HIM NOT TO, Fang said.

I glanced down. I'd been stomping so hard in my boots that I hadn't even heard the clicking of his nails as he caught up to me. "That's no excuse," I muttered, and hated the fact that tears choked my throat and threatened to spill from my eyes.

WHAT'S WRONG?

Damn it, we just had our first fight.

AND IT PROBABLY WON'T BE THE LAST, Fang added wisely. DON'T WORRY, HE STILL LOVES YOU.

I sniffled. *You sure?*

I'M SURE. AND MAYBE IT'S FOR THE BEST AFTER ALL.

How do you figure?

WELL, YOU WANTED TO STAY AWAY FROM HIM FOR AWHILE. HERE'S YOUR EXCUSE.

Maybe. But I hadn't wanted it to be like this . . . . My shoulders sagged and all of the mad went out of me. Dang. Now I was going to have to walk home.

CHAPTER EIGHT

I glanced around, trying to get my bearings. Where was I? Somewhere on the west side of San Antonio, far from anywhere I wanted to be. Not exactly the best neighborhood. Creepy, in fact. I looked down at my feet. Dang. These boots weren't made for walking, either. And my side was still too sore to be doing much hiking. Losing my temper . . . not the brightest thing to do.

Fang clicked along beside me. YOU WON'T HEAR ANY ARGUMENT FROM ME.

I glanced down at him. "Say something helpful," I challenged him. HOW ABOUT CALLING FOR A RIDE?

I doubted Alejandro would be very happy with me if I asked someone to pick me up after I'd already given away the keys to one of his cars.

THEN CALL MICAH OR THE SCU.

I was kind of on vacation from the SCU, and many of them still saw me as a monster. I didn't even know if they'd come. Maybe Dan would, but he might ask questions I really didn't want to answer. Telling an ex about an argument I had with my current boyfriend just seemed . . . wrong.

I glanced at my phone. Almost two in the morning. Micah would still be at the club. I called his office at Club Purgatory and his assistant Tessa answered.

"This is Val. Is Micah there?"

"Sorry, he's on stage for his last set right now. Can I have him call you?"

I squirmed. Seeing Micah dance on stage for women made me uncomfortable. That's how he fed his incubus lust demon—by drawing small bits of energy from the women he seduced every night in his dance. I understood it, but watching it made me feel like a voyeur since I was the only woman not affected by his act. And, obviously, even thinking about it made me squirmy. "Uh, maybe you can help me," I told Tessa. "I'm stuck on foot out at Wolff Stadium. Is there someone who could come out and pick up Fang and me?"

"Sure. The club is about to close and it's pretty quiet here tonight, so I'll send Ludwig."

"Great," I said with relief. The water demon, who also worked as a bouncer at the club, didn't talk much. "Thanks—I appreciate it."

"No problem. Where exactly will you be?"

I gave her instructions on where to find us in the stadium parking lot, then sat down under a light pole to wait. Fang flopped down beside me and closed his eyes. WAKE ME WHEN HE GETS HERE.

It was pretty dead here at this time of morning. Not even the undead or the gangs were hanging around to disturb the peace. Just as well—I wasn't in the mood to mix it up right now. Instead, I wanted to figure out what had happened tonight. Why did Shade trust Trevor when I didn't?

I thought back to our encounters. What had Trevor done to make me suspicious? The fact he didn't let us know what kind of demon he was? No, not really. A lot of demons in the Underground preferred to keep their powers secret, and I didn't suspect them of anything nefarious.

Maybe because Trevor was so arrogant about being a keeper? No, that didn't make sense either. Being arrogant made me annoyed at him, not suspicious. Then what?

Was Shade right? Was I jealous of Trevor? He had oodles of charm, made friends easily, totally won over Shade without hardly trying, and even I had to admit the guy was totally hot.

A good reason to hate anyone.

Okay, maybe I was a tad jealous. Maybe I *wanted* to find something wrong with him. And maybe I was annoyed by his confidence. He thought he could just take the books like they really belonged to him, without anyone telling him no.

Was that it? I should probably give him the benefit of the doubt. Stop getting in his face and cooperate more. Assume he was innocent until proven guilty.

Yeah, a dark part of me agreed. Give him enough rope to hang himself.

Okay, even discounting possible jealousy on my part, I still didn't trust him. But I didn't know why. Maybe something I'd seen and noted unconsciously?

I sighed. If I didn't want to look like a jealous fool—and who would?—I needed to pretend to believe him, especially around Shade. I spent the rest of the waiting time musing on how to go about faking my cooperation.

It didn't take long for Ludwig to show up in Micah's car. As he drove us back to the club, I decided to concentrate on learning more about Trevor, without alerting the guy that I was still suspicious.

The club had just closed, so it was a lot quieter than usual. Fang and I made our way to Micah's office, decorated simply yet elegantly in burgundy and silver for the holidays, and found him and Tessa there. He'd already showered and changed after his act, so thank heavens I didn't have *that* embarrassment. They were counting the night's receipts when I came in, so I sat down and waited until they were done.

"What's up?" Micah asked. "How did you get stranded? Did your bike conk out on you?"

"No. I—" Too humiliating to go into details. I shrugged. "It's not important." Changing the subject before he could say more, I asked, "How do you know Trevor Jackson is who he says he is?"

Micah glanced at his elfin-looking assistant. "Tessa confirmed his credentials."

"Not exactly," Tessa said. "I tried to call the Los Angeles Underground, but no one was there. It is headquartered in an acting studio, so it's usually closed for the holidays. But Trevor had information about the Los Angeles Underground, knew Micah was the leader here, and knew about the books. I figured he had to be one of us."

Micah asked, "Do you have reason to think he might not be, Val?"

"Not really. But do you know what kind of demon he is? Fang can't read him, and I don't think that's ever happened with a demon before."

NEVER, Fang confirmed.

Micah looked thoughtful. "No, I don't. But since you had the *Encyclopedia Magicka* for so many years, a lot of knowledge has been lost." When I grimaced, he added quickly, "I'm not blaming you—you didn't know what your father had given you. I simply mean we don't have enough information to make an assessment."

I glanced at Tessa. "I don't suppose you got a read on him?" If the soothsayer demon had a prophecy, that might tell us something.

She shook her head. "Afraid not. Touching him didn't awaken my gift."

Oh, yeah, that reminded me. "But touching Alejandro did. Why did you tell him that I was his only hope for getting accepted when he has his coming-out party?"

She raised her eyebrows. "I didn't know I did. You know I can't control my prophecies . . . or remember them."

"I know." It just irritated me that her prediction had bound me to the vamp for a while.

Fang poked me in the leg. FOCUS, VAL. YOU WERE ASKING ABOUT TREVOR.

Oh, yeah.

But Micah remembered. "Why do you think Trevor isn't who he says he is?"

"Just a gut feeling. He's too polished, too slick. I don't trust him. And have you ever even heard of a keeper before?"

"No, but that doesn't mean one doesn't exist." Micah thought for a moment. "How would he know about the books if he wasn't?"

Oh yeah, I forgot Micah didn't know what I'd learned. "He says his father was trapped inside them by a mage demon." When Tessa exclaimed in surprise, I quickly explained what I'd found out that evening.

"That does make it sound as if he knows what he's talking about," Micah said gently. "I've never even heard of a mage demon before."

"Maybe." I was still doubtful.

"I could try to contact the Los Angeles Underground again," Tessa offered. "Maybe if I leave a message about how important this is, someone will call back."

"A good idea," Micah said. "I trust Val's gut more than most people's."

That gave me a warm and fuzzy feeling. Now I remembered why I liked the folks in the Demon Underground so much—they appreciated the things that made me different from the rest of the world, the things that made me Val Shapiro.

LIKE THE FACT THAT YOU HAVE THE WORLD'S BEST HELLHOUND AT YOUR SIDE, Fang added.

Yep, like that, I agreed, scratching his ears.

"Since he's visiting, I've invited Trevor to the Underground's Christmas party tomorrow night," Micah said. "Maybe we can learn more about him there."

Christmas party?

Fang snorted. SHE FORGOT.

Oh, yeah, I vaguely remembered something about a party . . . just not when and where it was happening. Parties, with all those people, made me uncomfortable. "I only forgot for a moment," I said defensively. "But don't worry, I'll be there. And that's a good idea, Micah. He might talk more to you."

"Do you really believe he wants the books because his father is trapped in them?" Tessa asked.

I shrugged. "I don't know. Probably. But he admits he's never actually been a keeper, so I'm not sure why he thinks he'll be able to control the books if his father couldn't." I thought for a moment. "And I don't buy his explanation of why they never tried to control me." I glanced at Tessa. "You held them for awhile, right? What did you feel?"

Tessa shrugged. "I didn't have them for very long—only long enough to bring them from the bar to this office. I do remember sensing the dark magicks. They didn't try to control me, though. Maybe I didn't have them long enough."

"I never felt anything like that. Maybe I'm not sensitive enough?" I was grasping for any explanation.

"I doubt it," Micah said. "More likely it was because they'd been with you for so long."

"Maybe." I thought for a moment. "Trevor said he could sense the books if he got within five hundred feet of them. Tessa, do you think you could sense them if you got that close, since you know what they feel like?"

The soothsayer demon shook her head. "No, I only felt them while holding them. But you had them for what? Thirteen years? Maybe you could sense them."

"I doubt it. I don't remember ever noticing that before."

"Are you sure?" Micah asked. "Have you tried?"

Fang broadcast his thoughts to the room. IT'S WORTH A SHOT, BABE. I KINDA REMEMBER FEELING LIKE YOU HAD A SMALL PIECE OF YOURSELF MISSING WHEN YOU GAVE UP THE BOOKS.

I stared at him in surprise. "Really? Why didn't you say something?"

AT THE TIME, I THOUGHT IT WAS BECAUSE YOU AND DAN BROKE UP. NOW, I'M WONDERING IF IT WAS THE BOOKS.

"It might be," Tessa said eagerly. "Why don't you see if you can sense them—find them before he does?"

Micah nodded. "I would like to have a look at them before Trevor claims them as their keeper. You might even have a wider range than he does."

I spread my hands, feeling inadequate. "I don't even know where to start."

MAYBE THAT CANDLE THING, Fang suggested.

Candle thing? Oh yeah, Micah had taught me to go to a still inner place by staring at a candle. He'd done it to help me learn to control Lola, but maybe it would work for this, too. "Okay, I'll try it." It wouldn't hurt. Besides, this way, I'd have a good reason to tell Alejandro why I wasn't accompanying Trevor on his search. Otherwise, the vamp leader might not be too happy with me.

He wasn't. Especially when Micah returned me to the mansion, and I arrived without the car and without Trevor. Alejandro sat in his throne-like chair behind the massive desk in his study and regarded me with his eyes narrowed and his mouth set in a grim line. Hmm . . . maybe if I pissed him off enough, he'd fire me.

DON'T PUSH IT, BABE, Fang advised.

Unfortunately, Fang was right. Alejandro might still be one of the "good" vamps, but that didn't mean he couldn't lose his temper. I hadn't seen that yet and wasn't sure I wanted to.

"There are times when I forget how young you are, Slayer," he said with a frown.

At his age, I probably did seem incredibly young. I wasn't sure exactly how old he was, but from a few things he or the others had let slip, I believed he'd arrived in the Americas almost five hundred years ago with the Spanish conquistadors. But, just as you didn't ask a member of the Underground what kind of demon they were, you didn't ask a vamp how old he was.

"What does my age have to do with it?" I wanted to add, "oh ancient one" but thought better of it.

WHAT DO YOU KNOW? Fang snarked. YOU ARE DEVELOPING SOME MATURITY AFTER ALL.

I ignored him. They were probably both jealous of my youth. Not that I had any idea how old Fang was, either.

AND YOU NEVER WILL.

A bit touchy about our age, are we?

Alejandro interrupted our private chat. "With youth comes impetuosity," the vampire said wearily. "Age and wisdom grants the ability to think something through before jumping headlong into an ill-considered action."

"I gave Shade the car keys," I said defensively. "And Trevor will be just fine, I'm sure." Before he could chastise me further, I added, "Besides, after talking with Micah, I realized I might be able to find the books myself." I explained why.

Alejandro thought for a moment, rubbing the head of the small bronze bust on his desk. From the shininess of Cortes' dome, it looked like the vamp leader did this a lot. "I would like to see you recover the books before Mr. Jackson does," he said. "But what if he finds them first and you aren't present? I have no confidence he will share this information with us."

I shrugged. "You could continue to have Shade escort him. Or Rosa. Trevor needs someone who knows the city and he likes the two of them."

"Perhaps. Then again, perhaps it would be better if all of you accompanied him."

I suppressed a grimace. That didn't sound fun. "Wouldn't you rather have me help with fighting the unaffiliated vamps? I hear that's not going so well for you." One of the vamps had let it slip when I arrived.

Alejandro shook his head. "We have it under control. I believe you would be best utilized in finding the books. For the rest of the night, why don't you put some effort into locating my vehicle and Mr. Jackson, then attempt to see what you can do on your own in finding the books?"

I was on his payroll until dawn, so I nodded and left to find some privacy. The dining room was the best bet, since they rarely used it. I sighed. I wasn't quite ready to call Shade just yet, not so soon after our argument. I could text him, but if he was driving, that could be dangerous. I'd text Andrew instead.

Fang snorted. COWARD.

I ignored him and sent a note to Andrew, asking where they were and if they were returning the car. He texted back right away, letting me know that they were returning to the mansion. They planned on being back before dawn and had talked to Trevor who intended to return to the mansion the next day.

Well, Alejandro would be happy. But I really didn't want to see Shade again this evening, so I gave Alejandro an update and headed home, telling him I was going to try to find the books on my own.

The townhouse was quiet, so Gwen must either be asleep or working. I could never keep track of her crazy hours at the ER. But wherever she was, she'd been busy. The living room now looked as though Santa's workshop had exploded in it. Okay, slight exaggeration, but apparently Gwen really liked Christmas. With my father being Jewish, my mother raised Catholic, and her tending toward New Age spiritualism when I was growing up, I was pretty open to whatever kind of celebration people wanted to make this time of the year.

Fang headed out the doggie door to get a little alone time, and I set up a candle on my nightstand. I lit it, then relaxed and stared into the flame. Finding that calm, centered place inside myself was easier now, but I usually just stayed there, enjoying the freedom from Lola's needs and resting and rejuvenating myself. Today, however, I planned to look for something specific.

I hesitated, unsure how to go about it. First, I pictured the books and tried to put them in different settings in my mind, hoping something would click. Total failure.

Next, I thought about sending out one of Lola's tendrils to find the man trapped in the books. But since this place inside me was free of Lola, that wouldn't work. I tried and failed at several other approaches, then gave up for the night.

However, I wasn't willing to give up on this lovely feeling, this wonderfully quiet, serene place. I let myself drift and just be, with no worries, no quests, no squabbles.

There, deep inside myself, someone abruptly spoke to me. *Find me!*

CHAPTER NINE

I jerked out of my trance. Whoa. There *he* was again. Who was it?

Quickly, I tried to re-enter my trance, find that thread of thought and follow it to its owner, but it was no use. My mind whirled with so many questions that I couldn't get back to that still, quiet place.

Finally, I gave up, but the speculations wouldn't stop. It was difficult to analyze with only two words, but this time the voice had definitely sounded male . . . and stressed out. Let me think . . . I'd been trying to find the books. Could it be them, reaching back to me? It didn't seem possible that books could talk, but Josh and Andrew had claimed they did. Then again, these books contained some kind of dark magick and were supposedly written by a mage demon. Who knew what all they could do?

Or maybe the voice was Trevor's father, still trapped within them. That made more sense than talking books. But if it was him, what did it mean that he was reaching out to me? Why not directly to his son? Well, maybe Trevor couldn't hear them, because of his shield. But how could he sense the books through that shield if he did come close to them? And if Trevor's father was talking to me, why would he urge Josh and Andrew to do evil then reach out to me to save him?

None of it made any sense. Maybe the voice was someone else entirely, unassociated with the books. But whoever it was, they had to know me to reach out to me. So far as I knew, all my friends and family were accounted for—no one was missing. Who else knew me well enough to contact me deep within my inner self?

I thought for a moment. The first time the voice had reached me, I'd been pretty drugged up. The second, in kind of a Zen state. That was probably the only way he could contact me.

Shoot, there were so many unanswered questions, it made my head hurt. I'd try again tomorrow. For now, it was time to sleep.

When I woke around noon the next day, Fang was cuddled up next to me. I petted him for a moment, trying to figure out what to do with my day. According to Micah, the Underground's Christmas party was today. What time?

Fang yawned. THE INVITE IS ON YOUR DRESSER.

Oh, yeah. I'd skimmed it, then tossed it there and forgot about it. I read it now. Six o'clock tonight at the club, and I was supposed to bring a wrapped ornament to exchange. What was that for?

IT'S FOR FUN, VAL, Fang said, peering out of the bedcovers at me. EVER HEARD OF IT?

Ignoring his caustic comment, I asked, "What should I get?"

USUALLY THE ONES THAT ARE REALLY ORNATE OR REALLY FUNNY DO BEST.

"Okay, I guess I'm going to the mall then."

Fang jumped down from the bed. IT'S ABOUT TIME. YOU HAVEN'T BOUGHT ANYTHING FOR YOUR FAMILY AND FRIENDS YET.

Crap. He was right. I really needed to do some serious shopping.

DON'T FORGET YOUR FAITHFUL HELLHOUND. SOME NICE MEATY BONES WOULD BE GOOD. OR A PORTERHOUSE STEAK.

I laughed. "And what are you planning to give me?"

He bowed to me, one fuzzy leg stretched forward. MY UNDYING DEVOTION.

He even managed to say that with an earnest expression. I grinned.

The bow turned into an opportunity to scratch his ear. C'MON, BABE. HOW COULD I GET YOU SOMETHING? NO MONEY, NO POCKETS, NOT ALLOWED IN STORES . . .

"I know. I was just yanking your chain."

WELL, YOU CAN STOP NOW AND OPEN THE DOOR, OH SHE OF THE OPPOSABLE THUMBS.

I let him out, then showered and dressed. Fang stayed home while I went to Rivercenter Mall. It wasn't the closest, but since I'd been there with Gwen before, I was a little familiar with the layout. Besides, it was at my favorite place—the River Walk. Even though it was a weekday, the place seemed packed with Christmas shoppers.

I got most of my shopping done and found an ornament I really liked—a gingerbread man that said "Bite Me." It amused me, anyway.

I went home and dumped the gifts on my bed, then found Fang watching television on the couch. He might not have thumbs, but he was a wizard at using his claws on the remote control. He liked to watch Cesar Millan, the dog whisperer, especially the part where Cesar trained the humans to do what their dogs needed.

I rubbed his fuzzy little head. "Let me wrap this and we can go to the party."

Fang turned off the television and jumped down from the couch. YOU'RE NOT GOING LIKE THAT, ARE YOU?

I glanced down at my clothes. It was what I wore every day—jeans, a long-sleeved T-shirt, and a vest over it to hide the stakes. "What's wrong with what I'm wearing?"

IT'S A PARTY, VAL. DRESS UP A BIT. I grimaced and Fang added, YOU DON'T WANT TREVOR TO SHOW YOU UP, DO YOU?

Now that was a low blow. Trevor would show me up no matter what I wore. I sighed. "Okay, what should I wear?"

Fang fancied himself a fashion connoisseur, and the worst part about it was that he was far better at choosing clothes than me. He nosed through my closet and chose an outfit Mom had bought me last year for Christmas—black slacks, a satiny white blouse, and a black vest with white and red embroidered flowers. I'd never worn it because I hadn't had an occasion—it was too dressy to wear hunting vamps.

IT COULD BE WORSE, Fang reminded me. IT COULD BE A DRESS.

Good point. Not that I owned one—they didn't ride well on a motorcycle.

I wrapped the ornament, then futzed with my make-up and hair in the way Gwen had showed me. It didn't look as good as when she did it for me, but at least it looked like I'd made an effort. I even tied a festive red bow around Fang's neck. Surprisingly, he didn't object.

As we drove to the club on my bike, I reminded myself that I needed to get on Trevor's good side, so I probably needed to apologize. To Shade, too.

Tessa and Micah had done their best to transform the club into a festive Christmas atmosphere with lots of twinkling lights and bright decorations, despite the dark walls and club lighting. I was about a half hour late, so the party was already in full swing, with liquor flowing freely and people laughing and dancing. Tessa hovered near the door, greeting guests. I drew her aside. "Learn anything about Trevor yet?"

She shook her head. "Not yet. The LA Underground hasn't gotten back to me." She made a shooing motion. "Go. Mingle. Enjoy yourself. You can put your ornament under the tree."

Mingling. Great. I glanced around and saw I actually knew more people than I had at the previous party, but most of them were in the same cluster as Shade . . . all but Josh and Andrew, of course, who were still being punished. Trevor was holding court among them, and since I wasn't quite ready to join them, I put the ornament under the tree with the rest of the small packages and looked around for the food.

We hadn't eaten, and Fang insisted he was starved. I filled a plate for each of us and took it to a corner where we could eat in peace. Micah had catered the dinner—turkey, roast beef, and ham with all the fixings. Delicious. I was leaning down to wipe some gravy off Fang's fuzzy beard when someone stopped in front of me.

I looked up. Shade.

All of a sudden, the food I'd just eaten started whirling as fast as the swirls on his face. Gee, I really wished I could see his expression, get a clue as to what he was thinking and feeling. I stood, figuring that whatever he'd sought me out to say, I needed to be on my feet.

I'LL JUST LEAVE YOU TWO ALONE, Fang said, and trotted off to join the rest of the party.

Shade stood there, all swirly and enigmatic. "Val, I'm sorry. I acted like a jerk."

Relief flooded through me, making me feel light-headed. I hadn't realized how much I regretted our fight until he apologized. I shook my head and took his hands, looking into his beautiful blue eyes. Eyes that showed no blame. "No, it was me." I swallowed hard and somehow found the guts to say, "You were right. I-I was a little jealous. I'm sorry I took it out on you."

He smiled, looking as relieved as I felt. "Good. Uh, do you realize where you're standing?"

I glanced around. "You mean the corner—I put myself in a time out?"

His grin widened. "No . . . you're right under the mistletoe."

I glanced up, but before I could spot it, he kissed me. He missed the first time, hitting my chin, but the awkwardness soon turned into something much nicer as our lips meshed and Lola rose between us, sparking all kinds of illicit thoughts. I beat her back down. Shade was mine, not hers, and I didn't want her to mingle tonight.

The kiss broke off, and Shade said, "Come on, join—"

But I didn't hear what he was about to say because Micah used the microphone to call for attention and start the ornament gift exchange. Shade led me to one of the tables near Trevor and his court, and we listened to the instructions for the exchange.

Seemed it was to be a different kind of gift opening, where people could open an ornament from under the tree or steal one from someone else. It was as fun as Fang had promised, lots of laughter and joking as people stole the most coveted ornaments. Mine was pretty popular, but the one everyone seemed to want was the one Trevor brought.

He must have had it made, because it pictured a slayer shoving a stake into a vampire's heart. The slayer resembled me, and the vamp looked a great deal like Alejandro. I wasn't sure I cared for it or its message, but everyone else seemed to really enjoy it.

At the end of the exchange, Shade had the slayer ornament while I ended up with a pretty silver and blue one that would look great in my bedroom.

The music started up again, playing an old favorite—*White Christmas*—and Trevor came over to where Shade and I sat. I plastered a smile on my face and he acted like nothing had ever happened. Good. I really didn't want to apologize to him—he didn't deserve it.

Trevor slapped Shade on the back then held out his hand to me. "Would you like to dance?"

Embarrassed, I said, "Sorry, I don't know how." Getting close enough to dance with a guy meant he'd be inside my energy field . . . and easy prey for Lola. So, I'd never learned.

"No problem," Trevor said with a wave of his hand. "Just follow my lead and you'll have no problems."

"But it's a slow dance." I wasn't sure I wanted to do that with him. And I had a good excuse. "You know, lust demon and all."

"Won't affect me a bit," Trevor declared, and this time I smelled the whiskey he must have been drinking.

Shade said, "Go ahead," so I didn't see how I could refuse. And maybe a slow dance coupled with his drinking would give me the opportunity to find out more about him. I forced a smile and took his hand.

He swept me out onto the floor, and I stumbled a couple of times until I got the hang of it. All I had to do was relax and let him push me where he wanted me, and we did just fine. Slayer reflexes didn't hurt either.

Once I felt more secure, Trevor glanced down at me and asked disarmingly, "Why do you dislike me?"

That was certainly blunt. "Maybe I just don't know you," I said evasively.

"What would you like to know?"

I thought for a moment. I wasn't real good with small talk. "Um, how about your family?"

"Well, you know about my father. My mother died in an

earthquake right after I was born."

"I'm sorry," I said. "Do you have any brothers and sisters?"

"No. No other family. The Underground raised me."

"That must have been tough," I said, meaning it.

"No tougher than what I hear you went through," he said, raising an eyebrow.

Sheesh. The Demon Underground, strangely enough, was no place to keep secrets among its members. Was he trying to say we were two of a kind? I was so not buying it. I shrugged. "My family is doing just fine now." We were having civil conversations and everything.

"Someone told me your parents own the Astral Reflections bookstore."

His harsh tone surprised me and I missed a step. "Yeah, they do. So?"

"So why didn't you mention the store as a possible hiding place for the books?"

I shrugged. "I didn't even think about it. I guess because Andrew trashed the store once looking for them without any luck. I don't see why they'd want to hide somewhere obvious like that." At his disbelieving stare, I added, "I can take you by tomorrow when they're open, if you like." I really didn't think he'd find the books at the store. "Or Shade can. He knows where the store is."

He seemed to relax. "Okay, let's do that."

As the song segued into a medley of classic Christmas songs, I took the opportunity to continue questioning him. "I didn't know there were other Demon Undergrounds. Is the one in Los Angeles a lot like this one?"

He shrugged, looking indifferent. "I don't know anymore. It's been awhile since I needed their services. I have my own business."

I hadn't even thought about what he did for a living. "Oh, what kind of business?"

"Hair salons."

"You're a hairdresser?" I asked in surprise. Though I had to admit it did fit.

"No," he said, sounding annoyed. "I *own* upscale hair salons in Los Angeles, Beverly Hills, and Hollywood. My flagship salon is on Rodeo Drive." He glanced down at me. "If you ever make it to California, stop by for a free hairstyle."

He didn't actually say I looked like I could use one, but it was implied in his tone. "Yeah," I sniped back. "I guess people out there obsess about hair." When slaying vamps, not so much.

Trevor looked at me thoughtfully, then spun me in a whirling circle that left me confused and feeling klutzy. "We're not so different, you know," he said.

Be nice, Val, I admonished myself. I didn't want this guy to see me as a threat. "Oh?"

"No, we're not. We both want the Demon Underground to remain hidden, don't we?"

I had to agree with him there. I didn't care for the idea of witch hunts, which is where I figured revealing ourselves would end up. I nodded.

"And we both would just as soon have all vampires vanish from the face of the Earth?"

Okay, I had to agree with him there, too. While I might believe Alejandro wholeheartedly believed in his Movement, would his followers revert to bloodsucking fiends given the chance? I was mostly human, and I didn't want to see any more of us die at their hands. "True." Where was he going with this?

"Don't you think it's unwise for the vampires to reveal their presence by coming out to the population?"

"I don't know. Alejandro's ideals are good—he's hoping to regulate vamps through the laws, make it safer for humans."

Trevor sneered. "Humans will never be safe around them. Why are you helping them?"

Gee, he'd never acted this way around Rosa or the other bloodsuckers he despised. Two-faced much?

"I had no choice." I explained my promise that demons wouldn't harm vampires, Josh and Andrew breaking that promise, and having to work for the Movement to make it up to them. "I'm under contract now with Alejandro."

"Does that mean you have to persuade the Underground to come out with them?" he persisted.

"Not at all. I'm not sure that's such a good idea." I'd thought about it and realized that with each generation of demons interbreeding with humans, the demon strain was getting more and more diluted, our powers weaker. In a few generations, they were likely to be totally gone, so long as no more full demons found their way into our world. Why reveal ourselves when our numbers were dwindling so fast?

"Good," Trevor said. "I—"

He broke off when the music stopped and Fang shoved his way between us, his red bow looking a little bedraggled. HATE TO BREAK UP THIS LOVE FEST, BUT MICAH WANTS TO SEE YOU.

Good—I was tired of being on my best behavior with this guy. *Thanks,* I told Fang, and relayed to Trevor what he'd said. *I appreciate the rescue.*

NOT REALLY A RESCUE. MICAH REALLY DOES WANT YOU.

Oh. Fang led me to him, and Micah pulled me out into the hall. "Bad news," he said, looking worried.

"Did you find out about Trevor? Did you find the books?"

Micah grimaced. "No, nothing like that. Alejandro's been trying to call you."

I checked my phone. Dead. I'd forgotten to charge it. "It isn't midnight yet. My contract says I work for him midnight to dawn."

"I know, but his mansion is under attack."

Of course it was. When could I get a break? "By who?"

"The unaffiliated vamps who oppose the Movement. Apparently, they've banded together and decided to take Alejandro down."

I sighed. "Well, fewer bloodsuckers in the world isn't a bad thing." Maybe they'd take each other out and end this. But Micah looked worried. "Why does this bother you?" I asked.

Fang barked at me, sounding impatient. BECAUSE JOSH AND ANDREW ARE STILL THERE, he said.

Oh, crap.

CHAPTER TEN

I might be annoyed at Andrew and Josh for pulling their stupid stunts, but I didn't want them killed. "I'll go."

"Why?" someone asked behind me.

I turned around. It was Trevor. He and Shade had followed me to see what Micah wanted.

"He never answered your question," Trevor continued. "Why does this bother you? Do you and the vamps have some sort of alliance?" he asked Micah, looking disgusted by the idea.

"Not really," Micah said with an impatient frown. "Not officially. But Alejandro and I agree the free agent vamps aren't good for either organization. Not only do they murder humans, but they have the potential to turn the world against us. Do you want to see another Inquisition . . . or Salem witch trials?"

"No, but—"

Micah cut Trevor off with an impatient gesture. "Two of our own are at the mansion tonight. We're going to help them."

Trevor looked annoyed, but he couldn't argue with that. He compressed his lips into a thin line and nodded.

Relieved that Micah was going to provide some backup, I signaled the DJ to turn off the music and handed the mic to Micah.

Nodding his thanks, Micah spoke into the mic, glancing around at the curious crowd. "I apologize for interrupting your good time, but Andrew and Josh are in trouble. They're at the Movement's mansion, which is being attacked by the independent vampires. We need to help them. Who's in?"

About two-thirds of the crowd volunteered, including Shade and Trevor.

Uh-oh. Some of them had no business battling bloodsuckers. I grabbed the mic. "This isn't a picnic, people. Some of you will get hurt, maybe even killed. If you're not accustomed to fighting vamps or don't have a power that will help, stay here." Some of them looked mutinous, so I added bluntly, "We don't want to get hurt because we're worried about protecting you."

Micah took the mic back and was a bit more diplomatic. "The Slayer has an excellent point. I don't want anyone hurt. I commend you all for wanting to go, but please don't unless you have a good reason to be there. I wouldn't want to have your injuries on my conscience."

That was a better way to phrase it. I guess that's why he was the boss and I wasn't.

YEP, Fang agreed, then poked me hard with his nose. LET'S RIDE.

Just a sec. I had one more thing to take care of. "Shade, you stay here, too."

I couldn't see his expression, but his voice was hard as he said, "I may not be able to fight, but I can heal others."

"I know, but you can do that here, after it's over. Remember what happened the last time we fought at the mansion?" He'd lost his temper and almost lost control of his interdimensional energies. If I hadn't distracted him with Lola, he would've let more full-blooded demons pour into our world through the rift he created. With no human blood to give them compassion, they'd wreak havoc on San Antonio and the rest of the world.

Shade had vowed to kill himself rather than let that happen. "It's too dangerous," I reminded him. And I couldn't be of any help if I had to worry about him.

Trevor slapped him on the back with a rueful look. "Val's right. I'll stay here with you, Shade. I won't be of any use there either, but I can help you get ready for any wounded."

I felt pulled in two directions. I needed to leave and help the two demons at the mansion, but had to make sure Shade stayed here. As Fang almost vibrated with the need for us to be on our way, I waited anxiously for Shade's answer.

He took a quick step forward then grabbed me by the shoulders. "Okay, you're right. But I don't have to like it."

Relieved by the resolve in his face, I said, "Thank you."

"But be careful, damn it," he muttered. "Come back to me." With that, he gave me a hard kiss.

Lola wanted to stay and linger, but now was *so* not the time. I kissed him back fiercely, a promise to return and pick up where we left off. "I will." I gave him another swift kiss for good luck, then ran like hell out of there to grab my Valkyrie, Fang hot on my heels.

The hellhound jumped into his seat behind me and we didn't bother with his goggles—it would take too much time. I gunned it out of there and broke more than a few speed limits as I headed for the mansion. I passed a few of the other demons who'd left immediately and, because I could weave in and out of traffic on my bike, I was the first one there.

The iron gates had been smashed and lay broken off their hinges to either side of the entrance. Three vamps stood in the space between them, as if they'd been waiting for us. They snarled when they saw me and rushed forward, fangs gleaming. Okay, obviously *not* part of the Movement. That made things easier.

Lola's lust for the fight sizzled in my blood, and I quickly sent Fang a mental picture of what I intended to do. As we got close, he leapt off the bike, launching straight into the face of the one on the far right. I turned my bike into a skid and leaned over parallel to the ground, right in the path of the two on the left.

They screamed as the Valkyrie's wheels hit them in the shins and flipped them, the bike going down hard. I scrambled off and grabbed my stakes out of my back waistband, cursing the pain in my side. Sure, they might not be going anywhere on those legs anytime soon, but two less bad ass vamps in the world was a Good Thing. I staked them, putting them out of their misery, then turned to see how Fang was doing.

He'd used teeth and claws to make the guy's face pretty well unrecognizable, and was now leaping up to take bites out of anything he could, while the bloodsucker screamed like a sissy, trying fruitlessly to kick Fang away. Another stake took care of him. So far, so good.

You okay? I asked Fang.

I'M GOOD, Fang said immediately. IDIOT COULDN'T EVEN AIM. His gaze focused beyond me. WATCH OUT!

Another bloodsucker, who must have been hiding in the bushes, tackled me on my injured side and took me down. The pain almost crippled me, and all I could do was lie there and fend him off as he lay on top of me, scrabbling to find my neck with his fangs. Then, as Lola's energy field took effect, he tried to feel me up even as his fangs scraped my neck, seeking my jugular.

The guy must be nuts. Repulsed and pissed off, but unable to breathe well, I gathered all of Lola's force and thrust it at him. "Stop!" I controlled his mind utterly, so he had no choice but to do what I told him to. Annoyed, but stakeless at the moment, I snarled, "Go kill yourself."

He immediately stood, then took a running jump and leaped up with his arms spread wide toward one of the broken gates and smashed down hard on several of the *fleur de lis* spikes, impaling himself. He must have hit his heart, because he went limp and our connection faded and broke.

Ohmigod, I hadn't thought he'd actually *do* it. I stared at his body, horrified that Lola could compel someone to do something like that.

I heard a motor behind me and someone said, "Interesting. I didn't know you could do that."

I turned around to see Ludwig and several others staring at me from inside a car. Some looked as appalled as I felt.

"I didn't either," I snapped, struggling to my feet and trying not to show how much my side hurt. "But the other option was to tell him to go screw himself." I paused to gasp for breath. "And who wants to witness that?"

Ludwig gave me a lopsided grin as the others chuckled nervously. "Out," Ludwig told the others. "Let's clear this garbage out of the way. The others are right behind me."

As Ludwig and his helpers pulled the vamps to the side, I grabbed my bike and sped up the long driveway to the house, Fang running alongside. This time, I babied the Valkyrie, letting it down easy onto some grass on the side of the drive, and paused to assess what was going on in the chaos outside the mansion. I could see pretty well under the full moon.

Dozens of vamps fought other bloodsuckers fang to fang all around the house. Without a scorecard, I couldn't tell which were the good guys and which were the bad. Either way, it didn't matter. I needed to make sure Micah's guys were safe. Were they in the house?

As I watched, a vamp tried to climb in a shattered window and a fireball blew him back out, the intense heat engulfing him in flames instantly. Since there were several other crispy critters on the ground near him, it looked like Andrew had been busy. Josh popped his head out and quickly blasted the flames licking around the window frame with a fire extinguisher, then ducked back inside. Ah, good. They were both still alive.

Determined to keep them that way, I ran over to the door, Fang right on my heels. Dang. The thing wouldn't budge.

THEY PROBABLY HAVE IT BLOCKED, Fang said.

Of course. Turning to the side, I yelled, "Josh, Andrew, let me in!"

Josh looked out at me in surprise, then nodded and disappeared. I heard a thump, then Rosa opened the door and gestured me in urgently. Three vamps with stakes in their hearts lay scattered among the Christmas decorations in the great room, broken glass glittering on the floor. Luis guarded the window on the side next to Andrew and Josh, while two other vamps I didn't know covered the windows on the other side. I don't know if Luis even realized he had a bloody shard of glass sticking in his back.

Rosa pushed the door closed and dropped a large wooden bar into the iron brackets on either side of the door. It settled with a thunk. Sheesh—now I realized why that door was so massive. It could withstand a siege . . . and probably had. I'd never noticed the bar before.

"Josh, Andrew, are you okay?" I asked.

They gave me a thumbs-up then quickly returned their attention to what was going on outside.

Rosa said, "They are fine. Come, Alejandro needs you."

"But I have to—"

"We will protect them." She tugged on my arm. "Please, you must see Alejandro now. The prophecy said you must be by his side."

Sheesh, they were taking it a bit literally, weren't they?

Go, Fang said. THE BOYS ARE OKAY AND I'LL WATCH, TOO. I'LL CALL YOU IF WE NEED YOU.

They'd kept Josh and Andrew safe so far, so I guessed it was all right. "Where is he?" I asked her.

"At the back of the house."

"Okay, I'll go. You stay here." Then, hearing a pounding at the front door, I remembered Ludwig and his friends. "Some of the Underground are right behind me. If you let them in, they'll help you defend the house. We can't tell friend from foe out there."

Rosa nodded, then pushed me toward the back of the house. "Go quickly."

I went.

Alejandro was at the more vulnerable back door, barricading it with the dining room table and the help of Austin and two other vamps. Something thumped against it and the door bulged inward. "Hold fast," he shouted. "Do not let them have our home!"

A fist smashed through the top half from the outside, splintering the heavy wood. Sheesh, I knew they were strong, but that had to hurt. Why were they so desperate?

Alejandro cursed, and Austin said, "They must be crazy."

As two hands tore at the hole in the door, I asked, "How can I help?"

Alejandro glanced at me in surprise. "Slayer—excellent. Perhaps you would be so good as to use your powers to stop these creatures?" Even hard-pressed as he was, he still had time to be gracious.

I hesitated for a moment. Use my powers? I didn't care to dip into that well too often. Not only because I feared one day I would go too far, too deep, and Lola would take over forever, but also because I hadn't wanted to undermine Alejandro's authority again. "But there are some women out there, not all our side." There weren't that many, but what if I enslaved the men and left the women free to murder at will? "My powers only work on men."

"But mine work on women," Micah said from behind me.

I whirled around. He certainly had gotten here fast.

"Excellent," Alejandro said with a grim smile. "Between the two of you, you can contain this."

"Okay," I said, "but it's difficult to be selective. It'll affect everyone," I warned him. Including Alejandro. Again.

"I know, but please, do it quickly."

I glanced at Micah. "You ready?"

He nodded. "Let me know when you're ready so we can do this simultaneously."

I'd never tried to enslave this many before. I braced myself in a wide stance, closed my eyes, and dug down deep. Lola was ready, waiting in anticipation. Knowing how many men were out there, I couldn't do this piecemeal, couldn't let her out slowly through my barriers. It had to be all or nothing.

Yet still I hesitated, unsure how to maintain control.

A loud crash sounded from the area near the door. "Ms. Shapiro, please," Alejandro pleaded.

Oh, crap. Guess I just had to let go and find out what happened. "Now!" I told Micah.

I let loose and Lola exploded from my core, blasting out tendrils of energy like heat-seeking missiles, each honing in on a prime lusty male. As Lola found each one, she hooked into their sacral chakra, the center that housed the source of their sexuality.

I was spread too thin to let the energy reach out into their other chakras, so I had to be content with this one. Lola certainly was, and she was soaking up their energy like she was a dry shriveled-up sponge. It became strangely quiet inside and outside the mansion as Micah did the same.

I fought against Lola, struggling with the tightrope act of trying to hold onto them all while simultaneously trying *not* to draw in too much of their energy. I fell to my hands and knees with the effort, feeling like a black widow at the center of her web. I tried to isolate the sticky strand holding Alejandro hostage, but I had so many threads going in so many directions, it was impossible. The sheer vitality flowing into me, from all around me, was intoxicating and distracting. Besides, I feared if I let one go, I had to let them all go.

I felt Fang lick my face. ARE YOU OKAY IN THERE, VAL?

I couldn't spare any effort for speech. *Not . . . really.* I was barely holding onto control, trying to throttle Lola's siphoning down to a trickle as I desperately tried to figure out what to do. They were immobilized all right, but how could I sort friend from foe when most of them couldn't even see or hear me? All they knew was that they were drawn to me, completely enthralled by the succubus inside me.

VAL, Fang said urgently, MORE DEMONS HAVE ARRIVED. THEY'RE ATTACKING ALL OF THE VAMPS, NOT JUST THE BAD ONES. YOU HAVE TO STOP THEM.

No way. I was already feeling the strain of holding onto too many men. *Get . . . Micah . . . to help.*

I DON'T THINK HE CAN. HE HASN'T DONE THIS BEFORE LIKE YOU HAVE. HE CAN'T MOVE FROM WHERE HE IS WITHOUT RELEASING SOME OF THE WOMEN UNTIL HE FIGURES OUT HOW TO HANDLE IT. THE DEMONS ARE ALL MEN—YOU CAN DO IT.

Oh, crap. I had to. I stretched myself and found a small bit of unused capacity. Peeling it away from my core, I thrust it toward the front of the mansion. Unerringly, Lola found the chakras of nine more males and locked on like a vacuum cleaner on maximum suction.

It was overwhelming . . . it was wonderful. It was oh so right. More . . . I needed more. Their energy made me feel as if I were crackling with vitality, wildly alive. I opened the floodgates and let it pour in.

VAL, STOP. YOU'RE TAKING TOO MUCH!

No. It felt so good. It was my right, my destiny, my—

I felt a blow to my head and the tendrils all spasmed in surprise. No, I was losing them! I tried to gather up my errant strands, but another blow to the head made all my lovely threads snap. The incredible pain of the recoil sent me spiraling down into oblivion.

CHAPTER ELEVEN

I rode my Valkyrie around San Antonio, desperately looking for the books, but having no success. Trevor had searched the whole city and so had I, but neither of us had been able to sense the encyclopedia. Maybe we were wrong. Maybe the books weren't in the city. Maybe Andrew had time to take them to Lytle or Castroville.

Maybe they're still in San Antonio and you're searching in the wrong place.

I seized on that thought as if it were my own. But what could we possibly do differently?

Look somewhere else. Look up—

The voice abruptly cut off. Look up what? What am I supposed to look up?

The next thing I knew, I was riding on a rough dirt road on a balmy Spring day, the tall grass of a prairie skimming by in a blur of motion on either side of me. Nothing to see for miles and miles except the grass and a small wooden house set back a short distance from the road. And best of all, my worry was gone.

Suddenly noticing I was thirsty, I brought the motorcycle to a halt next to the well on the property. I brought a dipperful of cool water to my mouth, reveling in the way it quenched my thirst completely.

Fang wandered out onto the porch from inside the house. WELCOME HOME, VAL.

That's right, this was my home. I moved leisurely into my house and stopped inside the living room. From the outside, you wouldn't know that this elegant powder blue and chocolate brown oasis waited inside. I had everything I needed here. Computer, Internet, television . . . and no men. None for many, many miles. I sank down onto the luxurious couch and relaxed when it cradled me perfectly. Here I could be alone, be myself, with nothing and no one to bother me.

Fang curled up beside me. LIFE IS VERY, VERY GOOD, he said with a sigh.

Huh? What was wrong with Fang? And who wanted to be alone?

Something unseen soothed me, made me settle back into the

couch.

"Val, you're home," Tessa exclaimed as she came into the room. "Come on, everyone, the party's on!"

I glanced up, surprised to see all my female friends coming in through the door. Gwen, Mood, Shawndra, my sister Jen, Lt. Ramirez's wife—even some female demons from the Underground I'd seen but never spoken to. They poured into the room and filled it up, each one bringing something to eat.

"What's going on?" I asked with a smile.

"It's a girl's night out," Tessa said. "We're going to pig out, have facials, give each other manis and pedis, and gossip to our heart's content."

I clapped my hands. "That sounds like fun."

Insert record-scratching noise here. Huh? Had I been lobotomized . . . or Stepfordized or something? What the heck was wrong with me? This dream sucked.

I forced myself to consciousness. Pain awaited me there, but it was so much better than this disturbing dream.

"I'm losing her," I heard someone say.

For a moment, I lay there, fuzzy but awake, trying to figure out what was happening. My head felt tender and pain pricked along my nerves, but I was lying on something soft that cushioned me, with Fang curled up beside me. What was going on?

I blinked open my eyes and stared into a familiar face. His name escaped me for a moment then the fog cleared from my brain and I remembered. "Kyle." The dream demon. "What were you doing inside my dream?" I asked indignantly, then winced as pain shot along my abused nerve endings.

Kyle looked rueful. "Trying to help."

I gaped at him. "By giving me longings for manis and pedis?"

Fang chuckled beside me. GIVE THE KID A BREAK. HE WAS TRYING TO KEEP YOU IN A HAPPY DREAM SO YOU WOULDN'T WAKE UP. NOT HIS FAULT HE DOESN'T KNOW YOU VERY WELL.

I guess. I glanced around, noticing that I was in my own bedroom, with Kyle, Shade, Micah and Gwen all standing around, staring down at me. *Wizard of Oz* time again.

Gwen busied herself by my bedside table then handed me some pills and a cup of water. "Here, take these. It'll help with the pain."

I took them gratefully then settled back on my pillow.

Shade squeezed my hand, looking anxious. "Good. Now that

you're conscious, I can heal you. A lot of people have volunteered to let me use their energy to heal you and can be here in a matter of minutes."

"No, wait," I said as my last conscious moments started to come back to me. "First, tell me what happened." I lifted my hand to my head, wondering why it didn't hurt more. "Did someone break free of my hold and wallop me?"

"No," Micah said. "That was me."

That didn't make sense. "*You* hit me? Why?"

His mouth formed into a grim line. "Because you lost control. You were in the process of totally draining every man there but me. Someone had to stop you, and only Fang and I could do it."

I gasped as the full memory of what I'd done filled my mind. Ohmigod. I covered my face with my hands, too ashamed to look them in the eyes. I'd become what I most despised. The worst part of it was, I couldn't even blame Lola for this. As Micah constantly reminded me, there was no Lola. There was no separate demon hiding inside me. It was all me—and when it came down to it, I'd enjoyed the hell out of being a succubus. "I'm a monster," I moaned. How could they even stand to be around me?

Fang snorted in disbelief.

Micah echoed him. "You are *not* a monster. Because if you are, then I am, too, and I refuse to believe that."

Surprisingly, another voice joined the party. Don't be silly. You're nothing of the kind.

Princess, Fang's part-hellhound girlfriend, jumped up on the foot of the bed. And Princess was always blunt, more so than even me. What she thought—and sometimes what other people thought—came right out of her mouth. I guess if Princess said I wasn't a monster, then it must be true. And no one else looked horrified, just concerned.

The painkillers Gwen had given me kicked in and the pain eased, helping me relax a little. "Maybe not," I admitted. "But why not? What happened? I know I lost control. Did I . . . did I . . . ?" I had to know if I'd sucked everyone dry, but I just couldn't form the words.

Micah glanced uncertainly at Gwen. Good point—she didn't need to hear this.

She patted my arm and smiled, saying, "I'll just go fix you some soup."

Kyle patted me awkwardly on the shoulder. "I'll help."

Strangely, his touch made calm spread through me. When they

were gone, I was left alone with Shade, Micah and Fang. I gulped. "What happened? Is it bad?"

Micah pulled up a chair next to my bed as Shade sat next to me and took my hand again. "Not as bad as it could have been," he said. When I bit my lip, he added hastily, "You didn't kill anyone. Fang alerted me to the problem so I could stop you. Sorry, I didn't know any other way except to knock you out."

"Don't apologize," I said hurriedly. "You did the right thing—and thank heavens you did." The relief was incredible. I didn't want to kill anyone in that way. I thought for a moment, then clutched Shade's hand tighter. "Are you sure I didn't drain anyone?" It had seemed awfully close.

"Not a one. But you did bring them to the brink. They're all exhausted, but they'll live."

Fang snorted. ALL BUT THE ONES THAT WERE EXECUTED, YOU MEAN.

"Executed?" I said in surprise.

Shade frowned. "She doesn't need to know about this right now."

"Yes, she does," I insisted. "Tell me what happened. I need to know."

When Micah hesitated, Fang said, SHE HAS A RIGHT TO KNOW. He snuggled closer. RELAX, AND I'LL SHOW YOU HOW IT WAS.

I relaxed and closed my eyes, anxious to know what had happened. Suddenly, it was as if I was seeing through Fang's eyes. We were back in the mansion, and I saw myself drop to all fours on the floor, looking strained and haggard. All of the colors seemed washed out, and everything looked about four feet higher than I expected. Wow—I was really seeing this from Fang's perspective. *I didn't know you could do this.*

QUIET, WOMAN, AND LET ME SHOW YOU, Fang said tartly. THIS AIN'T EASY, YOU KNOW.

I shut up and relaxed into the experience. I did want to know what had happened.

Fang resumed the vision with me on all fours, my face stretched in a ghastly smile.

Fang skipped out of the way and Micah, looking determined, walloped Val upside the head with his fist. She fell to the floor and flopped like a fish on the line, but didn't let go of her prizes. Micah hit her again and she went limp and still.

SHE'S OUT, Fang confirmed, feeling worried. BUT SHE'LL LIVE.

HOW ABOUT THEM?

Micah was bent over with his hands on his knees. He gasped, "Just a moment. I can't . . . lose control either."

Leaving Micah to regain control of the chicks he had under his incubus spell, Fang trotted over to where the vamps lay still and poked Alejandro with his nose. The vamp leader wasn't breathing, but bloodsuckers didn't have to. Who knew if he was dead or not? They could take a lot of abuse, so he was probably still alive. Fang hoped so—he knew Val would be upset if she'd killed her boss.

What about the demons? He went to the living room and stuck his nose in Andrew's face. Still breathing. Good. But since Micah was bound to release the female bloodsuckers sooner or later, the boss needed to know who was good and who was apt to separate his blood from his body.

THE BABE IN HERE IS ONE OF THE GOOD GUYS, Fang called out mentally. WHY DON'T YOU LET HER GO SO WE CAN SORT THE GOOD FROM THE PUTRID?

Micah came stumbling back in, the strain of holding the women on his face. It had to be what? A whole dozen? Val could do far more than that with nothing but the power in her pinkie, Fang thought with pride. Then again, Micah hadn't had as much practice.

THIS ONE, Fang said, poking his nose into Rosa's ankle. LET HER TELL YOU WHICH WOMEN YOU CAN LET GO AND WHICH ARE TOAST.

Micah nodded, and released Rosa alone with a visible effort.

She came back to life with a start and stared around herself in disbelief.

"I have all of the other women under my control," Micah said, his voice strained. "I'm drawing them in. They're . . . at the door. Can you . . . let them in?"

She did and fourteen of them filed in, staring at Micah like he was all that and a bag of chips.

Micah grimaced. "Tell me which . . . ones are on your side . . . I'll release them."

Rosa nodded grimly then picked up three crossbow darts from the floor and bam, bam, bam, slammed them into the hearts of three vampires. They crumpled to the floor.

Fang scratched his ear. WELL, THAT'S ONE WAY TO DO IT.

Micah jerked, looking horrified. In his shock, he must have released the other women in his power, because they suddenly looked less like adoring groupies and more like vengeful harpies.

They grabbed crossbow bolts and stakes from the supplies on the floor. Some even grabbed glass icicles from the tree. They all headed for the door, murder in their eyes.

"Wait," Micah said. "You can't do this when they're helpless."

Rosa turned and glared at him. "Of course we can. When better?"

" It's not right. I-I can stop you."

She frowned. "Why would you? They are filth, scum, nothing but rabid dogs."

Another woman spat on one of the stakees. "They are worse than that. Do you know what they did to one of your own?"

"No, what?" someone asked from the doorway—Jacob, one of the older demons, who'd arrived too late for the main event. "What did they do?"

Rosa stalked to the study and flung open the door. "See for yourself. We tried to rescue her, but it was too late."

Fang pushed through a forest of legs to see who was inside. All he could see was a body sprawled on the floor, pale arms outflung, her head facing the doorway. A head with green hair. *Oh, damn*, he thought with regret.

"Shawndra," Jacob cried out, falling to his knees beside the demon girl. "My God, there are bite marks everywhere. They drained her dry!"

"Why?" Micah asked in despair. "She wouldn't harm a fly . . . ." He glanced up, suddenly alert. "But that doesn't make sense. Demon blood makes vampires crazy."

Rosa nodded grimly. "And so it did. They dragged her to our front lawn and ravaged her with much joy, shouting that demon blood would make them invincible." Her fists tightened on the weapons she held. "Even if they wake, they will still be mad."

No wonder the vamps had all seemed so nutso.

Micah nodded grimly. "I won't stop you from doing what you have to do."

With that, the women gathered up all the weapons they could and left the house to do some selective termination.

Fang stopped his memories there. THEN WE DRAGGED ALL THE GOOD GUYS INSIDE, LEFT THE BADDIES TO FRY IN THE MORNING SUN, AND BROUGHT YOU HERE.

I'd seen a lot of carnage in my day, but I thanked Fang for not showing me the rest. Yes, it needed to be done, but it was still horrifying. "Poor Shawndra." I'd hardly known the girl, but she deserved better than that. To have her life cut so short was a tragedy. "Where is she now? Is she still at the mansion?"

Micah shook his head. "We buried her yesterday."

"Yesterday! How long have I been out?"

"Three days," Shade said, squeezing my hand. "You see why we were so concerned?"

Micah nodded. "Shade and Fang never left your side. Fang knew how much pain you were in, so Kyle tried to keep you in healing dreams for as long as possible."

"And now that you're awake, *I* can heal you," Shade said once again.

Shade shot Micah a stubborn look. Wonder what that was about?

Princess spoke up again. MICAH SAID HE HAS TO ASK YOU, THAT YOU WOULDN'T WANT TO BE HEALED, the part hellhound, part Cavalier King Charles Spaniel said, letting everyone in the room hear her. WHY WOULD YOU *WANT* TO HURT?

"I don't. But when Shade healed Josh, he almost lost control. He'd rather kill himself than let that happen. I don't want him dead. Do you?" That wasn't the only reason, of course, but it was all she had to know.

Princess jumped up to place her front paws on Shade's chest and stare into his face. DON'T HEAL HER, she ordered. OR ANYONE ELSE.

Now *that* she could have kept private, but obviously chose not to. Fang snorted, though whether in amusement or disgust, I wasn't sure.

Shade patted Princess on the head then put her paws gently back down on the bed. "You're overdramatizing this, Val. You're not hurt as badly as Josh was, so it will be easier on me. There's no danger. Besides, you and Micah are here to help me recover afterward."

I smiled at him, to take the sting out of my words. "If I'm not hurt as badly, then I really don't need healing, do I?"

"What?" he challenged. "Do you think you deserve to suffer or something?"

I patted his hand. "Now who's being overdramatic? I'm not suffering, especially after the pills Gwen gave me."

THAT'S RIGHT, SHE'S FINE, Princess said with finality.

SHE REALLY IS, Fang added. AND SHE'D BE EVEN BETTER IF YOU'D STOP PUSHING.

I rubbed Fang's head. *Thanks for the support.*

DE NADA.

Shade looked taken aback, but Micah dropped a hand on his

shoulder. "They're right. We all appreciate your offer, but it isn't necessary."

Shade's mouth firmed into a line. "I just wanted to help."

"I know," I said, rubbing his arm to soothe him. "I'd feel the same way. But it's not necessary. I'm not feeling all that bad. Just a little weak . . . and hungry." I added the last to refocus his attention elsewhere, but I realized it was true. After all, I'd been in bed for three days without, I assumed, anything to eat.

Right on cue, Kyle knocked on the door, then pushed it open to admit Gwen, carrying a tray. "You should eat something," she said with a stubborn look around the room, as if daring one of them to argue with her.

Shade hurried to take the tray from her. "Yes, you should," he said.

He waited while Micah helped me sit up and Gwen fussed with the pillows behind me. When they were done, Shade placed the tray gently in front of me.

"Smells great," I said. And it did. A hearty beef soup with chunks of potatoes and vegetables, with a side of crusty French bread and creamy butter. Boy, did I have a great roomie or what? I took a bite. "Delicious as always." I glanced around. "Have the rest of you eaten?"

Micah nodded. "Just before you woke." He smiled at my roomie. "Gwen always takes good care of us."

She shrugged. "One of my few accomplishments. I'm just glad to have someone to cook for."

I'M HUNGRY, Princess complained.

Fang scrambled to his feet on the bed. I COULD EAT, TOO.

"The dogs want food," I translated for Gwen.

"Oh, I'm sorry, I forgot," she said with a smile. "I'll get them something."

Both hellhounds jumped down off the bed to follow her. THAT SOUP SMELLS GOOD, Princess said, hinting strongly as she left the room.

I grinned then glanced around at the guys who were left. "So, instead of watching me eat, why don't you tell me what's been happening." Besides Shawndra's death and the Christmas massacre. "Did Trevor find the books?"

"Not yet," Shade said. "He's been calling me every day to check on you, and each time, he tells me he hasn't found them yet."

To check on me? Yeah, right. More likely he was checking on

Shade to see when he'd be free to come out and play. I thought about telling them about the voice I'd been hearing, but decided not to. It would be too easy for Shade to let it slip to Trevor, and for some reason, I didn't want to let the visiting demon know about it.

"Where has he looked?" I asked, then continued to slurp up the soup.

"Everywhere," Shade said. "He's going to check the whole city again, in case he missed something the first time. Then he's planning on moving to some of the nearby towns that Andrew would have had time to get to."

I nodded then got busy finishing the soup as I thought about that voice again. What did it want me to look up? I didn't have a clue to even go about it, but I knew someone who would—Rick, my stepfather.

I paused with the spoon halfway to my mouth as I remembered something. Oh, crap. Would Rick still be speaking to me? I'd sicced Trevor on him, so to speak. "Did Trevor visit Astral Reflections?" I asked in trepidation. "He seemed convinced the books would be there."

"Yes, he did," Shade confirmed.

I set my spoon down. "Oh, no. Did he tear the place up?" Would Mom and Rick ever forgive me?

Micah shook his head solemnly. "It's worse than that."

"What?" I demanded. "Did he hurt them?" If he harmed a single hair on their heads—

"Nothing like that," Micah said with a grin. "They think he's wonderful and invited him to join you for Christmas dinner."

CHAPTER TWELVE

I closed my eyes, my appetite suddenly gone. "They invited Trevor to our family Christmas? You're kidding me." Please, goddess, let it be a joke.

"Nope," Micah said. "Afraid not."

Damn. "Since when are Mom and Rick so gung-ho about associating with demons?"

"They invited me, too," Shade said stiffly. "Is there a problem?"

"Of course not." Shade had spent Thanksgiving with my family and they really liked him, swirls and all . . . but Trevor? He was so not their new age-y type. "I was just surprised, that's all," I fibbed. And I had a couple of weeks to make sure Trevor was *un*invited.

"He's really a good guy once you get to know him," Shade said. "He's been worried about you."

I didn't want to start a fight again, so I said, "Okay," and changed the subject. "Uh, what am I wearing under here? I kinda need to use the bathroom." I raised the covers and saw I was wearing a sleep T-shirt. Good. But . . . "Who undressed me?" I wasn't wearing a bra anymore so I kinda wondered who had seen me partially naked.

"Gwen and Tessa," Micah told me. "After we brought you back from the mansion."

Good. It would have kind of weirded me out to know it was Micah . . . or Shade, when I wasn't even conscious. I threw back the covers and scooted to the side of the bed then dangled my legs over the side. The T-shirt came down to mid-thigh, so I felt covered up enough. I stood and immediately, all three guys moved forward, arms outstretched to help.

"I'm good," I told them. A little wobbly, but I could stand and was sure I could move on my own. "Remember, I heal pretty fast. Since you kept me out of it for so long, I was able to heal more than I thought. And the soup helped, too."

It really had. I just had a bit of jangling along my nerves and some pain in my chakras from the backlash of Lola's tendrils. Even that was easing with the painkillers Gwen had given me. And my side didn't hurt at all.

"Okay," Shade said, handing me my robe. "But I'll stay close, just in case."

Whatever it took to make him happy. I smiled at him and slipped on my robe, then made my way slowly to the bathroom. I gained confidence with each step. No problem. I was a bit weak still from so many days in bed, but a little food and time would take care of that.

I closed the bathroom door gently in his face, relieved to be away from so many pairs of staring eyes. I took longer than I needed, just to have some alone time, and looked at myself in the mirror. Good grief, I looked ghastly. My normally tamed shoulder-length brown hair was tangled and messy, and my face was creased and as pale as a vampire's, with dark smudges under my eyes.

I stuck my head out the door. "I feel okay, so I'm going to take a shower," I told Shade.

"Okay, but don't lock the door, and yell if you need help."

"I will," I said. As if.

I enjoyed the hot pounding water for a few blissful minutes, then checked my side and my head. I had a couple of round, pink scars where the crossbow bolt had skewered me, but otherwise, I was totally healed. And I had a sensitive spot on my head where Micah had hit me, but no bump or gash. What were they all worried about? I was fine.

But how was Lola? Had the recoil whiplash fried my succubus circuits, so to speak? Checking deep inside, I could sense the succubus still there. Hiding and hurting, but with enough sucked-up sexual energy to power her for days. I didn't know whether to be glad or sad that I still had her around.

Then again, she was probably the reason I was healing so well. Remembering how alive and vital I'd felt the last time she gathered up that much energy, I realized that without it, I'd probably still be in a world of hurt. I might even miss her if she was gone.

Not that I'd admit it . . . .

I got out of the shower and was glad to see someone had slipped in and left me some clean clothes. Good—the T-shirt I'd been wearing was grungy after so many days of wear, even in bed. I dressed and checked myself in the mirror. I had more color in my face and my hair looked better now that I'd shampooed it, so I toweled it as dry as I could and combed it free of the tangles.

Feeling more human, I left the bathroom to find Shade waiting to escort me back to bed and the other two hovering in the hallway. I passed my bedroom door and headed for the living room.

"Where are you going?" Micah asked.

"I'm not an invalid," I told him. "I just want to sit up for awhile."

They followed me into the bright, cheerful living room where Gwen was watching television and eating popcorn with both hellhounds lying on the couch next to her. Both watched her every move.

Mooch, I accused Fang with a grin.

SO? I LIKE POPCORN, he said. ESPECIALLY WITH ALL THE GOOD STUFF GWEN PUTS ON IT.

It was a good thing hellhounds had a constitution of iron and the metabolism of a hummingbird. He jumped down and nosed Princess to do the same so I could sit next to Gwen.

"Feeling better?" she asked.

"Much." I smiled at the guys, as if to say, "See, the nurse isn't concerned. You shouldn't be either." Out loud, I said, "While I was in the bathroom, I realized the energy I took in boosted my healing more than usual, and I still have more to draw on."

Micah and Kyle sat in the two club chairs, and Gwen scooted over so Shade could sit next to me. He twined his fingers with mine. "Good," he said with a sigh and finally seemed to relax.

Nice. I let myself slump against him, enjoying the feel of his warm body next to mine, knowing that Lola was too out of it to attack him. I needed to enjoy this while it lasted.

"What time is it?" I asked, noticing it was dark outside. "Is Alejandro expecting me?"

"It's past midnight," Shade told me. "And you're not seriously thinking about going over there tonight, are you?"

"No need," Micah broke in before I could say anything. "I talked to him while you were in the shower to let him know you're up and about. He knows you need to recuperate and told me to tell you to take all the time you need. He isn't expecting you back for days. And, when I visited him yesterday, he told me how much he appreciates what you did for him. Besides, he and his people need some time to recoup as well. You really took a lot out of them."

I grimaced. "And he *appreciates* that?"

"Yes," Micah said in a firm tone. "You brought the carnage down to a manageable level and ensured he didn't lose any more people . . . at great cost to yourself. He's very grateful."

"But doesn't this make him more vulnerable?" I asked.

Micah shrugged. "It might have, but the women weren't affected, so they've been in charge while the men recharge."

Fang chuckled on the floor beside me. I BET ROSA'S LOVING THAT.

Micah grinned. "You could say that. She's certainly protective of the men, and has all the women in the Movement cleaning up the mansion, inside and out. It's spotless." He paused, then said, "At least one very good thing has come out of this."

"What's that?" I couldn't imagine what it could be.

"Luis told us how well Josh and Andrew helped them defend the mansion, so they all agreed the boys have served their allotted time and released them."

"Luis said that? Will wonders never cease . . . . "

Shade squeezed my hand. "So what are you going to do with your free time? I hope you're planning on taking it easy."

"Oh, yeah." I mulled it over for a moment. "I think I'll just veg, maybe spend some time with Mom and Rick. They could use some help at the store this time of year, and it sounds like a nice change." Shade tensed up beside me. "Don't worry—I'll take it easy. I might do some research on the books, too, while you help Trevor search for them."

There. That ought to appease him. Not that I wanted those two becoming buddy-buddy any more than necessary, but someone should be with Trevor when he found the books . . . and Rosa was obviously busy.

Shade nodded. "Sounds like a plan."

Kyle and Micah left then, to go to the club, and the rest of us watched a silly movie about zombies. When it was over, Shade and Princess left, and Fang, Gwen and I all hit the sack.

I felt even better the next morning when I woke up. I tried lying in bed for awhile and encouraging the voice to come back to me, but no luck.

Now what? I could probably go back to work this evening, but heck, I'd been given the option of a few days off and I planned to take them.

WE DESERVE IT, Fang declared.

We do indeed.

So we goofed off for awhile and headed over to Astral Reflections at noon. Mom, Rick, and Jen were all there, and the store wasn't too crowded.

"Val!" Rick exclaimed and came over to greet me. "What a nice surprise." Mom and Jen, who were ringing up customers, smiled and waved at me as Fang found an out-of-the-way corner and flopped down, for all intents and purposes your ordinary, average mutt.

Knowing Lola was out of it, I did something I was so rarely able to—I hugged Rick. It felt good. Tall, blond, and handsome, he looked just like his wife and daughter . . . and nothing at all like me, since I took after my demon dad. But he was the only father I'd really known and had treated me like his own. I sighed, feeling safe and secure in his hold. It would be nice to stay here for awhile.

When I didn't let go, he asked, "You okay, hon?"

"Fine," I whispered. "Lola's taking a break so I can enjoy this without worrying." I gave him one last squeeze, then let go.

"Ah, good. Did you need something?"

"Not really. I have a few days off and thought I'd come by and see if you need any help."

Rick glanced around. "No, we have it under control. People aren't buying as much this year, unfortunately."

I nodded. Even I'd heard about the economy. "So, I hear Trevor Jackson came by the store."

Rick nodded and smiled wide. "Yeah, what a nice guy. We invited him for Christmas dinner."

"Is that such a good idea?" I asked. "You don't even know him."

Rick's smile faltered. "But you and Shade do, and we figured since he was all alone in town for the holidays . . . We invited others, too."

That's right—Mom and Rick enjoyed having a big crowd at Christmas. They use to invite everyone they knew who had nowhere else to go . . . and even other families. Except for the last few years when I'd developed my powers and hadn't been able to handle them all that well around strangers.

Really, inviting others was a vote of confidence in me. I hesitated. Should I push this? I didn't want to—I'd been trying very hard to play nice with Mom . . . so long as she was nice to me, that was.

BETTER SUCK IT UP THEN, Fang advised.

Dang. He was right. Giving Rick a smile, I said, "That'll be fine. What time do you want us there and what do you want me to bring?"

We talked arrangements for a few minutes, then I said, "You know, there is something I'd like to ask you. Can we go to the office?"

"Sure. Let me just tell your mom."

I gave Mom and Jen each a brief hug as Rick explained where we were going, then I followed him to the office upstairs. Fang, who was getting all kinds of attention from the customers, elected to stay downstairs.

We entered the cramped space, filled with piled boxes, stacked papers, file cabinets and packed bookcases lining the walls. It was a mess, but an organized one. Somehow, Rick knew exactly where everything was.

He leaned back in his creaky office chair as I took the bare metal chair next to the desk. "What do you need, Val? Is it money? We're not doing that bad—"

"No, no, nothing like that. Did, uh, Trevor mention what he was looking for?"

"Yes, he said something about three old books, an encyclopedia of some sort. I haven't seen them."

Just as I thought. "We're all looking."

"What's so important about them?"

I shrugged. "Remember the books my father gave me?" Rick knew about them—they were the only thing I'd ever had from my real father except my demon nature.

"Of course. Is that what you're all looking for?" At my nod, he asked, "How did you lose them?"

"It's a long story. But now they're hidden somewhere in San Antonio and no one knows where they are."

"Sorry, hon. If I had them, you know I'd give them to you. But I haven't seen them."

"I know, but I wondered if you could help me find them."

Rick crinkled his nose like he always did when he was confused. "How can I help?"

"I'm not sure, but I keep hearing this voice in my head. I think I'm supposed to look something up, do some research to find them."

Rick didn't even blink at the notion that I was hearing voices. He'd been around enough demons to not question anything weird. "What do you think you need to look up?"

I thought for a moment. "I'm not sure. Uh, maybe . . . do you have any references to old books, something that might mention the encyclopedia? Or anything about keepers . . . or mage demons?" I didn't need to tell him I was looking for real accounts, not the product of someone's imagination.

"Maybe." He stood and perused the books shelved above the old metal desk, then pulled down a thick one. "This one has a listing of old magick books, but I'm going to have to think about the keepers and mage demons. Have you tried the Internet?"

"Not yet."

"Why don't you do that, and I'll see if I can find anything here." He handed me the book, then snapped his fingers "Wait. Don't I remember seeing some spells in those books?"

"Yes, in the second two volumes."

"Then maybe it's similar to a Book of Shadows."

Why hadn't I thought of that? It was how Witches recorded their spells and kept track of the rituals and other information pertinent to their craft. "Yeah, maybe it is."

"If you don't find anything on the Internet, you might check with one of the local Wiccans."

"Okay . . . . " I knew from working here that most of them had a lot of desire, but very little actual power. "Is there one you'd recommend? Maybe someone who knows a lot about this kind of stuff . . . or some real magick?"

He thought for a moment. "Marina Lester might be the one you want. She's in the book . . . and she takes appointments as a psychic. Maybe even walk-ins. I've heard she's extremely accurate, if she's able to give you a reading."

Wondering what that meant, I thanked him, then looked her up in the phone book. I called her, and since she had an appointment available in an hour, I wrote down her home address. Taking the book Rick had given me back downstairs, I chatted with Mom and Jen a little then asked Fang, *You ready to go?*

He scrambled to his feet. YEAH. THIS LYING AROUND STUFF GETS OLD AFTER AWHILE. WHERE ARE WE GOING?

"To see a psychic."

OOOOKAY. WELL, IT'S DIFFERENT, ANYWAY. NEVER GET BORED AROUND YOU, BABE.

Yeah. Kind of like that old Chinese curse, "May you live in interesting times."

Marina Lester was nothing at all like I'd pictured. I should have known better than to buy in to stereotypes, but I'd expected an old crone or, at the very least, an overweight poser with heavy eye shadow and a dimly-lit space draped with acres of colorful shawls. Instead, this Witch was tiny, petite, and maybe a few years older than me. She wore everyday clothes just like mine and led me into an ordinary family room that looked a lot like Mom's. The only thing that looked remotely witchy about her was her hair—long red ringlets bounced around the delicate features of her face as if they were springs.

She didn't even raise an eyebrow at Fang's presence, but offered me a seat and came right to the point, smiling and speaking in a confident tone. "This is how I work. It's twenty dollars for a reading, but only if the spirits speak through me. I'll need to hold your hands and concentrate. Sometimes the spirits come through, sometimes they don't. If they do, I won't remember it, but I'll record what they say on tape. I can discuss it with you, but I won't necessarily understand it, and the message is often very brief and cryptic. If they don't come through, there's no obligation and you don't owe me a thing. Okay?"

Weird, that was very similar to the way Tessa operated, though Micah's assistant had never claimed the voices were spirits.

Duh. I should have seen it before—she looked just like Tessa, except for the hair. Without thinking, I blurted out, "You're a soothsayer demon, aren't you?"

WONDERED IF YOU'D PICK UP ON THAT, Fang said with a grin. SHE'S DEFINITELY SOME KIND OF DEMON—I CAN HEAR HER THOUGHTS.

Her face paled and she jumped out of her chair, her hand at her throat. "Wha-what are you saying?"

"It's okay," I soothed her. "I'm a demon, too. And my dog is a hellhound."

She glanced wildly between the two of us. "You need to leave now."

WHOA, BABE, Fang cautioned me. I'M NOT SURE SHE KNOWS WHAT SHE IS.

I worked on looking as unthreatening as possible. "I'm sorry, I guess I made an assumption. Don't you know what you are?"

"I'm a Witch, and a psychic," she said with an unsteady laugh. "There's no such things as demons."

From the nervousness in her voice, I gathered she did know what she was, but didn't want to admit it.

OR SHE'S BEEN TOLD TO KEEP IT HIDDEN, Fang suggested.

Definitely a possibility. How could I convince her I knew what I was talking about? "It's okay," I said gently. "There are a lot of other demons in San Antonio. In fact, I know one who has the same gift you do."

"That's not possible," she said, "Mama said we're the only—" She broke off and covered her mouth, looking as though she regretted revealing her secret.

Fang trotted over to place a gentle paw against her calf. MAYBE YOUR MAMA DIDN'T KNOW.

She stared at him in disbelief, then at me, her eyes wide.

"I did mention he was a hellhound," I reminded her. "That means he can telepathically connect with demons."

She sat back down gingerly, as if she were afraid her world would shatter if she moved too fast. "I—I don't know . . . "

" . . . what to say?" I guessed.

She nodded, still looking stunned.

SHE CAN'T BELIEVE SHE CAN ACTUALLY TALK TO ANYONE ABOUT THIS. SHE HASN'T BEEN ABLE TO TALK TO ANYONE SINCE HER MOTHER PASSED AWAY, Fang told me privately.

"You don't need to say anything," I told her. "Have you heard of the Demon Underground?"

She shook her head.

I grinned at her. "Well, it's full of people just like you and me."

"You're a soothsayer?"

"No, I'm a succubus, but I have a friend who's a soothsayer. She's in the Underground, too."

"I don't understand," Marina said, looking as though she were having a hard time taking it all in. "What does the Underground do?"

"We help other demons keep their presence a secret, help them find jobs, and generally give them someone else to talk to about what it's like being part demon in a human world. Oh, and I haven't been in it for very long, but they seem to have lots of parties."

She sighed. "It sounds wonderful." She glanced back and forth between us. "You aren't putting me on, are you?"

NOPE, Fang confirmed. IT'S ALL TRUE.

She jumped, seeming unnerved whenever Fang spoke to her. "Hold on," I said. "Let me call Tessa and she can give you some more info." I dialed the club and was glad when Tessa answered. "Hey, Tessa, I think I found your long-lost cousin or something."

"My what?"

"Hold on." I didn't want Marina to think we were trying to scam her or anything. "I'll hand the phone to her and you can tell her what you are."

"Are you sure?" Tessa asked.

"Yes, I'm sure. Just trust me, okay?"

"Okay," Tessa said.

I handed the phone to Marina and said, "Ask her what she is."

Marina took the phone gingerly. "He-hello?"

Wanting to give her some privacy, I wandered over to look out the window as she held a conversation with Tessa.

Fang joined me. I CAN TELL YOU WHAT THEY'RE SAYING.

I know, but I prefer to give her the illusion of privacy, okay?

YOU GOT IT.

After about half an hour of me pretending to stare out the window and trying *not* to listen to their conversation, Marina finally handed me the phone and said, "Thank you. Tessa explained all about the organization and invited me for dinner at Yule. It was wonderful to talk to someone else who understands."

"You're welcome," I said and took back my phone. "I remember how glad I was to find other people like me. It's a relief."

"Yes. I'm sorry I was so skeptical at first."

We both sat back down. "Not a problem. I totally get it. I'm just sorry I hit you with it like that."

She shrugged. "It worked out. So, I assume you didn't come here to invite me to join the Underground. Do you still want a reading? It's on the house."

"No, actually, I wasn't looking for a reading. I was hoping to get some information." She looked surprised and I hurried to assure her, "I was planning on paying you for it."

She waved that away as if it were inconsequential. "Don't worry about that. I owe you. What do you need to know?"

"You practice Wicca?"

She nodded. "I do. I really resonate with the beliefs. Plus, it's helped me . . . blend in to a community."

She'd been luckier than me in that respect. "Do you have a Book of Shadows?"

"Yes, of course."

"We're looking for some information on three books that are something like a Witch's Book of Shadows. Have you ever heard anything about the *Encyclopedia Magicka*?" I explained what I knew of it.

She thought for a moment, then shook her head. "I don't remember anything offhand. I've become a bit of a scholar on Wiccan ways, and I don't recall ever seeing anything like that mentioned."

Rick *had* sent me to the right person. "Maybe it was called something else?"

She thought for a moment. "I don't think so . . . but I can look."

"How about a keeper or a mage demon?"

"Not that I recall, but let me do a little research and I'll get back to you." She looked chagrined that she couldn't help me.

"Okay," I said, trying to mask my disappointment. "Here's my number." I scribbled it down. "Call me if you find anything out, or if you just want someone to talk to."

I handed her the piece of paper with my number on it and our hands brushed. As they did, Marina's eyes went flat and blank. Grabbing my wrist, she uttered a prophecy . . . the second one I'd ever received in my life.

CHAPTER THIRTEEN

An hour later, I was home, still puzzling over the prophecy. "Seek not, lest you find more than you bargained for. Keep not, lest you are prepared to meet your destiny."

It seemed to tell me I shouldn't look for the books unless I was prepared to accept the consequences, and I shouldn't keep them unless I was okay with meeting my destiny. What did that mean? Was that a veiled way of saying I'd die if I found and kept the books? Or was my "destiny" something else?

That was the problem with these soothsayer prophecies—their meaning was never clear until after the prediction came to pass. I sighed. I couldn't be sure what it meant, so the best thing was to ignore it and continue on like I'd never heard it. I looked through the book Rick had given me. No listing for the *Encyclopedia Magicka* and nothing useful. So, I booted up Gwen's computer in the corner of the living room and tried to figure out what the voice wanted me to look up.

I tried an Internet search for "*Encyclopedia Magicka*" first, and the only things that came up were references to role-playing games. I searched again for people trapped in books and got nothing but fiction. A search for "mage demon" brought more game stuff. And searching for a keeper of books was hopeless—scads of listings about accountants, but nothing about a keeper for magickal books.

I kept trying different combinations and different ways of saying the same thing, plus any other word combinations even close to what I was looking for, but it seemed to all be fiction, no fact. Then again, did I really expect to find factual accounts of demons on the web where anyone could see it?

Searching for "Book of Shadows" gained me a lot more information, including a mention of grimoires. Since both these types of books contained magickal spells, they were close to the *Encyclopedia Magicka*. But while reading about how to create them was interesting, I didn't see anything that would help me find the ones that were missing. And there was nothing about mage demons writing their own grimoires.

Fang yawned, bored with the hours I'd spent searching. MAYBE THIS GAME STUFF IS A DECOY, OR A CODE TO MAKE PEOPLE THINK IT'S ONLY FICTION.

I shrugged. Couldn't hurt to check. I pored over the rules of a bunch of games, trying to find one that fit the way the real demon world worked, but no luck. Each seemed to have inconsistencies that made me cross it off the list.

Finally, feeling eye strain—not to mention butt strain—I quit for awhile. Sheesh, this was harder than hunting the streets.

Fang stretched. I'M BEGINNING TO THINK THIS VOICE OF YOURS IS BOGUS. WHY DIDN'T IT SAY *WHAT* YOU WERE SUPPOSED TO LOOK UP?

"Because Kyle interrupted it when he messed with my dreams."

THEN MAYBE YOU SHOULD TRY DREAMING AGAIN.

Maybe. But the voice only seemed to be able to reach me when I was doped up or unconscious . . . or hanging out in that still, private place within myself.

SO USE THE CANDLE, ALREADY.

"I will . . . but let me give my butt a break first."

I got up and stretched, then searched for leftovers in the kitchen. With Gwen doing most of the cooking, there was always something good to eat in the fridge.

After we ate, I decided to try using the candle again. It was dark, so I set the candle on my nightstand, lit it, and turned off the lights. Sitting on the bed where it was softer on my backside, I stilled my mind as Micah had taught me and stared into the flame.

It became easier each time to go to that still, quiet place deep inside me. Without Lola to distract me, I visualized my favorite place in the world. In my mind's eye, I pictured myself sitting on the banks of the San Antonio River on the River Walk. The place was all mine, free of tourists, partiers, or people of any kind. I watched as the lazy waters of the jade green river flowed by, the soft breeze caressing my skin.

Peaceful, quiet, serene . . . perfect. I stayed there for awhile, just enjoying the unaccustomed tranquility. When I felt it was time, I opened my mind and my heart to receive any messages that might be waiting for me. After a time, I heard a whisper, so faint I almost didn't catch it.

Tell me what you want me to know, I urged.

But though the voice became a little louder, I couldn't catch every word. *Must . . . me . . . before . . .*

What? I concentrated harder, hoping the voice would become more clear.

The voice tried two more times before I finally got the full message. *You must find me before Trevor Jackson does.*

So it *was* the books talking to me! *Where are you?*

In the—

The voice abruptly cut off. This time, the sudden termination wasn't me, wasn't anything I'd done. I was still in the trance. What had happened to cut our communication? I stayed by the river in my mind a while longer, open and receptive, but the voice didn't return.

Disappointed, I finally withdrew and brought myself back to awareness of the here and now. And, as I lay back on the bed, I became aware of all my aches and pains. The wound in my side was almost healed, but still ached. My head still hurt a bit from where Micah had walloped me, but the worst part was the energy conduits that Lola used and my abused chakras. They still felt seared and overly sensitive. And I was still weaker than normal, not quite back up to full slayerish capacity.

So this was what it was like to feel human . . . vulnerable . . . fragile.

I wasn't sure I liked it much.

Lola was hiding down deep somewhere, which was odd but good. I couldn't remember a time when she hadn't been ever-present, always empty, always seeking more male energy, even when she was totally satisfied. But now, it was as if she was curled around the pain of the backlash, hiding from the boogie man, afraid to come out.

And, speaking of that backlash and what had caused it, why wasn't I more upset? This wasn't natural. It wasn't like Mood was around to control my emotions. Or was she? Upset, I sat up, prepared to call Micah and demand to know what was going on.

Fang spoke from beside the bed. CHILL. IT'S NOT MOOD—IT WAS KYLE.

"The dream demon? What did he do to me?"

HE PLANTED A SUGGESTION IN YOUR DREAMS SO YOU WOULDN'T FREAK OUT ABOUT WHAT YOU DID. HE TRIGGERED IT BY PATTING YOU ON THE SHOULDER WHEN HE SAW HOW UPSET YOU WERE.

And now that I knew that, the dam broke and the emotions poured back in. "Damn it, he had no right."

MICAH ASKED HIM TO. HE DIDN'T WANT YOU WORRYING ABOUT IT UNTIL YOU WERE ABLE TO HANDLE IT.

For some reason, that just ticked me off. "I can handle it just fine."

NOT FUN WHEN YOU'RE ON THE RECEIVING END, IS IT?

I glared at him. "Shut up."

IS THIS YOU HANDLING IT? 'CAUSE I GOTTA SAY, BABE, IT SURE DOESN'T LOOK LIKE IT.

I closed my eyes and took a deep breath. Why was I letting the hellhound get to me? Maybe because the sudden flood of overflowing emotions needed some outlet? Hell, I couldn't just sit here and let them overwhelm me. I had to deal with them somehow.

Grabbing my stakes, I headed for the Valkyrie.

Where you going? Fang asked as he trotted close behind me.

"I don't know. Out."

WELL, YOU'RE NOT GOING WITHOUT ME. SOMEONE NEEDS TO KEEP YOU GROUNDED.

"Whatever," I muttered. At the moment, I didn't care. I just needed to deal with these emotions churning inside me. Fear . . . shame . . . anger . . . they all warred for dominance.

Fang jumped up into his sheepskin-lined seat on the back of the bike. CAN YOU HELP ME WITH THE GOGGLES? I THINK I'M GONNA NEED THEM.

Impatiently, I strapped the goggles on over his head to keep the wind out of his eyes, then swung my leg over the seat and started the bike, revving the engine. I poured all of my frustration into gunning it the hell out of there, and as soon as I got on Highway 10, I sped up until I barreled along at breakneck speed, blowing the last of the cobwebs out of my brain. I couldn't worry about the emotions. All my concentration went to controlling the bike, fighting the wind and dodging other drivers on the dark highway.

I did just fine until we came up on the town of Seguin, and Fang warned me the police would likely be patrolling near the town. His warning came just in time. As I slowed to the speed limit, I saw a cruiser parked alongside the highway.

FEEL BETTER NOW? Fang asked.

Since he wasn't snarky for a change and actually sounded like he cared, I said, "Not really."

DID YOU HAVE, YOU KNOW, AN ACTUAL REASON FOR COMING HERE?

I sighed. *No, I just wanted to clear my mind.* But it hadn't gotten us any closer to finding the books.

MAYBE YOU SHOULD TALK YOUR PROBLEMS OUT WITH SOMEONE INSTEAD OF STEWING ABOUT IT, HE SUGGESTED.

I thought about it. "Maybe." Yeah, I should talk to Micah. He'd be the most likely to understand, since he had the same kind of issues I did.

Fang nuzzled me. IT'S WORTH A SHOT. I HATE IT WHEN YOU'RE OUT OF SORTS.

I smiled. So now I was supposed to do it for the hellhound's sake? I could deal with that. I pulled off the highway to get gas and something to eat and drink, then headed back to Club Purgatory.

On the way, I tried not to dwell on the fear lurking within me, thinking instead how nice it would be to take a vacation. I preferred taking a cruise to somewhere they didn't have demons or vampires, but Fang claimed that kind of place didn't exist. Besides, dogs weren't allowed on cruises, and he deserved a vacation too. We batted some other ideas back and forth, agreeing to avoid long flights when he'd have to be caged, and opting to go somewhere we'd never been. Since that was pretty much everywhere outside of Texas, there was lots to choose from. Maybe San Francisco, Taos, or Colorado Springs. They all sounded like great places.

When we arrived at Club Purgatory, we'd finally agreed to take a long driving vacation and make a loop to wander through New Mexico, Colorado, Utah, California, and Arizona to see the sights. It sounded like fun, but now that I was at the club and off my bike, I was wrenched back into the everyday world. Taking off Fang's goggles, I said wistfully, "Maybe someday."

Fang nuzzled against me for a moment. LET'S PLAN ON IT . . . ONCE YOU'VE MET ALL YOUR OBLIGATIONS.

Yes, that was the problem, wasn't it? My obligations. Sheesh, I was only eighteen. I wasn't *supposed* to have this many obligations. Not only was I contracted to the Movement until the books were found and the vamps came out, but the demons seemed to want to use me as a sort of enforcer, the Special Crimes Unit still wanted me to train vampire hunters, and my parents thought I should set a good example for my half sister. Would it never end?

Fang jumped down off the bike. HEY, THAT'S WHAT IT'S LIKE TO BE A GROWN-UP.

Even grown-ups get vacations, I reminded him, feeling sulky.

THEN LET'S FIND THE BOOKS AND HELP THE MOVEMENT COME OUT TO THE WORLD SO WE CAN TAKE ONE.

Good plan. But first, I needed to talk to Micah. I went in through the back and headed through the fake flames and hell theme of the club to his office, feeling the deep, thrumming beat of the music in the club. I'd never really been drawn to that scene, maybe because none of my friends were. But the clubbers all seemed to be having fun . . . I envied them for that.

Micah's office door was open, so I went in. He was working on some kind of paperwork. The simplicity of his office was a nice contrast to the drama of the club.

"Hi," he said. "Come to visit?"

I shrugged. "Just kind of need someone to talk to. Do you have time?"

"Of course," he said, and came around the desk to close the door, then sat in one of the side chairs. "What do you want to talk about?"

"I just realized Kyle made me . . . stop feeling things."

Micah grimaced. "I'm sorry. I knew you'd be upset, but I figured it was for the best at the time. Fang said you'd blame yourself for losing control."

I glanced down at Fang, but he gave a sort of doggie shrug and laid down with his head on his paws. Oh well, it didn't matter. I was all over my mad, and I knew they were just trying to help. "Who else is there to blame?"

"Blame for what?" Micah asked softly. "You saved a lot of lives that night . . . vampires and demons alike."

"I lost control, Micah. I *enjoyed* it. If you hadn't stopped me, I would have killed all the men there."

"But I did stop you."

"What if you hadn't been there?"

Micah shook his head. "You don't get it yet, do you?"

"Get what?" What was there to get?

"That's what the Demon Underground is *for*. Sure, we help each other find jobs and provide others to socialize with like ourselves, but we're here primarily to help each other deal with our gifts." He could obviously tell I was puzzled, so he added, "You're not alone, Val. There's not one of us here who hasn't been tempted to use our powers in a way others would find unacceptable. We help each other to be strong, to get beyond that temptation, to be better people."

"I—I didn't realize."

"What it means is that you don't have to go it alone, that we're here to back you up . . . just as you back us up."

Sheesh, and here I'd been whining about my obligations to the Underground. Made me feel kind of stupid.

YOU'RE TOO HARD ON YOURSELF, Fang said. LISTEN TO MICAH.

"I get what you're saying," I told Micah. "But that doesn't change the fact that if you hadn't been there, I would've killed a lot of people."

"I doubt it. If I hadn't been there to control the women, they would have stopped you. Or Fang would have found a way."

YEAH, Fang said. IF ROSA HAD CAUGHT YOU ABOUT TO DRAIN ALEJANDRO DRY, I DON'T THINK SHE WOULD HAVE BEEN AS GENTLE AS MICAH IN STOPPING YOU.

I hadn't even thought about that. For some perverse reason, that made me feel better. Fang was right—Rosa and the other women would definitely have kept me from taking everything. Grimacing, I said, "I guess I owe you one, cuz."

He grinned. "I don't think so. After all, you saved my life and have helped the Underground in many other ways. I probably still owe *you.*"

I waved that away. I wasn't interested in keeping score. It was enough to know we'd be there for each other.

And what he said was beginning to sink in. It wasn't all one way— I didn't have to be the savior all the time. Wow, I'd never really had anyone who'd be there for me like that. And, I now realized, any of the other demons would have probably done the same thing for me that Micah had. Kind of like a family. For the first time since I joined the Underground, I actually felt like I belonged somewhere. Nice.

But that didn't change certain other facts. "I appreciate that, really I do, but what happens now that I've let the genie completely out of the bottle? Can I ever stuff her back in?"

Micah gave me a half smile. "I think you can do anything you set your mind to."

I shook my head impatiently. "Thanks for the vote of confidence, but I don't need that rah-rah stuff. I need to know if I can trust myself to ever use my powers again."

"It's not 'rah-rah stuff' as you call it. It's the honest truth." Micah leaned forward, his expression earnest. "Val, you are one of the strongest people I know—"

"That's not important—"

"I'm not talking bodily strength, but strength of conviction, strength of purpose, strength of character."

Whoa. Was he really talking about me?

HE IS, Fang confirmed. NOW SHUT UP AND LISTEN.

"You kept your succubus side suppressed for a very long time, longer than I thought possible. You were getting a handle on it with Shade's help. You did it once—you can do it again."

I shook my head. "But what if I can't control it? What if I . . . suck him dry?"

"You won't."

"How do you know that?" I wanted to believe him, but the evidence didn't support it.

"Succubi and incubi were designed to enthrall one person at a time. I had a very hard time controlling the small number I held, and you had what? Four times that? And you didn't lose control until you tried to take on too many."

"Maybe."

"Think about it this way. You've been out and about all day. Have you had the urge to consume anyone yet?"

"No," I admitted, "But my succubus circuits are fried—I couldn't even enthrall a horny teenager right now. But when they're healed . . . "

"Then now is a good time to work on getting control, don't you think?"

"I guess," I said doubtfully.

"I *know* it is." He leaned back in his chair. "Val, what choice do you have? You either need to learn to control it, or it will control you. And I'm betting on you."

I shook my head, not entirely convinced.

Looking exasperated, Micah said, "This time, try something radically different. Something way out of character for you."

"Like what?"

"Like asking for help."

"I asked for help with rescuing Josh and Andrew," I protested.

"Yes, but that was for other people. You don't ask for assistance when you need it, personally."

Whoa. Was I really like that? Did I really try to do everything myself without asking for help?

PRETTY MUCH.

Well, crap. He wasn't the first one who'd said that, either. Maybe Micah was right. Maybe if I had help with this, I could figure out how to *not* lose control of Lola ever again.

Micah continued, "People like to help others. They'd love to help you if you ask for it. They just don't know what you need."

I nodded. "Okay, I'll think about it." I rose to give him a hug. "Thanks for pounding some sense into my head."

"No problem." He grinned. "Next time, I'll try not to be so literal."

I laughed, and a knock sounded on the door.

IT'S TESSA, Fang said. SHE'S BEEN WANTING TO COME IN, BUT I ASKED HER TO WAIT UNTIL YOU WERE DONE.

"Come in," Micah called.

Micah's assistant opened the door and smiled at me. "I'm glad you're here. I finally got the call back from the Los Angeles Underground."

"Good," Micah said. "And . . . ?"

"They never heard of Trevor Jackson."

CHAPTER FOURTEEN

The LA Underground had never heard of Trevor? Didn't surprise me at all. "Ha, I knew it."

"Knew what?" Micah asked.

"Knew he was lying about being a member of the Underground," I said triumphantly.

Tessa shook her head. "Actually, he never said he was a member of the Underground. But since he knew of their existence and ours, I just assumed he was. But he's not in any of their records."

Back to square one. "But doesn't it seem odd that they don't know anything about him?"

"Maybe," Micah said, then asked Tessa, "Did they give you any other information?"

She nodded. "I asked about mage demons, keepers and the encyclopedia. My contact said the LA Underground is well aware of mage demons, and the word is, when encountering one, to shoot first and ask questions later." Tessa gave Micah, Mr. Dudley Do Right, an apologetic look. "Apparently, a mage demon caused the 1906 San Francisco earthquake that took over three thousand lives and left three-quarters of the population homeless. The Underground there has never forgotten it."

Micah shook his head, whether in disbelief, denial, or disgust, I wasn't sure.

"And keepers? What about them?" I asked.

"She wasn't so sure of that part, but their history says that's when the Underground got together to find a way to control the mage demon. Keepers came into being about the same time, so are probably related. She doesn't remember hearing anything about the books, but knows their predecessors did something to control the mage." Tessa shrugged. "I figured it was the keeper. She admits she isn't the most knowledgeable person there, but said she'd see what she can find out and call us back."

"That wasn't real helpful," I said. I'd hoped to find some kind of evidence that would prove who Trevor really was.

"More than you think," Micah said. "Now we know mage demons do exist, and keepers were probably developed to control them. Maybe we'll learn more after the holidays."

"That's too late," I protested. "We need to find those books now."

"I'm glad you agree," someone said from the doorway.

I turned around. Trevor and Shade stood there. How much had they heard?

NOT MUCH, Fang said. THEY JUST GOT HERE.

Gee, thanks for the warning.

He shrugged. WASN'T NECESSARY.

"But what brought you to that conclusion?" Trevor continued.

Taking the offensive, I said, "We just learned the LA Underground doesn't have you in their records."

"Of course not."

Trevor looked so calm about my dramatic revelation, it really took me aback. I'd kind of hoped he'd come up with a lame excuse that would prove he was trying to deceive us. "What do you mean, of course not?" I tried not to sound too challenging, since Shade was standing there, looking all enigmatic and swirly. Sure wished I could see his expression about now.

Trevor shrugged. "I never joined."

"Why not?" I asked. After all, he'd been a real social butterfly in our Underground.

"Things are different in LA. They're more focused on other things."

"Like what?" Micah asked. "I've never really talked to the Undergrounds in other cities much."

Micah gestured us all to take a seat, so I grabbed one on the couch next to Shade while Micah and Trevor took the armchairs. Tessa perched on the arm of Micah's chair.

Trevor settled in, looking very comfortable. "The LA Underground seems to be more concerned with finding jobs in the entertainment industry, making sure their people are able to pass as human. I've never had a problem passing, so I didn't see any point in joining."

After what Micah had just told me, I bet there was more to it than that.

Trevor wrinkled his nose. "We had nothing in common, so I didn't socialize with them either."

Yeah, right. The metrosexual hairdresser was soooo not the Hollywood type.

Was Micah buying this? I couldn't tell.

HE'S RESERVING JUDGMENT, Fang said. GIVING THE GUY THE BENEFIT OF THE DOUBT.

Shade touched my arm and I glanced at him. He was giving me a warning look. Okay, so maybe I should pretend to believe Trevor, too, and wait for him to slip up.

"They did confirm that letting mage demons have control of the books is a bad idea," I conceded.

Trevor gave me a half smile. "You didn't believe me? Or Shade? He said the same thing I did."

"That's not what I meant. I was just trying to show you that I agreed with you." When he gave me a knowing smile, I said screw it. This wasn't me and no one would believe it. "You know, if you gave us something we could use, I might be less skeptical. Like that shield you have. It would come in real handy for some of our folks."

Everyone turned to look at Trevor and he grimaced. "I wish I could help you, but it's not something external that anyone can use. It's something internal, peculiar to me and my needs."

"Oh? What are those needs? What kind of demon are you, anyway?"

"Val, really," Micah protested.

Okay, yeah, I knew that was supposed to be the height of rudeness in the Underground community, but how could I find out if I didn't ask?

Trevor's smile disappeared. "I prefer to keep that private. It's necessary to protect myself."

"I thought so," Shade said.

Huh?

My guy smiled. "I've figured it out. There's only one type of demon I've read about who needs to keep up a constant shield like that. Add that to your ability to sense magick, and I know what you are."

Trevor looked apprehensive, but silently, I urged Shade to tell all.

Shade's grin widened. "You're an empath demon, aren't you?"

Some emotion flickered across Trevor's face, but it was gone so fast, I didn't know what it was. He gave Shade a rueful grin. "You figured it out."

Micah and Tessa looked enlightened, but I still didn't have a clue.

"What's an empath demon?"

"Sort of the opposite of Mood," Shade explained. "They can sense the emotions of everyone around them to know what they're feeling, but can't influence them. If he didn't have his shield to keep the emotions out, he'd probably go crazy." Shade looked at him with compassion. "Are you ever able to use your gifts?"

"Only as a keeper," Trevor said. "My ability to sense when the books are getting dangerous is invaluable."

"But if you can't influence emotions, how can you control the books?" I asked.

"An empath has other abilities as well, plus the training I received as a keeper gave me the control I need." Trevor raised an eyebrow. "It doesn't take an empath to see that you don't believe me. What have I done to merit your suspicion?"

"Act suspiciously," I shot back. "Keep secrets, let us believe things that aren't true, like your membership in the Underground."

"I've explained all that," Trevor said mildly, apparently refusing to let me bait him. "But I think I know why you're so suspicious when it's so unwarranted."

Unwarranted? Ha! "Oh yeah, why?"

"I think it's your prolonged exposure to the books."

"What do you mean?" Shade asked, looking interested and not at all like he didn't believe the creep.

Addressing me, Trevor asked, "How long did you have the books? About thirteen years?"

I nodded warily, not sure where he was going with this.

"How do you know they haven't influenced you against me?"

"That's ridiculous."

"Is it? They knew a keeper would come for them eventually. What would keep them from influencing a young, susceptible mind? Make that young mind believe that keepers are bad and shouldn't be trusted?"

Dang. He made it sound so plausible. "I think I'd know if that happened."

"Would you? Would you really?"

This guy was beginning to get on my nerves.

"Andrew didn't remember where the books told him to hide them," Shade reminded me.

"But he did remember that the books told him what to do."

Trevor shrugged. "The books didn't have as much time to work on him as they did on you." He cocked his head and gave me an insincere smile of concern. "I wonder why they programmed you that way. And what other things did they plant in your impressionable mind?"

Damn, he was good. He almost had me wondering. And from everyone else's speculative expressions, he was well on his way to convincing them, too.

ASSWIPE, Fang said with a growl. HE'S TRYING TO TURN THEM AGAINST YOU, MAKE THEM QUESTION YOU.

Yeah, I got that. "Don't be ridiculous," I all but spat out. "Remember who's in those books? Your *father*. Why would he hide from you?"

"He wouldn't. He's not in control—the books are. Maybe they're asserting undue influence over you even now."

"Oh yeah? Then why is it so hard for them to reach me? Why can I only hear them speak when I'm damn near unconscious?"

I was gratified by the stunned look on his face until he said, "What? They *talk* to you?"

Oops.

CHAPTER FIFTEEN

"What do you mean, they talk to you?" Micah asked, indignantly echoing Trevor.

Crap. I really wished I hadn't let that slip. Wonder if I could pretend like I was joking and laugh it off.

NO WAY, Fang said. YOU'RE NOT EXACTLY KNOWN FOR BEING A CUT-UP. BETTER TELL 'EM THE TRUTH.

Okay . . . some of it anyway. I shrugged like it was no big deal. "Something or someone is trying to reach me. I thought it might be the books."

Trevor's eyes narrowed. "Are you sure?"

"No, I'm not. That's why I didn't say anything." That, and the fact the books wanted me to find them before *he* did.

"How did this happen?" Micah asked.

I sighed. "Look, it only happened when I was unconscious or deep in a trance. It's like that's the only time the voice could reach me."

Shade linked his fingers with mine, his frown becoming visible. "That doesn't sound good. What did the voice say? Is it trying to control you?"

"No, the only thing he's said so far is to find him, and that we're looking in the wrong place."

"He?" Micah said.

"Well, it sounds like a man's voice. Do you think it might be your father?" I asked, trying to deflect the attention back on to Trevor.

"Perhaps," he said, but from his suspicious expression, I could see he doubted it. "So where did the voice say we *should* look?"

"I don't know. Every time it tries to tell me something, we get cut off or interrupted, like we have a bad connection. Really, I don't know anything or I would've found them by now." *Lay off, dude.*

Trevor relaxed then, and I wondered what I'd said that had caused that reaction.

"Can you tell where the voice is coming from?" Micah asked.

"No. I hear it in my head."

Trevor glanced at Shade with an I-told-you-so look which ticked me off more.

"No, it's not all just in my head," I snapped at him. "I heard what I heard."

Shade still frowned, and Micah glanced back and forth between Trevor and me uncertainly. "Fang, can you add anything?"

NO, SORRY. He gave me an apologetic look. I WASN'T CONNECTED IN WHEN SHE HEARD THE VOICE.

I hated the way that sounded. Damn it, I wasn't hearing voices. Well, okay, I was, but it wasn't just my imagination . . . was it?

"Maybe the blows to your head . . . " Trevor said suggestively.

"Nope. The voice tried to contact me *before* Micah hit me." Sheesh, I hated how defensive I sounded.

"Of course you'd believe that now." Trevor's expression held a fake look of concern that might fool everyone else, but it didn't fool me.

Why was he trying to discredit me? Come to think of it, why wasn't he pressing me harder to help him find the books with the voice's help? Did he really believe I was crazy? Or faking it? Once again, I really wished Fang could read the guy's mind.

Fed up, I said, "You know what? Never mind. Forget I said anything. If you want to believe I'm delusional, I'm cool with that. I'll just find the books before you do."

Shade gave me a one-armed hug. Normally, I'd love that, but right now I'm sure I felt stiff as a stake in his hold. "Val, no one believes—"

"Let's drop it, okay?" I said. "So, why did you two come here? Did you have an appointment with Micah?"

Most of them looked like they wanted to say something else to me, but they let me change the subject.

Shade squeezed me. "I was worried about you. I asked Micah and Tessa to let me know if you blamed yourself for what happened. I wanted to make sure you're all right."

"It's okay," I said. I wondered how to explain that Micah had talked me down from the ledge, so to speak, and I was feeling much better.

I'LL LET SHADE KNOW, Fang said.

Thanks.

Shade squeezed my arm a little. He'd gotten better at not reacting to Fang's mental invasions. He probably had a lot of practice with Princess.

"How are you feeling?" Shade murmured, as if it was only the two of us in the room.

"Almost healed, but a little tired," I admitted. I still wasn't back up to a hundred percent.

"Then why don't you let me take you home?"

I thought about denying I needed help, but getting Shade away from Trevor's influence held a lot of appeal . . . and besides, it was past ten and I had nothing else planned for the rest of the night. "Okay," I said softly.

GOOD CHOICE, Fang said. LET HIM BE THE STRONG ONE FOR A CHANGE.

Yeah, I guess guys liked that sort of thing. And I had to admit, it was nice to have someone who actually wanted to take care of me.

No one objected, so we left on the Valkyrie. It was a tight fit with Shade driving and me squished between him and Fang's seat, but very cozy. I snuggled my arms around him, laid my head on his back and enjoyed the ride home. It was really nice to have an excuse to hold onto Shade, especially with Lola out of commission. Made me feel like a normal girl on a normal date with her boyfriend. Even Fang was quiet for a change. Closing my eyes, I enjoyed the sensation of being warmed against Shade's body, feeling safe and cared for.

When we arrived at the townhouse, I didn't want this lovely, serene feeling to end, so I invited him inside, into the bedroom. Fang headed outside as I ditched my jeans and got under the covers, patting the space beside me invitingly.

Shade hesitated. "I'm not sure this is such a good idea."

"It's okay," I assured him. "I just want to cuddle for awhile, no Lola involved." When he hesitated, I added, "I feel better just being around you."

"All right, then." Toeing off his shoes, Shade started to join me on the bed.

"Wait—don't you want to take off your jeans? Get comfy?" Yes, I was pushing the limits a bit, but I'd been living most of my life on the edge lately.

He paused for a moment, then shucked his jeans and joined me under the covers.

I snuggled up to him, laying my head on his chest and throwing my bare leg over his. Oh wow, this was great. Sighing, I closed my eyes and let the feelings roll over me. He made me feel . . . I couldn't even describe it. So good. Like my bones were melting and fizzy water ran through my veins. And warm, really warm. Though I felt a much milder version of the slamming need that Lola forced me to feel, it was so much better. It felt . . . real, genuine. Truly me.

Shade squeezed me tight. "Maybe this isn't such a good idea," he whispered.

"Feels pretty good to me," I whispered back.

He chuckled softly. "That's the problem. It feels too good." He released me.

"Is that such a bad thing?" I asked wistfully.

"I'm sure it won't be," Shade murmured. "But I don't want you to do something on the spur of the moment that might affect you for the rest of your life."

"But—"

"No, I want you to be sure. This is something you won't be able to take back."

Dang. "Why are you so darned sensible?"

He laughed. "Someone has to be. And if it weren't for the fact we need you as you are right now, I wouldn't hesitate."

"Really?" I asked, trying not to sound pitiful and needy.

He kissed me on the nose. "Absolutely. You can tell I want you. I've always wanted you."

He turned me over so we could spoon. I don't know if he thought it would help or not, but it left me with a heightened awareness of him. But the guy was a gentleman, darn it, and did nothing but smooth my hair back, then lay his arm across my waist.

"So," Shade said, "did Micah really help you understand that no one blames you for what almost happened?"

I guess it was time to talk. Holding back a sigh, I said, "Yeah. Actually, he helped me to see that someone would have had my back, no matter what."

"Good. Because it's true, you know. Any one of us would have helped."

"Even Trevor?"

"Of course. He respects you. He's mentioned it several times."

To Shade, maybe. But in my world, actions spoke louder than weaselly words. But I had to know . . . "Why do you like him so much, Shade? Maybe if I could see what you see in him, I might think differently." Well, not really, but I did want to know the appeal.

I felt him shrug. "I don't know—he's a friend. I just like the guy. He understands me, what it's like to be a shadow demon. He knows a lot about other things, too."

"Like what?"

"Guy things."

I wasn't sure I wanted to know what that meant. "Really? He owns hair salons, for heaven's sake."

"That doesn't make him any less a man. He's not gay, you know."

No, he didn't seem to discriminate at all between the sexes. "But he's not exactly contributing to society in a meaningful way, now is he?"

"He's not a slayer, you mean?" Shade asked, an edge to his voice.

"No, that's not—"

"He contributes in other ways. He's a keeper, remember?"

Maybe. I wasn't entirely convinced of that, either.

"What do you have against him, Val?"

I thought for a moment, trying to find a way to sugar-coat it, but nothing came. "I guess I just don't trust him. There are too many unanswered questions. Too many secrets."

"Maybe he has just as much reason as I do to keep some things quiet. I prefer to let him keep his privacy." When I didn't say anything for a moment, Shade added, "Are you worried that I'm spending too much time with him? That he's taking your place?"

The jealousy thing again? "No—"

"Because if you are, don't worry. If it ever comes down to a choice between him and you, there's no question. It's you, Val. It's always been you."

Feeling suddenly overwhelmed, "Oh" was all I could say.

He squeezed me lightly. "I've been waiting for the right moment to tell you this, a time when you knew I wasn't under Lola's influence." I heard him take a deep breath. "I love you, you know."

I inhaled sharply, then couldn't breathe for a moment. Oh, wow. I didn't know why people did drugs—this was the biggest high I could imagine. I turned to face him. "Seriously?"

"Seriously." He kissed me softly on the lips. "Don't worry, you don't have to say it back."

"But I do. I-I think I love you, too."

"You think?" he teased.

Thank goodness he was amused, not offended. "Well, I've never been in love before, so I'm not sure. Is it love when you see someone and you feel all mushy inside . . . sometimes sick to your stomach or like you're really dizzy?"

"I think so. I feel that way, too."

I ran my hand under his shirt, feeling that need rising again. "Then you know what the logical next step is, don't you?"

"Going steady?"

Startled, I glanced up at him to see laughter in his gorgeous blue eyes. I hit him. "No, you know what I meant."

"Yes, I know. And I'd like nothing better, you know that. But I can wait. Forever . . . if it's for you."

Maybe he could, but I wasn't so sure about me . . . .

CHAPTER SIXTEEN

I woke feeling chilled, then smiled, remembering how nice it had felt to sleep spooned in Shade's arms. But when I groped to recover his warmth, I realized I was alone in the bed. The yummy aroma of frying bacon clued me in, and I realized Gwen must be cooking breakfast. Shade was probably in the kitchen with her.

YOU'RE HALF RIGHT, Fang said, speaking from another part of the townhouse. BUT IT'S SHADE DOING THE COOKING. GWEN ISN'T HOME YET. COME JOIN US, SLEEPYHEAD. IT'S ALMOST NOON.

WHY? Princess asked petulantly. SHE DOESN'T DESERVE IT. SHE KEPT MY HUMAN HERE *ALL NIGHT* AND LEFT ME *ALONE*.

NOT INTENTIONALLY, Fang soothed her. BESIDES, HE GOT UP EARLY TO GO GET YOU, DIDN'T HE?

YES, she grumped. BUT HE SHOULD HAVE DONE IT LAST NIGHT. HE FORGOT ALL ABOUT ME.

That last part sounded so forlorn, I almost felt sorry for the self-involved hellhound. But not quite. Shade indulged her too much. It was good for her to put someone else before herself for a change. Character-building, as Rick would say.

YOU'RE NOT HELPING, Fang reminded on a private channel. SHE CAN HEAR YOU, YOU KNOW.

Oops. I kept forgetting they could narrow their thoughts down to one person, but that I couldn't unless I concentrated really hard. Princess was as good as Fang at mind-reading and wasn't shy about using her abilities.

WHY WOULD I BE? the spaniel asked, sounding clueless.

No reason. Other than good manners, but I tried to keep that thought where she couldn't read it. *I'll take a shower then join you,* I told Fang.

Stretching, I realized that I felt a whole lot better this morning. Probably the fast healing that came with being a virgin succubus, but I wouldn't discount Shade's presence in my bed either . . . or the fact he'd said he loved me. As I headed for the shower, I couldn't stop grinning. Shade loved *me*, warts and all. Made me feel all warm and gooey inside.

When I finally looked presentable, I joined them in the kitchen and found Shade flipping an omelet at the stove with the two hellhounds watching his every move. There was no feeling awkward about whether or not to kiss him this time. Sure of my welcome, I slipped my arms around him from behind and hugged him, resting my head on his back. Love swelled within me, making me feel so full of happiness my body could barely hold it all. Wow—what a great feeling.

Shade turned in my embrace and gave me a kiss, looking all droopy-eyed and sexy.

"What a great way to wake up," I murmured. "I could get used to this."

He gave me a lopsided grin then turned back to the omelet. "Well, I'm not as good a cook as Gwen, but I do know how to make an omelet."

That wasn't what I meant, but I didn't want to chase him away by going all girly mushy on him. "Smells great," I said as my stomach growled.

He slid it onto a plate and nodded toward the table which was laden with toast, bacon, orange juice, and lots of condiments. "Sit," he said with a smile. "Eat."

Looked like my timing was excellent. Shade joined me at the table where three other omelets waited. He added bacon to two of the plates then slid them down to the hellhounds. I took a bite of my omelet. "Mmm. This is good." Delicious, in fact. I didn't know if it really was that great, or if it just tasted that way because all of my senses seemed to be bathed in a sort of love-stricken glow. It could have tasted like crap, and I probably would have still loved it, simply because Shade had made it for me.

GAG ME, Fang said from beneath the table. WHERE IS VAL SHAPIRO AND WHAT HAVE YOU DONE WITH HER BODY?

Making a pig of himself didn't hinder the mental communication one iota. I nudged him with my foot. *Quiet, beast. Don't make me remind you how sappy you get when talking about Princess.*

HE GETS SAPPY WHEN HE TALKS ABOUT ME? Princess asked, sounding self-satisfied and smug.

VAL, Fang whined. DIDJA HAVE TO?

Payback's a bitch, isn't it? Come to think of it, so was Princess.

Shade chuckled. Obviously, the hellhounds had shared their thoughts with both of us.

OKAY, OKAY. I'LL STOP IF YOU WILL.

Deal. I smiled at Shade. "So, what are you planning to do today?"

He shrugged. "Continue searching for the books with Trevor. The sooner we find them, the sooner we can get you out of your contract with the Movement."

I paused in mid-bite. Was that why he was so gung-ho about finding the books? That put a whole new light on things. "I appreciate you doing that, but doesn't it get boring, driving around all day while someone else listens for the books?"

"Not really. Trevor rented a comfortable car. Plus he has a lot of knowledge about other demons that he learned from his mentor and he's sharing it with me. I've been taking notes."

"Notes? Why?"

"To supplement the encyclopedia when we get it back."

"What a great idea. You could make it a living document—the encyclopedia part, I mean." There were gaps in the entries—serious ones—and having Shade fill them in would be awesome. But could we trust Trevor's information?

SHE THINKS TREVOR IS LYING TO YOU, Princess announced.

What the heck? I glared down at the spaniel. "I did not think that," I said aloud. *You're being petty, Princess. Not exactly royal behavior, is it?*

The dog sniffed and turned her head away, giving a great imitation of a spoiled brat.

"Why don't you two go outside for a while so we can talk privately?" Shade said. "We'll call you when we're ready to leave."

Since her human had suggested it, Princess was all for it. Their plates licked clean, the hellhounds wandered out the doggie door.

"Really," I assured Shade. "I didn't think that." And maybe my radar was wrong. Maybe Trevor was a good guy. But I was still cautious enough to keep to myself the fact that the encyclopedia didn't want Trevor to find it first.

Shade chuckled. "No worries. I plan to double-check all the information he gives me anyway. Details might have gotten garbled after they were passed from one person to another." Now that we were both finished eating, he reached for my hand. "What about you? Did the books talk to you again last night?"

I searched my mind, trying to remember what I'd dreamt. "Nope. Those dreams are usually pretty vivid, so I think I'd remember. The only thing I know I dreamed is that vamps and demons were searching everywhere for them, but it was a pure human who found them."

"Maybe your subconscious is trying to tell you something. Who was it?"

"Dan." I said it casually, hoping Shade wouldn't make a big deal out of the fact that I'd dreamed of my ex.

Shade nodded thoughtfully. "That's a good idea."

"What?" There was an idea in there somewhere?

"He's a good detective. Maybe he can, you know, detect or something to help you find them."

Shade didn't seem at all jealous. I didn't know if I should feel happy that he was so evolved, or upset that he wasn't the possessive type. Then I remembered he'd been jealous of Trevor at first, until he met the flirt. Maybe Shade was so confident of me because I'd admitted I loved him.

Yeah, I liked that answer. I was going with it.

"Dan might be able to help," I agreed slowly. "But I wouldn't know how to ask him. And, to tell you the truth, it would feel weird to beg a favor of him."

"Remember, as Micah said, people like to help. You ask so seldom, it'll be a novelty. Besides, he owes the Underground a huge favor after I healed him. Let him know this is how he can pay us back."

For some reason, that appealed to me, though I wasn't at all sure how Dan could help. "Okay, I'll do that. Thanks."

While Shade called Trevor to come pick him up, I did the dishes, then called Dan. He was at home, so after Shade and Princess left with Trevor, Fang and I walked over to see my ex-partner—and ex-boyfriend. Since he lived in the same complex, it was very convenient.

Dan opened the door and invited us in. Though the layout was a mirror image of our townhouse, his was decorated in Early Bachelor with a touch of College Dorm. He had the bare necessities as far as furniture went—dark, functional and comfortable, though not exactly stylish. But he'd spared no expense on the electronic equipment, which dominated the living room against one wall.

I suddenly felt weird. The last time I'd been here, we were kind of dating. I stood like a lump in the living room and wondered where to look, what to do.

AWKWARD MUCH? Fang quipped.

No kidding. I'd been sheltered all my life from the normal things people do. I probably ought to know how to act around an ex-boyfriend in the living room where we'd once made out, but I felt clueless.

"Have a seat," Dan said, and plopped down on the couch like nothing had ever happened.

Hmm, maybe in his view nothing had. It had been brief, though intense. I sat in the chair and relaxed. Okay, if that's how he wanted to play it, I would do the same.

When Dan looked at me expectantly, I figured I should make with the small talk first, so I said, "How's it going with you?"

"Good. The job keeps me busy."

"And Nicole?" I hadn't intended to ask about his new girlfriend, but it just sort of blurted out of my mouth.

SMOOTH, REAL SMOOTH, Fang said.

Leave me alone. I'm doing the best I can.

"She's doing better. Still not a hundred percent, but she's healing nicely."

"Good, good," I said, grateful that he'd mistaken my nosiness about their relationship for concern about her health. After all, a vamp had stabbed her in the shoulder with a chair. "She still in the Special Crimes Unit?" After her experience, I wouldn't blame her if she decided to have nothing to do with hunting vamps.

"Yeah. She's taken a desk job in the SCU until the shoulder heals, then we'll finish her training and assign her to a team."

I sat there, trying to think of something to say. Once again, my mouth opened and words came out that I hadn't really intended to say. "Shade and I are together now."

I cringed immediately. How lame was that?

VERY, Fang said with a snort.

Ignoring the hellhound, I added quickly, "Thanks for your advice there."

Dan nodded. "I'm glad it worked out for you." He paused, then said awkwardly, "I'm seeing Nic now."

"I figured." Oh, great. Now he'd think I was fishing for information. Okay, I was, but I didn't want *him* to know that.

Fang rolled his eyes. HUMANS MAKE EVERYTHING SO COMPLICATED. IF YOU WANT TO KNOW, ASK!

Like it's that easy.

IT IS.

The strange thing was, I didn't even know why I wanted to know who Dan was seeing. I just did. But learning the nitty gritty details . . .

not so much. How could I change the subject?

Luckily, Dan did it for me. "I hear you're working with Alejandro." He sounded disapproving.

I nodded. "I promised to work for him if any member of the Underground hurt any of his people. And since Andrew and Josh screwed up . . . " I shrugged. "Micah's lawyer helped me work out a contract so I only have to work with him until the encyclopedia is found and they have their coming out party."

"Any closer to finding the books?"

"No, actually, that's why I'm here. I was hoping you could help me."

Dan's eyebrows rose. "Me? How can I help?"

"As Shade reminded me, you're a darned good detective." I wasn't going to mention the dream. Didn't want him to think I was still pining over him or even thinking about him, because I wasn't. I had Shade now.

"What have you done so far?"

I explained about Trevor and how we'd been looking for the books with his senses and mine, plus the Internet searches I'd done.

Dan grilled me on everything I knew about the books, then nodded thoughtfully.

"Can you help me?" I asked when the silence stretched on too long.

"Maybe. Where were they last seen?"

"At Mood's house. Andrew hid them somewhere between the time he left Mood's and before he arrived at Alejandro's mansion."

"How did he leave there? On foot? By car? In a cab?"

"I don't know." And if it was in a cab, they might have records . . .

SORRY, BABE, Fang said. ANDREW HAS AN OLD BEATER CAR AND USED IT THAT DAY. I SAW IT IN HIS MEMORIES.

"Fang says he left in his own car." Something aligned just right in the old gray matter and an idea struck me. "Hey, you think it might show up on traffic cameras?" I asked eagerly.

My ex-partner smiled. "Maybe. Good idea. What kind of car does he drive?"

A 1967 BLACK MUSTANG, HELD TOGETHER WITH BONDO.

I passed the info on to Dan, then asked Fang, "How do you even know that?"

Fang laid his head on his paws and shrugged. ANDREW THINKS

ABOUT IT A LOT. ABOUT HOW MUCH IT COST TO BUY IT, ABOUT HOW MUCH IT COSTS TO FIX IT, HOW MUCH IT'LL COST TO BUY A HUMMER NEXT—

I get the idea. Turning to Dan, I said, "I can probably get a picture of it pretty easily. You think we could find it on the traffic camera tapes?"

"Maybe. Since you know the day and about when he arrived at Alejandro's, we can start from there and work our way back."

"Great!" Now we were finally getting somewhere.

Shaking his head, Dan said, "It still won't be easy. There are a lot of cameras and many routes he could have taken."

Feeling more optimistic now that there was a chance of finding the books, I said, "No problem. I don't mind looking. Can you set it up for me?" It would help me feel like I was actually doing something, making some kind of progress.

He pursed his lips. "I'm not sure. The guys in Traffic are kind of territorial, and they don't like the SCU much. And you're more of a civilian now—I don't know if they'd allow you to look at all."

"You think Lt. Ramirez might grease the wheels a bit? Especially if we explain why?"

"I don't know. If it's for the Movement, I'm not sure how well that will go over. And even if we get them to agree to release the tapes, I'd probably have to be the one to review them."

"But it's for the Underground, too, and you owe Micah a big favor . . . ." I hadn't wanted to play that card unless I had to, but it was looking that way.

Dan rubbed the shoulder Shade had healed for him. Sighing, he said, "Okay, I'll see what I can do and let you know."

WHADDAYA KNOW? Fang snarked. THE GUY ACTUALLY CAME THROUGH FOR US.

I knew he would. After all, he still had that hero complex and couldn't resist a damsel—or anyone else—in distress. He only needed to be talked into it. "Thanks, Dan. I really appreciate it. I'll get pictures of the car for you and Andrew's license plate number."

I was asking a great deal of him—it meant hours and hours of tedium. But he shrugged like it was no big deal. "I'll get Nic to help. It'll give her something to do besides paperwork."

Wow, not even a twinge of jealousy here. Looked like I was finally over him.

DATING A HOT NEW GUY WILL DO THAT FOR YOU.

I hid a smile. Yeah, it didn't hurt.

"Besides," Dan added, "I have more time on my hands since the bloodsucker population seems to have gone down quite a bit lately. It's not the SCU's doing, though we haven't been slacking on patrolling the streets. It's almost as if they're afraid to come out. Not that I'm complaining, but I wondered if we have some vigilantes out there among the Movement."

"Not that I know of. But we did send a warning to the rogue vamps, telling them to join the Movement or be fair game. Attacks on the blood banks slowed down after that."

Dan nodded. "We heard something about a big smackdown last week among the vampires, but we were asked to keep away so Alejandro could police his own. Did you have something to do with that?"

"Sort of. The Movement and the rogue vamps had a showdown. Alejandro won with the help of the Underground."

"Why didn't they want the SCU's help?" He didn't seem pissed about it, just curious.

"I'm not sure. Probably because it was impossible to tell the good vamps from the bad. We had to kind of incapacitate all of them and sort them out later."

Unfortunately, Dan picked up on the one weasel word I hadn't wanted to explain. "Incapacitate?"

I glanced away, knowing how he felt about my succubus. "You know . . . Lola. And Micah helped with the women."

Dan made a face but didn't comment on my lust demon. "And did you use, uh, drastic staking measures to do that sorting?"

I winced. "The Movement did, yes. I was kind of out of it by that time." Not that I was going to tell Dan I'd totally lost control of Lola as he'd always feared. But I did explain about Shawndra's death and warned him the SCU might encounter more crazy vamps, if the ones still alive believed demon blood would make them stronger.

"Why did they start attacking the Movement anyway?" he asked. "It doesn't seem rational."

"Because they don't want the Movement to announce to the world that vampires really exist."

"Why not?"

"Because when Alejandro makes his announcement, he'll also announce that any good vamps need to join the Movement, and he has legislation in place to administer the death penalty to any vamps who suck vein without permission. In Texas anyway." Though the rest of the states would probably follow. "That makes sense. And I wish Alejandro the best with it."

"Why?" I didn't think he wanted the world to know vampires really existed.

"It'll be a lot easier on the SCU if we're allowed to work out in the open . . . and execute fangbangers on sight."

"I hadn't thought about it that way." But he was right. "Then by helping us find the books, you'll be helping Alejandro come out that much sooner."

"Noted," he said with a nod.

Fang scrambled to his feet. CAN WE GO NOW?

I guess so. I rose, too. "We've taken up enough of your time. But thanks for doing this. You have no idea how much I appreciate it."

"No problem." Dan hopped out of his chair to open the door for us. "I'll do my best to find where Andrew hid the books and let you know as soon as I learn anything."

"Good." I just hoped I'd hear from him really soon. I had to find those books before Trevor did. I didn't know what would happen if he got them in his hot little hands, but whatever it was, it couldn't be good.

CHAPTER SEVENTEEN

I spent the next several days trying to figure other ways to find the books—something better than aimlessly wandering the streets or hoping they'd contact me again. Sending me a mental map with a big red X on it would be nice . . . .

But since there was no luck in that department, our best shot seemed to be the traffic cameras. I'd sent Dan pictures of Andrew's car and his license plate number, but the red tape in the department had slowed that down, and he wasn't even going to be able to start looking until tomorrow. The only bright side was that Shade reported Trevor hadn't found them either.

I slumped on my living room couch in the early afternoon, hoping a clue or the voice would magickally come to me.

HOW'S THAT WORKING FOR YOU? Fang asked beside me.

I pulled his fuzzy ear. "Not so good. Got any better ideas?"

HAVE YOU HEARD FROM THE WITCHY CHICK YET?

"Marina Lester? No. I guess it wouldn't hurt to talk to her again. Good idea. I'll try her." Maybe there was some kind of Wiccan magick she could use to find them.

I hadn't thought to keep her number, and it was probably better to do this face to face anyway. Sure beat hanging around home.

Jumping at the chance to do something, I took Fang and headed over to her house on the Valkyrie. We arrived just as she was opening the door and a client was leaving. Our pixie-like redheaded host smiled. "Come on in. I don't have another appointment for a couple of hours."

Just inside the door, another woman stood. Tall and thin with long wavy dark hair, she wore a purple caftan with shiny silver moons and stars all over it—a stark contrast to Marina's petite jean-clad form. "This is my friend, Erica Small," Marina said. "And this is Val Shapiro and Fang. I told you about them."

Really? How much had she revealed? We shook hands and I took a step back toward the door. "I'm sorry, I didn't mean to intrude."

"It's all right," Marina assured us. "I was just getting some tea and we were going to chat.." Marina waved us toward the living room, then asked over her shoulder, "Would you like some tea?" as she and Erica headed for the kitchen.

I was more of a Coke drinker, but when in Wicca land . . . "Sure," I called out, then took a seat in the living room. It had seemed pretty normal before, but now I realized it was decorated in soothing pastel shades of blue and green, with nothing harsh on the eyes, designed to put people at ease. The only things indicating her Wiccan background were a few subtle accessories—a yin-yang symbol on the pillows, pentacles on the coasters, that sort of thing.

Marina brought in the tea on a lacquered tray etched with a goddess symbol, and set it down on the coffee table. Erica added a plate of cookies that looked more healthy and good for you than good tasting. I decided not to risk it. "I hope you like chai," Marina said.

"I don't know. I've never had it." I took a sip. It tasted hot and sweet, with cinnamon and other spices. "Hey, this is good."

Erica smiled. "I'm glad you like it—it's my special blend. I made the cookies, too."

I glanced at Marina. "I wondered if you'd had any success in learning about that, uh, book I asked you about before."

Marina took a sip of her tea as well, then said, "I'm sorry, but I wasn't able to find anything on an *Encyclopedia Magicka* anywhere."

I gave Erica a dubious glance, but Marina waved that away. "Erica won't say anything. She's my best friend—we share everything . . . including a new membership in the Demon Underground."

Is that true? I asked Fang.

YEP. THEY'RE BOTH MEMBERS NOW . . . BOTH PART-DEMON.

"Really?" I asked with a smile, not sure how to respond to that . . . or how to ask exactly what kind of demon she was.

"Yes," Marina confirmed. "No wonder we always got along so well. Me with my prophecies and Erica with her ability to find things. We work together sometimes."

I perked up at that. What a useful talent. "That's great. Do you think you could help me find some lost books?"

Erica shrugged, looking embarrassed. "Maybe. The demon blood is pretty diluted in me, so it's not really easy. If my father were still alive . . . it was a lot easier for him."

"But she'd be happy to try," Marina said eagerly. "Wouldn't you, Erica?"

"Sure."

THANK YOU, Fang broadcast to all of us.

The two Witches jumped, and Erica's mouth spread in a delighted smile. "Wow, he really does talk. Where can I get a hellhound of my own?"

WELL, IF PRINCESS WOULD JUST COOPERATE BY GOING INTO HEAT . . . , Fang said suggestively.

We all laughed. "Princess is a Cavalier King Charles Spaniel," I explained. "And part hellhound. She and Fang have a thing." I glanced at Fang. "But she was a rescue dog. Wasn't Shade required to get her spayed in order to adopt her?"

HE WAS SUPPOSED TO, BUT WOULD *YOU* TRY TO DO ANYTHING TO PRINCESS AGAINST HER WILL?

He had a point. "I guess not. We'd hear about it for years." And it's not like we had an overpopulation of hellhounds.

Marina grinned. "I bet their puppies would be really cute."

I LIKE HER, Fang declared.

"Cute, yes," I agreed. "But I'm not vouching for the attitude in that mash-up."

HEY, Fang protested. YOU THINK I CAN'T TRAIN 'EM UP TO BE JUST LIKE ME?

"That's what I'm afraid of," I said drily.

We all chuckled at that. But I had to admit that having a bunch of diva dogs like Princess running around—-who figured the world owed them adoration—that would be even harder to take.

TELL ME ABOUT IT, Fang said. BUT YOU DO WHAT YOU GOTTA DO TO GET WHAT YOU WANNA GET.

Okay, TMI. *Way* too much information . . . . I shoved a cookie in his mouth to distract him and changed the subject. "Erica, you said you might be able to help us find the books. How would that work?"

"There are a number of ways I've learned over the years to find something. The best is through an affinity spell."

"What does that mean?"

"It means that like calls to like. Do you have any small portion of the books still? Like a page, or a bookmark, part of the binding? If so, we can use a spell to call the two together again."

"No, I'm afraid not."

"How about something the books were kept in, like a cloth bag?"

I shook my head. "No. I kept them mostly in a backpack but it was taken along with the books." I felt my shoulders slump in disappointment.

"It's okay," Erica said with a pat on my hand. "There are other ways. Have you tried looking for them with a map and a pendulum?"

"No. Do you think that will work?"

"One way to find out," Marina said. She cleared the tea and cookies off the coffee table and even discreetly picked up the cookie Fang had spit out and tried to hide under my chair.

THEY TASTE LIKE DIRT WITH MOLDY RAISINS, Fang complained to me alone. YOU TRY ONE.

I suppressed a grin. *I'll pass. But thanks for not spitting it out in Erica's face.*

HEY, I GOT SOME COUTH.

You do indeed.

I helped Marina spread out a map of San Antonio on the coffee table, and Erica drew a clear crystal out of a silk bag. The crystal looked like a fat stubby pencil, with five sides and a point at the end. The other end had a silver cap with a chain attached.

Setting the crystal down on the map, Erica explained, "This is a pendulum. If I hold it above a map and concentrate hard on something, the pointed end will land on the portion of the map where the object or person can be found."

"It's that easy?" I asked incredulously.

"It can be, if I know the object or person in question. To find something for someone else that I've never seen, I need to hold their hand and try to get a picture of it. Sometimes it works, sometimes it doesn't. It depends on how well you're able to concentrate."

"That's why we work together sometimes," Marina added. "Usually one or the other of us can answer a client's question."

That made sense.

"Let me show you how it works," Erica said. "Think of something you'd like to find. Something you know very well . . . and make sure you know where it is right now, so you can see that it works."

HOW ABOUT PRINCESS? Fang asked.

Well, we both knew her really well, and she was probably either at Shade's house or in the car with him and Trevor, so I said, "Okay, let's try that."

Erica gave us a slow grin. "I've never tried this with er, someone of the canine persuasion before. Let's try it with Fang by himself first and see what happens."

She held out her left hand, and Fang solemnly put his fuzzy paw in it. Erica then used her right hand to pick up the pendulum. Holding the chain so it swung loose over the map, she closed her eyes and said, "Okay, Fang. Think of Princess, wonder where she might be."

She moved the pendulum in a wide circle, skimming it barely above the map, then let it swing free on its own. Soon, the pendulum moved in tighter and tighter circles over one particular spot until it suddenly jerked to a halt and fell onto the map.

Erica opened her eyes and touched the crystal lightly. "Princess is located where the point of the crystal ends."

Fang and I leaned in to look at that point on the map. "That's where she lives," I confirmed.

SHE'S GOOD.

"Fang must have a very strong image of the subject," Erica said with a smile. She looked at me. "Would you like to try it?"

"Sure." If this would help us find the books, I'd be willing to do a lot more than play spin the crystal.

"Okay, let's start with something easy. What would you like to find?"

"Do I have to tell you what it is?"

She looked surprised. "Not really. It just helps me focus a little more."

"Okay, let's try it without telling you." I wanted this to be a real test. Now, what should it be . . . ? "I've got it," I said, and grasped her hand, closing my eyes and concentrated on finding Trevor. I put some oomph into it, not wanting Fang to be the only one who could do this. And before he could say anything, I added, *yes, I wanted you to hear that.*

After a few moments, I heard the pendulum thunk down on the map and opened my eyes to see it pointing to an address that looked vaguely familiar. Oh yeah, it was one of the blood banks.

"Is that right?"

"I don't know. It could be. He was driving around today with a friend."

"Oh," Erica said, sounding disappointed. "Maybe you can try to find something when you know where it is?"

Duh. Made me feel kind of foolish. "Okay, I've got something else."

We went through our ritual again and this time the pendulum landed on the hospital.

"Oh, no," Marina said. "I hope no one's hurt."

"No, it's okay," I assured her. "I was thinking of my roommate—she's a trauma nurse in the ER there. And that's exactly where I expected to find her."

Erica gave me a relieved smile. "Good. It worked for you, then. Would you like to look for the books next?"

Convinced this was for real, I said, "Absolutely." I rubbed my hands together, partially in anticipation, partially to ensure we would get a good connection. "Let's do this."

I placed my hand in hers, but this time I kept my eyes open and watched. The crystal spun in circles for several seconds, but didn't zero in on any one location. This was taking a lot longer than the others. "Is something wrong?" I whispered.

Erica opened her eyes and stopped the pendulum. "Are you sure the books are in San Antonio?" she asked.

"Not really. We just assumed there wasn't time to take them anywhere else."

"Okay, let's turn the map over."

On the other side, the whole state of Texas was laid out in the bottom right corner of the map. Holding the pendulum above it, Erica said, "Okay, concentrate once more."

It didn't take long this time for the crystal to land, its pointed end squarely on the dot representing San Antonio. Unfortunately, with the small scale of the map, it didn't give us much idea of exactly where the books would be.

"Hmm," Erica said with a frown. "They're here in town. How many books are there? Do you think they might have been separated?"

"There are three, but I doubt they'd be split up," I said. The voice didn't seem to indicate they were in pieces.

"Okay," Erica said with a sigh. "Let's try again." She turned the map back over and we tried again, but though the pendulum tried to waver over several different parts of the city, it gave up and just made big looping circles.

Erica stopped it, looking frustrated. "This may sound a bit strange, but I don't think these books want to be found."

I nodded. "You're right. They don't. But I was hoping we could force them to reveal their hiding place. Is there anything else we can try?"

Erica thought for a moment. "You know, I've never done this with more than one person, but given the power we hold collectively, maybe we could make it work if we all touched. Val, you and Fang hold my left hand and concentrate as hard as you can on the books . . . and Marina, if you would hold onto my left wrist and concentrate on amplifying their concentration, maybe we can make this work."

We did as she said, and the pendulum seemed to go crazy. It would swing above one space on the map only to suddenly jerk away and swing somewhere else. "Concentrate harder," Erica said with a grimace. "We've almost got it."

I leaned into it with everything I had, then felt Marina stiffen beside me. In her flat, prophetic voice, she intoned, "That which you seek reveals itself to a select few. If you are of good heart, you will find what you desire in—"

A bolt of electricity slammed through us, entering through the crystal and moving lightning-fast through Erica, then zapping the rest of us, blasting us violently apart. Marina and Erica cried out and even Fang yelped in surprise as we flew backward.

I'd tumbled over in the chair, then scrambled to right it and myself. I glanced around, feeling panicky. "Is everyone all right?"

I'M GOOD, Fang said. JUST A LITTLE SINGED. BUT ERICA, NOT SO MUCH . . . .

Erica was holding her hands before her, her eyes wide with horror. Everywhere she had been touching us or the crystal, her hands and wrists were blackened with the power that had just surged through us. The crystal lay shattered in jagged shards on the map, the chain black and partially melted. Holy cow, that was some power.

I glanced at Marina, but she seemed much like Fang and me, feeling singed and stinging a bit, but mostly startled, not injured. "Let's get you to the ER," I said. "My roommate works there."

Erica's mouth opened and closed, but nothing came out. She seemed to be in shock. "Marina, do you have a car?" I asked urgently. The motorcycle wasn't made for this.

She nodded, though she still looked stunned.

"Can you drive?" I persisted.

"Uh, yeah, I think so." She shook her head and seemed to get rid of whatever fog she was in. "Of course, of course. Let's go."

CHAPTER EIGHTEEN

We helped Erica into the car and headed off. She moaned and I cringed at the sound. The woman was hurting because of me. "Wait," I said. "I have a better idea. I know a demon healer. It'll be faster." And her injuries were minor enough that Shade wouldn't be endangered.

I called Shade and explained the situation. He agreed to meet us at his place since it was closest. I gave Marina directions, then explained about Shade and his appearance. Didn't want them freaking out at the guy who was about to be Erica's savior.

On the way, I told Marina, "That lightning bolt caught us just as you were giving us a prophecy about the books."

"It did?" Marina said. "No wonder I didn't see the strike coming."

"We didn't see it coming either. I don't suppose you remember the rest of the prophecy?"

She shook her head ruefully. "None of it, like usual."

Through gritted teeth, Erica added, "The timing seems suspicious. Like someone didn't want you to finish that prophecy or have us find those books. We almost had it . . . ."

Yeah, it did seem suspicious. But I couldn't understand it. I thought the books *wanted* me to find them. So what was this all about? Had we triggered an automatic protective spell of some sort? It was confusing.

We arrived at Shade's place just as he and Trevor drove up.

I introduced them. "Shade, Trevor, this is Marina and Erica. Erica is the one who's injured."

"What happened?" Trevor asked, looking at the two women with some annoyance.

I helped Marina get Erica out of the car. "She got hurt trying to find the books," I snapped at him. "Some compassion would be nice."

He held up his hands defensively. "Just asking." He darted a quick glance at Shade, but since he wore a deep hoodie and wasn't touching anyone, the shadow demon's features were inscrutable. "Do you need some help?"

That was obviously directed at Shade, as if Shade's opinion was more important than anyone else's. What was going on there?

Shade unlocked the door and directed them to his couch. His living room was a lot like Dan's, only with more gaming electronics and bookshelves. It was spotless as always, though.

Fang sniffed the air. I THINK PRINCESS IS GOING INTO HEAT. BUT SHE'S HIDING, THE LITTLE MINX. SEE YA.

Fang took off, following his nose. Sheesh. Males—always at the mercy of their gonads. Oh well, we didn't need him here right now anyway.

Erica half sat, half laid on the couch, her face twisted in a grimace of pain as she held her hands cupped in front of her.

"Are you sure this is going to work?" Marina asked in a worried tone.

"Don't worry, it will," I assured her. Then, turning to Trevor, I added, "You can leave to continue your search if you want. We don't need you here."

"No, that's all right," he assured me smoothly. "I'd like to see this."

Shade took my hand then threw back his hood. He probably wanted to reassure the Witches with his normality. "Do you know how this works?" he asked Erica.

Erica stared up into his face as if she'd suddenly seen her savior. With his head haloed by a lamp in the dark room, I could see where she might think he was an angel. "Sort of," she gulped out.

"I am part shadow demon," he said gently," and when I'm not touching a being of this world, I look like this." He let go of my hand, and Marina and Erica both gasped. They appeared fascinated instead of horrified by his swirls, thank goodness, or I would've asked Shade to stop.

He grasped my hand again. "I can channel healing energies from another dimension to heal Erica's injuries, but I need to use another person as a sort of template, to show the healing energies what a whole system looks like."

"I can do that," Marina said eagerly.

Shade smiled. "Thank you. However, I must warn you both that you will share a lot more than that. You will share memories, fears, hopes and dreams with each other, but not with me. I am merely a conduit for the energies. If you aren't ready for that, let me know and we can find someone else to be the template or take you to the ER."

Marina and Erica looked at each other and smiled. "We've been best friends forever," Marina said. "It's not a problem."

Erica nodded. "I agree. What do we need to do?"

"Just sit on the couch next to each other," Shade began.

Trevor interrupted him. "Are you sure this is wise? A good use of your abilities?"

Annoyed, I said, "I can't believe you're saying this. Who do you think you are? Shade's manager?"

Trevor scowled at me. "I'm merely concerned for Shade. He told me what happened the last time he healed someone. We almost lost him. I don't want that to happen again."

"I don't think her injuries are bad enough to be a danger to me," Shade said softly.

He was too nice to the creep. "Don't forget, this woman got hurt because she was helping us look for the books," I reminded Trevor.

"How?" Trevor asked.

"What does it matter?"

"It might matter to Shade in the way he treats her."

Dang it, he always made things sound so reasonable. But it wasn't my story to tell, or I'd reveal the Witches' demon powers. I looked at Marina and Erica to see what they wanted to reveal.

Marina sighed. "Erica is a finder. She was using a crystal pendulum over a map of San Antonio. We were close to finding the books when I, uh, went into a trance."

"A trance?" Shade repeated with a puzzled look.

"Soothsayer demon?" Trevor asked.

Marina nodded. "The books must be protected somehow, because as I was doing my prophecy thing and the pendulum was getting closer to finding the books, the crystal shattered and we got the backlash. It felt like lightning or electricity ran through us. Erica got the worst of it."

"What did the prophecy say?" Trevor asked, trying to sound nonchalant, but the eagerness on his face betrayed him.

"Nothing useful," I told him. "She wasn't able to finish it. Now, can we heal this nice lady?"

"Of course," Trevor said.

Soooo glad we had his permission. But I bit that back as I watched Shade position the women on either end of the couch.

He moved the coffee table out of the way and sat on the floor facing them, lightly touching their wrists near the injuries. "Ready?" he asked as he blipped into focus.

"Ready," they chorused.

"Then relax and try to stay conscious. This may hurt." Shade lowered his head, and his face flickered in and out of the dimensions, in and out of the swirls. The swirls moved faster and faster, like a tornado, with small flashes of purple lightning zinging through now and again. All normal . . . for him, anyway.

Erica grimaced and strained, but her fingers and wrist slowly turned from a blackened mess to pink, healthy flesh. I expected him to stop when they looked whole once again, but he kept going.

Trevor looked alarmed. "What's wrong? Shouldn't he be done by now?"

"Yes," I said, hating to agree with him.

"Then why isn't he?"

"I don't know," I said in exasperation. "You're the guy with all the answers. You tell me."

"He must be healing more than her hand," Trevor whispered in horror. "What else is wrong with her?"

"I don't know—I just met her." I stared at Erica, who was bent over double now, writhing in pain. "You think she has cancer or something?" That would be bad. Very bad.

"Shit. I hope not. Shade can't handle that much." Trevor took a step toward Shade, looking anxious. "We have to stop him. I need him."

I blocked him with my body, maybe a little more forcefully than I had to. "Leave him alone. You don't know what will happen if you touch him at this point."

Trevor shoved me backward with both hands. "We both know what will happen if we don't."

I slugged him back, right in the shoulder, just to relieve some of my pent-up anger at the creep. "I can handle it. I can help him. I did it before."

He got right up in my face and yelled, "If we stop him now, you won't have to."

I was prepared to yell right back, with my fists if necessary, but he darted around me and grabbed Erica's hand to pull her away from Shade.

But Erica's hand wouldn't pull away. It was as if a circuit had been completed with the four of them, and Trevor stood there, jerking spasmodically, his eyes wide open and his mouth drooling. The others mirrored him, even Shade.

Oh crap, oh crap. This couldn't be good. What could I do?

I couldn't grab hold of anyone or risk being pulled into that myself. Should I wait it out? I was afraid it wouldn't let up. Force wouldn't work, reason wouldn't work . . . all I had left was Lola. And since the only one in that unholy circuit she would affect was Shade, I concentrated on him, reaching out with all my might to grab onto his chakras.

But I couldn't get a grip. I couldn't snag his attention, not with all of his will focused on the healing.

Uh oh. Was that a green cloud forming above his head? That couldn't be good. Was it one of the other dimensions? Was he about to lose control and let more demons into our world?

Crap. Maybe if I distracted him . . . But how could I do it without touching him?

I couldn't touch him with my hand, but I could distract him by hitting him with something else. I glanced around the room and grabbed the first thing I found—a book—and threw it at him. It didn't seem to do anything, but something must have worked, because Shade moaned, "Stoooop meeeee . . . . "

Okay, maybe if I threw something harder and knocked him out. It had worked on me. Another book didn't do it, so I picked up a large crystal paperweight and threw it at his head. But he was jerking, so it missed and hit him in the shoulder instead.

Energy flashed from Shade into the crystal, turning it a virulent purple before it overloaded and exploded, sending the four of them flying apart. Trevor and the two women lay unconscious, but Shade was still alive and shaking, curled into a fetal position with that green cloud growing slowly over his head.

No, no, no. This couldn't be happening. I ran to him and helped him to his feet. He staggered toward the bedroom, and I followed him, wondering what he planned to do.

He pulled a knife from his nightstand, and I suddenly knew what he intended. Fear poured through me. No, I couldn't lose him. I'd just found him. I yanked the knife out of his hand and sent it spinning to the other side of the room.

Hugging him fiercely, I said, "I'm sorry, Shade. What can I do?"

"Kill me. Now." His voice was muffled in my shoulder, but I could hear him quite well.

"I can't do that. You know I can't." But the green cloud was growing above him.

Lola helped last time, so I hoped she could again. She wasn't quite back up to full force, but it would have to do.

Wrapping myself around him, I pulled Shade down onto the bed. His body was so tense, so concentrated on controlling his abilities, it was as if he didn't even know I was there. Instead of shoving Lola into him, I eased her in slowly through the cracks in his defenses, letting her gradually take over his body. This way he didn't slam up his defenses.

It worked, but that green cloud continued to grow, creepily silent, and it didn't look good for the home front. I needed more ammunition, needed to give Lola more room to work. Skin to skin, that was the ticket. I let go of him long enough to try to strip off his clothes, but he struggled against me.

"I'm trying to help you, damn it," I muttered. "Work with me here."

Though he was still gritting his teeth, Shade helped me remove his clothes, then I whipped off mine as quick as I could and wrapped myself around him, urging Lola in through all his pores, filling up every one of his chakras, willing her to leave no room for anything else . . . like pesky alternate dimensions.

Though Shade remained rigid in my arms, I could see the cloud getting smaller. It was working! Together, we were getting a hold on his sanity. I pushed harder, urging him to stay with me in the here and now, here in this flesh, together.

"Val," Shade groaned and buried his head in my neck. "Don't stop."

No problem. I couldn't stop for anything. I didn't want to. It was as if something else outside myself had control of my body, something freeing all of my inhibitions. Lola pulsed through us, raising our awareness higher, until there was nothing left in the universe except Shade, me, the slide of skin against skin, and an incredible pent-up passion. His scent was so delicious, so yummy—like some primeval musk—I just wanted to eat him up.

Oh wow, this was . . . amazing.

Wait, a little voice inside me said. *Stop and think about this.*

Who needed little voices? Not me. Not Lola. Right here, right now, I no longer cared about my powers, no longer cared about being the Slayer. All I wanted was to be normal, like any other girl loving her guy.

At last, I gave in to temptation.

CHAPTER NINETEEN

Afterward, as we lay entwined together, Shade murmured nonsense about how much he adored me and covered my neck with kisses. I sighed and rested my head on his chest, happy and content. For the first time in my life, I felt really loved. It wasn't how I would have planned my first time, but it was still wonderful, without the awkwardness I'd expected.

I explored my body and senses mentally, probing for any changes beyond the incredibly obvious one. Nope, not a thing different—I still felt like me. My hopes rose. Maybe Shade was wrong. Maybe I wouldn't lose my powers.

I didn't regret finally doing the deed, but I did wish it hadn't happened like this. I'd really wanted to make our first time special, at a time and place of my own choosing, with candlelight, roses, and the whole schmaltzy deal. Us both losing control of our powers . . . *not* my go-to choice. But it was as if something outside me—outside *Lola* even—had grabbed hold of my emotions and driven me out of control. Something like an empath demon, maybe? I went rigid at the thought.

"Are you okay?" Shade murmured.

I gave him a quick squeeze to reassure him. "I'm good."

"Are you worried about not having . . . you know, protection? Remember, different kinds of demons can't interbreed. And I'm clean."

"I know. I'm just trying to understand how it happened."

He levered up onto one elbow to look down at me and smoothed the hair from my face. "I'm sorry. I didn't intend for our first time to be like this."

"Neither did I," I assured him. "It wasn't your fault. But did you sense anything . . . odd . . . going on?"

"You mean like the spooky green cloud above my head?" he asked wryly.

"No, actually I meant someone manipulating our emotions . . . making it impossible to . . . er, stop."

146

He frowned. "You mean that wasn't Lola?"

"No. Trust me, I know the difference."

Fang scratched at the door. LET ME IN AND I'LL EXPLAIN.

He'd *explain*? It was getting dark outside, so I turned on the light. We dressed hurriedly—not that Fang would care, but I did—and opened the door. Fang trotted in and looked up at me with those big brown eyes, then lowered his head, looking guilty as hell . . . a classic hang-dog expression.

"Explain what?" I asked.

IT WAS ME, he said, sounding miserable. PRINCESS AND ME, I MEAN.

"I don't understand," Shade said.

That made two of us.

Fang heaved a doggie sigh. IT WAS AN ACCIDENT. YOU SEE, PRINCESS IS IN HEAT, WHICH MEANS SHE'S PRETTY HARD TO RESIST. He shrugged. SO I DIDN'T.

When I stared at him blankly, he added, YOU KNOW, WE DID THE DEED, HOOKED UP, STUFFED THE MUFFIN—

"We get the idea," I said, holding up my hands to stop the flow of unwanted images. "What does that have to do with Shade and me?"

WELL, I DIDN'T REALIZE IT AT THE TIME, BUT YOU AND I ARE PRETTY HOOKED IN TOGETHER. SO ARE PRINCESS AND SHADE. SO WHEN THE EMOTIONS RAMPED UP, WE ALL, UH, KIND OF . . . SHARED IN THE GOOD TIMES.

I cringed at his wording, but that made sense. Looks like I'd mistakenly accused Trevor.

"Like a feedback loop," Shade said.

EXACTLY, Fang said, and I got the distinct impression he felt no shame for sharing in our "good times," but was definitely sorry he'd caused this to happen.

I wasn't sure how I felt about that sharing myself . . . . Talk about TMI. And how about the other guilty party? "Where's Princess?" How did *she* feel about all of this?

HIDING, Fang said. SHE'S EMBARRASSED.

Really? I didn't think that word was even in her vocabulary.

I JUST HAVE ONE QUESTION, Fang continued.

I wasn't sure I wanted to hear it, but Shade asked, "What's that?"

WHAT'S WITH ALL THE STIFFS IN THE OTHER ROOM?

Stiffs? Oh, crap, I'd forgotten about the others. Shade and I shared a mortified glance, then rushed into the living room.

Shade turned on a light, and Trevor rose unsteadily to his feet. Relief surged through me. Sheesh, never thought I'd be so glad to see him alive.

Marina and Erica were still passed out on the couch. Shade felt for their pulses and nodded. "They're okay. This is the normal unconsciousness after a healing. It's best to let them come to by themselves."

I glanced around, expecting to see crystal shards littering the carpet, but the paperweight had broken into four irregular lumps and lay blackened on the carpet.

WHAT HAPPENED HERE? Fang asked, sniffing at it.

I answered, since I was probably the only one who knew all of it. Stabbing a thumb toward Trevor, I said, "Genius here tried to stop the healing by grabbing Erica and pulling her out of the loop. He ended up getting sucked in instead." I grimaced. "Then they all went into convulsions."

Trevor, still a bit shaky, glanced at the broken crystal and the books strewn around the floor. "So you threw things at us?" he asked in an incredulous tone.

"Well, your idea didn't work out so well, so I had to find some way to break the connection." He glared at me, and I added, "Hey, *my* idea worked."

Shade looked up from his examination of Erica, still touching her wrist. "I'm glad it did, Val. I always wondered what would happen if someone interrupted a healing. Now I know."

"But how could the crystal stop you when the books didn't?" I asked, confused.

Shade thought about it for a moment as he perched on the back of the couch and kept his fingers lightly on Erica's pulse. "I guess the crystal was able to absorb some of the energy. It interfered with the circuit just enough to destroy it."

"It shouldn't have been necessary," Trevor said impatiently. "It shouldn't have taken that long to heal her burns."

Shade's expression turned sheepish. "The damage *was* confined to her arms and hands, but she had . . . something else wrong with her."

"What?" Trevor demanded.

Shade shook his head. "I'm sorry, but that's private . . . her choice whether to reveal it or not."

What a great guy—and he could *heal* people. It made me so proud of him. I moved behind the couch to hug him and give him a kiss.

"Did you completely cure her?" I asked, hoping their pain hadn't been in vain.

Shade smiled at me. "Yes."

"What does it matter?" Trevor bit out. "Shade, you took too big a risk. And for what? To cure someone you don't know? For a problem she didn't even ask you to fix?"

WHOA. Fang rocked back on his haunches. ISN'T THIS DUDE SUPPOSED TO BE AN EMPATH DEMON? SHOULDN'T HE HAVE SOME, YOU KNOW, EMPATHY? WHAT'S UP WITH THE ATTITUDE?

Exactly what I was wondering.

"It was my risk to take," Shade said softly. "And I judged I could handle it."

"Obviously you couldn't," Trevor retorted, and flung his arm out to point at the women on the couch. "Look what happened."

Shade tensed. "It wouldn't have happened if you hadn't interfered."

"I had to do something." Trevor ran a hand through his hair, messing up his immaculate hairdo. "You're too important to risk like that."

THAT'S INTERESTING, Fang said. WONDER WHY MR. PERFECT IS FALLING APART?

I was afraid Shade would go all mushy with Trevor's compliment, so I challenged Trevor. "You said that before you grabbed Shade—that you needed him. For what?"

Shade grew very still. "That's a good question, Trevor. Why am I so important to you?"

The empath demon froze for a moment as well, but recovered quickly. Giving us his practiced smile, he said, "Hey, buddy, you know how it is. I don't have many male friends, and we've become like brothers in such a short period of time. I'd hate to lose you."

I wanted to call him on his crap, but Shade squeezed my hand, so I kept quiet instead and let him handle it.

Keeping his voice even as he released my hand and went all swirly, Shade said, "Oh, I think it's more than that. You glommed onto me when you realized I'm part shadow demon, and you've been all buddy-buddy ever since."

I blinked at Shade, surprised. Then again, my guy was no dummy. I should have given him more credit.

YES, YOU SHOULD, Fang agreed.

"No, no," Trevor protested. "I—"

"You had me fooled for a while," Shade admitted. "But you became even more friendly when you learned I was the only known shadow demon in existence. You do need me for some reason. Does it have something to do with the books?"

Fang's ears perked up. GO, SHADE!

Trevor stared at Shade, his fake smile fading as he tried to weigh Shade's reaction. But the whirls revealed nothing as Shade waited for a response. Trevor glanced at me warily, but I worked on keeping my face relaxed. I really wanted to hear the answer to this question.

Trevor sighed and sank down onto a chair, bending over to stare at his clasped hands. "Shadow demons can reach across dimensions, open portals to other realities."

So far, he wasn't telling us anything we didn't know.

"The books aren't just an encyclopedia," he explained. "They've also been spelled to be a portal. That's how my father was trapped."

"Oh, I get it," Shade said. "You need my help in getting your father out of the books."

Trevor winced. "That's right."

Well, that was one of the few things that came out of his mouth that sounded like truth.

Sounding relieved, Shade said, "Why didn't you just say so?"

"Shade's one of the good guys," I added. "You didn't have to pretend to be his friend to get his help."

Trevor grimaced. "I wasn't pretend—"

Shade held up his hand to stop both of us. "Enough, please. Val is right. That's what the Underground is all about—helping each other."

"I didn't realize," Trevor said. "I've never really been part of it before. All I know is that the Underground in LA lost the books my father was trapped in. I had no reason to believe you would be willing to help me."

"Of course I will," Shade assured him.

JUST MAKE HIM OWE A FAVOR TO THE UNDERGROUND IN RETURN, Fang suggested. MAKE HIM APPRECIATE IT MORE.

Fang must have said that to both of us, because Shade took my hand and shook his head slightly at the hellhound. Too bad. It was a good idea.

"How would I go about it?" Shade asked.

Trevor appeared eager now. "I'm not sure, but there's some theory on the subject. I think it's a lot like what you do when you heal someone or bring demons through from another dimension. You know, transfer the energy from there to here."

That left another unanswered question. "So if you need a shadow demon to release your father, and there are no other known shadow demons, how were you planning on springing dear old Dad before you found Shade?"

Trevor shrugged. "I hoped there'd be a spell or something inside to tell me how to go about it."

I heard a moan from the opposite end of the couch, and Marina sat up, holding her head. "What . . . what happened?" she asked, her eyes wide.

We turned to her to reassure her everything was all right, and Trevor rose, looking all bouncy now that he was getting what he wanted. "I'll leave you to it, then," he said cheerfully. "I need to find my father."

Shade wished him good luck and Trevor left, shutting the door behind him. Erica groped her way to wakefulness, too. After we'd gotten them each a glass of water and they'd marveled at Erica's healthy unblackened flesh, we explained what happened.

"My energies don't discriminate one kind of injury from another," Shade said. "So when I found another, older, problem, it took longer than I expected. Trevor thought something was wrong, so he tried to stop it."

Erica covered her mouth with both hands, looking mortified. "I'm so sorry. I didn't even think."

Marina grabbed her arm and shook it, an expression of unholy delight on her face. "Didn't you hear him? He said he *healed* you."

Erica's mouth dropped open. "You mean . . . I . . . you . . . ?" The hope on her face as she stared at Shade was almost painful to see.

"You're whole," Shade said with a smile.

Erica threw her arms around him and beamed from ear to ear. "Oh, goddess, thank you. Thank you, thank you, *thank* you."

Marina joined her, and Shade was almost smothered by the two grateful women.

I THINK THAT MAKES HIM A SHADE SAND . . . WITCH, Fang quipped.

I laughed. Not at Fang's horrible pun, but I couldn't help but share in their joy.

"Do you know what this means?" Erica asked me, apparently unable to stop grinning.

I shook my head. "Haven't a clue."

"It means my husband and I can finally have a baby." She let go of Shade and put a hand to her chest as if to hold in the emotion. "Marina knows. We've been trying so long, but I couldn't—" She broke off and burst into tears.

Marina joined her and they let go of Shade to hug each other and bawl.

Pain, injuries, death . . . these I could deal with. But two ecstatic, sobbing women? I was way out of my league. I stood there feeling helpless, not knowing what to do.

DON'T WORRY ABOUT IT, Fang said, sounding unconcerned. THEY'LL COME UP FOR AIR SOON.

And so they did . . . eventually. Wiping tears from her eyes, Erica said, "I can't wait to tell my husband." Turning to Shade, she said, "How can I ever repay you?"

Shade shook his head. "Just pass it on. Help someone else from the Underground when they're in need."

"Is that all?" Erica asked in surprise. "It seems so little compared to what you did for me."

"It won't seem that way to the other person," I reminded her. "Besides, you got injured trying to help us."

She tried to get to her feet, but the deep couch seemed to hold her captive. I held out a hand to help her, but misjudged my strength and almost fell on top of the tall woman. Bracing myself, I tried again, and was able to assist her up off the furniture.

For some reason, that apparently meant it was my turn to get hugged by both of them. I endured it with a smile, but was happy when they left. I was glad for Erica, but all those emotions could wear a person out.

Fang snorted. TRY LIVING WITH PRINCESS WHEN SHE'S IN HEAT.

Nope. Didn't *even* want to go there.

The hellhound sighed then added, I'D PROBABLY BETTER CHECK ON HER.

He trotted off and Shade and I collapsed back on the couch. He put an arm around me, snuggling me close. "Are you okay?" he asked.

"I'm not sure. When I tried to help Erica up right then . . . it was harder than I expected."

He squeezed me tighter. "You knew that would happen, didn't you? After . . . what we did?"

"I guess so. It just took me by surprise." And, though I hadn't really admitted it to myself, I'd hoped for a Hollywood kind of ending.

The kind where true love won out over everything else and allowed the heroine to keep her powers, win the hero, and live happily ever after.

Unfortunately, this was reality, not the movies, and I was screwed.

Wincing at the unintended double entendre, I thanked heaven that Fang was distracted by his girlfriend.

Unwilling to repeat any of that to Shade, I said, "It'll take some getting used to. I just need to figure out how to handle it." I needed some time to test my limits, find a way to deal with this new version of Val Shapiro. "I guess I can't be the Slayer anymore," I said, trying out the idea in my head. I didn't like it much. "What does that make me?"

"Precious," Shade said, and kissed me.

That was sweet, but not very helpful. "No, really. What should I do?"

"Do you really need to do anything?" he asked. "You can do what you've always done. You just need to be more careful."

I didn't think it would be that simple. "Maybe," I said doubtfully. "But how do I tell Micah . . . and Alejandro?" I couldn't imagine how to start that conversation.

"Why tell them yet? It's not like you're hitting the streets every night, staking vamps anymore. And the fewer people who know, the fewer attempts will be made to take down the Slayer."

A sensation like fear spiked in me. Would I become the target of a slayer hunt? "Yeah, there is that," I said slowly. "I guess I can wait until it becomes absolutely necessary." After I found a way to completely rearrange my life to accommodate this new reality.

I closed my eyes and rested my head on Shade's chest. I *so* didn't want to think about this now.

Lola perked up a bit, sending my body tingling and making a lewd suggestion as to how I could change the subject. I was considering it— great distraction—but as I ran my hand suggestively over Shade's stomach, it growled at me.

I couldn't help it, I chuckled.

"I'm sorry," Shade said, looking embarrassed. "I'm hungry."

Come to think of it, so was I. "Shall we go out and get something to eat, then?"

"Sure, after I take a shower."

We both got cleaned up, then headed for the front door. I slapped my pocket for my keys then stopped abruptly. "Uh-oh."

"What?"

"I left the Valkyrie at Marina's house."

Shade laughed. "And I left my bike at yours."

We grinned foolishly at each other. "Looks like we're ordering in," I said.

Fang came back in, his ears perked up. DID I HEAR SOMETHING ABOUT FOOD?

I rubbed his ears. "You chow hound, you. I thought you were going to check on Princess."

YEAH, WELL, HER PRECIOUSNESS NEEDS A LITTLE ALONE TIME RIGHT NOW, IF YOU CATCH MY DRIFT.

I did.

Shade chuckled. "Princess can be a handful at times."

I picked up my cell to call my favorite pizza place but paused when I noticed I had two messages. "Someone must have called while I was in the shower."

"Who?"

"Dan and someone else."

I dialed my voice mail and listened to Dan's message. Smiling, I told Shade, "He's narrowed down the area where Andrew must have hidden the books. He wants me to meet him downtown—at the Alamodome."

"Great," Shade said. "Call him back and tell him we'll meet him as soon as possible. I'll call a cab."

As he made his call, I talked to Dan and arranged to meet him right away at the stadium, then listened to my other message. It was Marina. I expected more gushing thanks, but that wasn't why she'd called. I frowned at the phone.

"What is it?" Shade asked.

"Marina says she has something very important to tell us, and we need to call her back right away. She sounded upset."

"We have some time before the cab gets here."

Shade slapped together sandwiches and grabbed Cokes and a bag of chips as I dialed her number. I held the phone so Shade could hear as we munched.

"Oh, good," Marina said. "I'm so glad you called back."

"Shade's here, too. What's up?" I asked.

"Erica and I were so distracted by her great news that we couldn't think about anything else. We were talking on the way home about what we experienced and compared notes." She paused. "Remember when Shade said we'd share thoughts and memories?"

"Yes," Shade said. "That's normal during a healing session."

"We did . . . but we also shared with someone else. Trevor."

"Trevor?" I repeated in surprise. "Oh, it must have happened when he got caught in the circuit."

"I don't know," Marina said, "but Erica and I compared notes and we both got the same thing from him."

UH-OH, Fang said. I HAVE A FEELING THIS AIN'T GONNA BE GOOD . . . .

I second that feeling. "What did you get?"

"Trevor has been lying to you."

Oh yeah? Go figure.

Shade pressed closer to the phone so we were cheek to cheek. "You mean about why he was being so friendly to me? We know that."

"You know that he needs you to get his father out of the books?"

"Yes, he told me that," Shade said, looking relieved.

Marina persisted. "And that he's not an empath demon or a keeper?"

"*What?*" Shade, Fang and I all exclaimed in unison.

"That's right," Marina said hurriedly. "The reason he's been keeping his nature hidden is because he and his father are both highly powerful—and highly *dangerous*—mage demons."

Well, I'll be damned . . . .

"It gets worse," Marina added. "His father caused the 1906 earthquake in California. That's why the keeper locked him inside the books."

"But Trevor isn't that old," Shade protested.

"Mage demons can live a very long time," Marina said. "Trevor is much older than he looks."

"That's right," I said. "He even told us that."

Shade stiffened as Marina continued, "With those books and the spells inside them, he and his father could control the entire world."

Oh, crap. I stared at Shade in horror, grabbing his hand so he didn't go all swirly on me. "We need to find those books before he does . . . . "

Shade closed his eyes, looking as if he were in pain. "And *I* just told him where Dan is meeting us to find them."

CHAPTER TWENTY

"You *what?*" I said, whipping my head around to stare him in the eyes. I had to grab his hand to see his expression, and smashed the bag of chips in the process.

He winced. "I'm sorry, but while you were talking to Dan, I also called Trevor."

"Why? You know the books told me to find them before he could."

"No," he said patiently. "You never told me that."

I closed my eyes and smacked myself in the forehead. "You're right, I didn't." I'd been too worried Shade would tell Trevor. Crap.

Marina was trying to get our attention on the phone. I held the cell so we could both hear again. "Sorry. Was there something else?"

"Yes," she said, as if she hadn't unloaded a big enough bombshell. "I didn't understand this, but you probably will. He convinced the freelance vamps to attack the Movement . . . and has been inciting the Underground to kill the vamps."

Must be the vigilantes Dan had mentioned. I *knew* Trevor was a total scumbucket. But it was no consolation to be right. We needed to stop him.

"But why would he *do* that?" Shade asked.

"Because he knows the Movement and the Underground both want the books, and he wanted to keep them off-balance, distracted," Marina explained. "Plus he didn't want any competition in his bid for emperor of the world."

Dang. I should have seen that—it made total sense. But we had to make sure he didn't do any more damage. "Thanks, Marina. We really appreciate the call."

"No problem. We owed you."

"Not anymore," Shade said. "This information wipes the slate clean. Thank you."

We gobbled down our sandwiches and waited outside for the cab. Thank heavens it showed up right away. Holding Shade's hand so his swirls wouldn't freak out the young driver, I got into the cab. "The

Alamodome, please."

The cabbie didn't even turn to look at us. He glanced in the rearview mirror. "Ain't nothin' goin' on there tonight, lady."

With that accent, he had to be straight from the Big Apple. A New York cabbie in San Antonio? Well, I guess that wasn't the strangest thing in this city. "Just take us there."

"Wait," Shade said. "I told Trevor we're meeting Dan there."

"That's right. But he doesn't know we're on to him," I whispered. "Maybe we should let him find them, then take them away from him."

"How?"

Good point. I had no idea how my lack of powers would work against a *mage* demon, fergawdsakes.

"I ain't got all night," the cabbie said. "Ya wanna ride or dontcha?"

"Yes, we do," I snapped. "Take us to . . . HemisFair Park." It was across the highway from the Alamodome, not far from where Dan had suggested.

The cabbie turned around to grimace at us. "Where? It's a big park, lady."

"Uh, near the Institute of Texas Cultures?" It was in the Southern part of the park, closest to the Alamodome.

"You got it." He glanced down at Fang who sat beside Shade. "Hey, wait. I don't allow no dogs in my cab."

"This isn't an ordinary dog," I said.

"Oh, yeah? He looks like a mutt to me."

Fang growled. I'LL MUTT HIM.

"That's it," the guy said as Fang bared his teeth. "Everybody out."

Dang. If only Fang had kept his muzzle shut. "No, wait." I hesitated for a moment. I hated to leave Fang behind but there was no time to call another cab. "We'll pay you extra."

"Nope. No dogs. I'm allergic. And he looks like he sheds."

"We have to go now," Shade whispered urgently. "Trevor can sense the books if he gets within five hundred feet, remember?"

Yeah, I did. And if the books were hidden somewhere in the center of the huge stadium or park, that might explain why he hadn't found them just driving around. But if he walked around those areas and the encyclopedia was hidden there . . . Damn. Still, I hesitated, not wanting to leave my best back-up.

GO, Fang said. YOU DON'T NEED ME FOR THIS.

Maybe. But I always wanted Fang, especially now that I was more vulnerable. I could use Lola to force the cabbie, but it was probably best to keep my trusty hellhound out of danger. Shade was my back-up now. Sighing, I kissed Fang on his fuzzy nose and let him leave.

"Okay, the dog's gone. Let's go," I said.

Good thing the cabbie didn't give me any more lip or I might've sicced Fang on him. But he set the car in motion, so I called Dan to let him know the change of plans.

It seemed to take forever to get there, but we finally did. I paid the driver—with a lousy tip because of his attitude—and got out at the plaza where two dozen or so flags flew, honoring the nations of all the immigrants who made up Texas' diverse culture. Above the Institute loomed the Tower of the Americas, a giant spear of light against the night sky with what looked like a UFO stuck on top. This object wasn't unidentified, though, it was a revolving restaurant and observation deck.

We found Dan in the far corner of the Institute's parking lot, leaning against the door of the SCU's Silver Dodge Ram.

"Why the change of plans?" Dan asked when we reached him.

I shrugged. "Because we accidentally told Trevor we were meeting you at the Alamodome, and want to find the books before he does."

Looking quizzical, Dan asked, "How do you do that accidentally?"

"Never mind," I said, not wanting to explain the whole thing or embarrass Shade. "Do you know where Andrew hid the books?"

"No, but I can narrow it down. We picked him up on cameras near Mood's house that day and followed the cameras until we saw him get off at an exit. I knew you'd want to see this, which is why I asked you to meet me." He opened the truck door and pulled something from behind the seat. Leaving the door open to provide more illumination, he showed us some grainy photos. "This is from the traffic camera at I-37 and Durango."

I peered at them. "Yep, that's his beater all right." Hope rose within me. We were finally getting somewhere!

Dan nodded. "It shows he got off at the exit, and this photo," he pointed to another one, "shows he didn't get back on until forty-five minutes later, at the same place. Time enough to park somewhere and hide the books."

That was the exit we'd taken to get here. Feeling excited, I said, "Awesome. You did a great job."

Shade's phone rang then and he checked the number. "It's Trevor. He probably wants to know where we are."

"Don't answer that," I said quickly. "Let him wonder."

"Right," Shade said and turned off the phone.

"Do you need me to distract the guy or something?" Dan asked.

I thought for a moment, but I didn't know what a mage demon could do and didn't want to embroil Dan in more Underground business. He'd helped enough. "No, we'll take it from here. Thanks a lot, Dan. We really appreciate it."

"No problem."

I suddenly remembered something. "Oh, and we found out who was inciting the vigilantes taking down the vamps. Don't worry, we'll take care of it."

"You're not going to tell me who it was?" Dan asked, sounding exasperated.

"No, sorry, I can't. Underground business. I have to let Micah know first, and if he wants to tell you . . . "

Dan rolled his eyes, but nodded. He respected Micah and knew the fine line the demon leader had to walk. "Okay. Give me a holler if you need a ride or something."

Oh, yeah, we might. "Thanks. We'll do that."

He got in his truck and left, and Shade said, "The park and Alamodome are both huge." He pulled his deep hoodie forward to hide his face from any passersby, then stuck his hands in his pockets. "Any idea where the books might be?"

"No, I don't, except maybe somewhere central." I shook my head. "Why would Andrew hide them here? There's lots of traffic through both areas."

"What does it matter?" Shade asked, sounding harried. "Can you sense them? If we look in the wrong place and Trevor finds the books before you do . . . "

"No, but I haven't tried. Let me find somewhere quiet." The traffic noise was a little distracting. Not to mention the Christmas lights everywhere which seemed sooo out of place with what I was feeling right now.

Shade followed me into the park on one of the concrete pathways. "Can we afford to take the time?"

"Can we afford not to?" I snapped back as I hurried along the path, then immediately felt bad. "Sorry, didn't mean to bite your head off. I'm feeling a bit stressed here."

"Ditto," Shade said grimly. "And I feel useless. I wish I could do more."

"You're not useless," I assured him as I continued looking for a quiet spot. "You're going to watch over me while I try to contact that voice."

I spotted one of the many fountains that dotted the park, one with a waterfall cascading over stone steps. No bum sleeping on the bench nearby, so I sat down, let the soothing sounds calm me and went deep into myself I dredged up all my self-control and forced myself into calm, reminding myself to be patient.

After a short while, I felt as if someone was straining to reach me. I don't know how I knew that, but I did. I concentrated harder and opened myself up as wide as I could. *Where are you?* I sent out into the universe. *There isn't much time.*

Nothing. And this was taking way too long. Sighing, I opened my eyes and glanced to the heavens for help. There, filling my vision, was the Tower of the Americas blazing against the darkness.

That's it! It had to be. Holy crap. The voice hadn't wanted me to look up something on a computer. It wanted me to look *up*. "Any idea how tall that tower is?" I asked Shade eagerly.

"Seven hundred and fifty feet to the top mast." He shrugged. "Sometimes trivia sticks in my brain."

"And to the bottom level of the restaurant?"

"I don't know . . . maybe six hundred feet. Why?"

"There," I said with excitement. "The books are there—in the tower. Out of Trevor's range."

"Are you sure?" Shade asked.

"Absolutely." I didn't know how I was sure, but for the first time, this felt really right. "Let's go."

"Not so fast," came a voice from behind me.

I jumped up off the bench and whirled around, my heart beating like a tom-tom. But it wasn't Trevor, just two baby vamps looking for a bit of fun. How did I know that? Because the pimply-faced idiots had flashed their fangs and made the mistake of trying to control my mind, so I could read theirs. And *that*, thank goodness, was not one of the powers I'd lost.

But I had lost my strength and probably the healing, too. Lola was still recovering, so I needed to get rid of them with the least amount of trouble. I grinned at them, which took them aback. "Seriously? You're trying to control *me*? Sorry, Benny and Fredo, isn't it? You may not realize it, but you're messing with the wrong people."

Shade threw back his hoodie and let his face show in all its swirly glory.

Benny and Fredo each took an involuntary step backward and, though I could read in their minds that they were frightened, they tried to hide it. "What *are* you?" Fredo asked.

My grin widened. "I'm the Slayer and this guy is a shadow demon. You know what will happen if you chow down a demon, don't you?"

"Or mess with the Slayer," Shade added, deepening his voice so it sounded more menacing.

From their appalled expressions and thoughts, it was obvious they did know, so I pulled two stakes out of my back waistband. "Your choice. Would you rather go mad from drinking our blood, or get staked in your black little hearts, hmm?"

They seemed rooted in place, not knowing what to do.

Shade took a step forward, flung his arms wide and yelled, "Boo!"

They ran.

I couldn't keep from laughing. "Boy, that was easier than I thought." Maybe I could still pull off being the Slayer without my powers.

"Yeah," Shade said, chuckling as well. "Now, let's go."

He grabbed my hand and we ran the short distance to the tower, which wasn't very far away. We had to pay to get in, then wait in line for the elevator. After what seemed like forever, we squeezed our way on, making sure Shade remained looking human, and the glass elevator started upward.

Instead of boring us with music, the elevator speakers droned on about the attractions here at the tower. Originally built in 1968 for the World's Fair, the tower now housed a 4D ride, restaurants, gift shops, and a magnificent view from the observation deck.

San Antonio spread out below us like a twinkling carpet of lights as we travelled high above the city. About halfway up, I somehow knew, without knowing how, exactly where the books were above me. The ride seemed to take forever, but couldn't have been more than a minute. I tried to enjoy the view—I hadn't been up here since I was a kid—but I was too anxious to get this over with. I promised myself to come back at some point and enjoy it when I had more time.

Finally, the elevator stopped and opened, and we followed the crowd to the glassed-in observation deck on the third level. That's where my senses—my homing beacon—were leading us.

Shade leaned close, whispering, "Do you know where they are?"

"Yeah. I'm heading directly for them." The slight pull on my senses led me away from the windows and toward three banquet rooms built inside the deck.

Two of them had noise coming from them—raucous holiday parties—but the third was quiet. With any luck, the books would be in the empty room. I didn't fancy the idea of braving a roomful of strangers to peek under chairs and tables. "Try that door," I said in a low voice, pointing to the quiet room.

Shade pulled on the handle. "Locked."

Well, shoot. I'd hoped this would be as easy as scaring off those baby vamps. As Shade leaned down to peer at the lock, I glanced around, looking for a waitress or someone in charge. "Maybe I can say I lost an earring and get someone to open the door."

"No need," Shade said, and I looked around to see something shiny disappear into his pocket as he turned the handle and opened the door a crack.

"You picked the lock? My, my, you have all kinds of talents, don't you?" I said with a grin.

"You have no idea." He grabbed my hand and maneuvered me so I blocked the door. "Look at me as if we're having a serious conversation. When no one's looking . . . Now, *go*."

We slipped through the door, and Shade closed it behind us. "Where did you learn this stuff?" I asked in the dim room. It was lit only by the lights from outside the panoramic window, but the strains of *Jingle Bell Rock* made it seem festive.

He shrugged. "Part of being a Watcher for Micah." When I reached to flip the lights on, he added, "Uh, maybe we should leave the lights off."

"No problem. We're in luck. I can feel the books on the far side of the room."

We made our way over there, and found a portable bar against the wall. Groping underneath, I found a lump the right size and shape. Smiling, I pulled it out and set it on the bar, careful not to knock over the glasses and decanter. The large lump had been shrouded in a dark tablecloth to keep it hidden in the depths of the bar. Pulling the cloth off as fast as I could, I saw my familiar backpack.

Finally . . . .

I reached inside and touched the books, to make sure they were real. "Wow," I whispered. "We really found them." It was sorta anticlimactic. I'd more than half expected to have to battle my way through a legion of the undead or something. But no, here they were, lying innocently—and quietly—under my hand.

"Great," Shade said. "Can you feel the dark magicks in them?"

"No, they feel the same as always."

Shade laid his fingers on them, then frowned. "I feel . . . something. Not sure what. Like dark whispers in my head." He jerked his fingers away. "Those things are dangerous. What are we going to do with them?"

I froze. "I don't know. I didn't think that far ahead."

"We have to take them somewhere Trevor won't find them."

"I know, but where?"

"Out of town somewhere. We should leave now, take them far away."

"Okay." I slung the backpack over my shoulder and started toward the door, then stopped. Deflated, I turned to face Shade. "We have a problem. Once we get downstairs, if Trevor is anywhere near, he'll sense them and be able to follow us."

"Maybe he's still at the Alamodome," Shade said in a hopeful voice.

"I doubt it. He probably left when we didn't show up." Something else occurred to me. "What if he realized Marina and Erica were able to read him?"

Shade slumped down on a chair. "He has to know. And he's probably figured out that they've told us everything they know."

Uh-oh. "You think they're in danger?" I asked.

"No. He knows Dan narrowed down the books' hiding place to somewhere near the Alamodome. I think he's searching for them as fast as he can. And it's probably only a matter of time before he looks up and makes the same connection you did."

The lights overhead suddenly flashed on, blinding me.

"He did," a voice said from the doorway.

I blinked. Oh, crap. It was Trevor, and he was pointing a gun . . . right at my head.

CHAPTER TWENTY-ONE

Run! the voice yelled.

It chose *now* to wake up? Too late. Nowhere to run, nowhere to hide. *Tell me something useful,* I shot back.

I stared at the weapon in Trevor's hand, noticing that he had a silencer screwed on to the end. With the noise of the parties and the tourists on the observation deck, no one would hear if he shot us. I ran through my options. My powers were gone, Fang wasn't here to distract him, Lola couldn't affect Trevor . . .

Damn it, I felt helpless. I hated it. I'd always said I wanted to be normal, but now that I was, I had to admit it totally sucked.

Now would be a really good time for some help, I sent to the voice, which definitely sounded like it came from the books.

Wait, it said, sounding strained.

Not helpful. Micah, Alejandro, Shade . . . they all expected me to retrieve the books, keep them away from the bad guys, and save the day. But what could I *do?*

Absolutely nothing.

Except maybe talk him to death. Hey, it worked for Fang . . . .

"You're not really a keeper, are you?" I blurted out.

Trevor grinned, looking cocky. "That's right."

"Is there really any such thing?"

"Oh, yes."

"Then how did the keeper get separated from the books?"

Trevor shrugged. "Does it matter?"

You're on the right tra—

On the right what? I demanded of the voice. *On the right track?* I had a pretty good idea of what that meant.

Shade took a menacing step forward. "You'd better run. We figured out what you were and called for help. The SCU, Underground, and the Movement are going to arrive at any moment."

He called? When?

Trevor laughed. "You are such a bad liar. Look at Val's face."

I'm an idiot. "Sorry," I muttered.

"I wouldn't have believed it anyway," Trevor assured me. "The Slayer would never call for help. She's a glory hound—she wants all the credit for herself."

Like hell. The way I remembered it, things had happened so fast, I hadn't even thought to call for help. Then again, Dan had offered . . . . And I had a good reason for turning him down. *Not* because I was a glory hound.

Trevor interrupted my self-reflection with a gloating, "Sorry, Val, you won't be taking *this* mage demon anywhere."

We had to keep him talking until I could come up with a plan. Luckily, Shade asked him a question. "Are you really a mage demon?"

Trevor inclined his head in a regal nod. "Indeed. Though it took you long enough to figure that out. I thought you were the expert on demons, Shade."

Shade let the taunt roll over him. "It was your shield," he said. "We should have known you were hiding something."

Looking as if he were enjoying this, Trevor said, "With the vamps and the hellhounds around, I had to block my thoughts. Couldn't let you know what I was really up to."

"And what *are* you up to?" I asked.

"Oh, the usual," he said, waving his gun airily. "Riches, power, world conquest. With the spells in those books, I can have anything I want."

The bastard was *enjoying* this.

"I thought you wanted to save your father," Shade said. "Was that a lie, too?"

"Oh, no, that was the truth. He's not really *in* the books, you know. They're just a portal to another dimension where he's been trapped. With your help, I can release him." Trevor's grin widened. "You did say you'd help me, remember?"

I clenched my fists, wishing I could strangle him, use Lola on him, stake him . . . anything to shut him up and keep him from using Shade that way.

Shade squeezed my wrist warningly. "Calm down, Val. Remember, he can use emotions to power spells and he no longer needs to hide behind his shield."

"Oh, stop," the metrosexual said with a pout. "You're ruining my fun."

"Really?" I asked. "I think you're bluffing. Your father probably put the shield on you as a kid—and you've already admitted you can't do spells without reading them from these books. That's why you brought the gun."

Trevor's grin faded. "Well, aren't you the clever one? But you know, I think the gun will suffice." He moved closer and extended the gun at full length, aiming right for my forehead. "And I don't need *you* at all. Shall we see how easily the Slayer can heal from a bullet in the brain?"

No one could heal from that. Fear skittered through me as alternatives ran through my mind. I tensed, preparing for action, hoping my instincts would help me do the right thing.

Shade jumped in front of me, spreading his arms wide. "No. If you kill her, I'll never help you. I'd rather die first."

How mortifying—someone was protecting *me* for a change.

Trevor lowered the gun to his side, looking exasperated. "What do you *see* in her?" Then, before Shade could answer, he said, "Never mind. I don't care. All I want is those books, and my father released from them." Waving the gun toward the bar, he said, "Put them down and I won't shoot you."

I hesitated, and he frowned. "Do it *now* or I might shoot out your kneecap, just for fun. Or Shade's."

Seeing he meant it, I backed up slowly and put the backpack on the bar, my mind whirling with plans to stop him. Shade moved with me, keeping his body between the gun and me.

"Take them out of that ratty bag and put them where I can see them," Trevor ordered.

I did as he asked, and Trevor seemed to relax. He gazed at the books and his eyes took on an acquisitive, unholy gleam. He moved closer until he was a few feet away. "Finally. I've been waiting for this moment over ninety years."

No wonder the Underground in LA didn't know who he was. "Gee, you don't look a day over eighty-two," I drawled. I couldn't help it. Sometimes my mouth just ran away with me.

"Very funny," he snarled. "Now release my father, Shade, or I'll hurt her."

Neither of us could see Shade's expression, but the shadow demon didn't move a muscle. What was he thinking? Was he going to try something heroic and get himself killed?

Do it, the voice urged.

"Do it now," Trevor unconsciously echoed. "And I'll let you both live."

I hesitated. Who did the voice belong to? I'd always thought it was the books, but could it be Trevor's father? Why else would the voice urge me to let another mage demon loose on the world? With the most dangerous books on the planet, no less.

Trust me . . . .

Shade wasn't moving and Trevor was looking even more pissed. Oh, crap. We were going to die. Could I trust this unknown voice?

Did I have a choice?

I had to prove Trevor wrong. I had to let go of my need to be the world's savior and trust in someone else. Taking a deep breath, I nodded at Shade. "Do it."

I still couldn't see his expression, but I'm sure he was confused. The ribbons of light where his face should be swirled faster.

"I don't know how," Shade said, sounding hesitant.

"Try," Trevor insisted. "It should be like what you did with the healing. But this time, you're not transferring healing powers from one person to another, you're transferring my father from one dimension to another."

Still, Shade hesitated. "I've been fighting all my life not to let other demons into this world."

Trevor grimaced. "Is that all? Don't worry. It's a barren plain of existence. He's the only demon there. You think I'd let you bring through *competition?*"

Now that sounded like truth. I nodded at Shade. "Try it." I just hoped I was right.

Tensing, I moved closer to Shade. I wanted Lola to be able to grab him and stabilize him if something went wrong.

Trevor moved closer, too, though he kept the gun trained on me. "Hold his left wrist," he told me. "I want to be able to see his face."

I wanted to see it, too, so I did as Trevor demanded.

"Now put your right hand on the books," Trevor said.

And repeat after me . . . my irreverent nature couldn't help but add.

Slowly, Shade rested his hand on the top book, his expression tense.

Do it now, the voice all but yelled at me.

Squeezing Shade's wrist, I whispered, "Go ahead. I'm here for you."

I don't know why, but that seemed to make up his mind. Nodding, Shade closed his eyes and I could almost feel him concentrating.

"No tricks now," Trevor warned.

"Shh," I said. "Don't distract him."

A small lime-green cloud, shot through with bright flashes of fierce lightning, appeared above the bar. "That's it," I whispered. "It's working."

I let go of Shade and backed away from that virulent, creepily silent maelstrom, and so did Trevor. We both watched as it grew bigger and bigger, until it was a round sphere of roiling energy about six feet across.

"Are you . . . sure about . . . this?" Shade gasped out.

"Bring him through!" Trevor said. With his tense attitude and eager, green-tinged expression, he looked positively diabolical.

"I don't . . . know . . . how."

Suddenly, a man flew out of the cloud as if he'd been thrown, landing face down on the ground between us. He rolled onto his back, looking *way* stressed out, but the spitting image of Trevor.

Mr. Jackson, I presume.

"Father," Trevor exclaimed.

Another man leapt out as well, landing on his feet, his fists clenched. This one looked just as wild-eyed, but bigger, meaner, like a huge lumberjack with a bushy black beard and veins popping out on his forearms. Oh, crap. How many more demons were going to come through? I should have known Trevor had lied about that.

"Keep him off me," the father shouted.

The other man pointed at Shade, yelling, "Don't close that portal yet. No more demons are coming through."

I recognized that voice. It was the one who'd been talking to me. "Do as he says," I told Shade. "He's on our side." I hoped.

"Shoot him," Trevor's father screamed as he scrambled to his feet.

But Trevor, caught off-guard by the appearance of the second man, didn't move fast enough. I grabbed the heavy decanter on the bar and whipped it at his gun hand.

Nailed it!

The pistol flew out of Trevor's hand. The big bear of a man muttered some words and made a throwing motion at the two Jackson boys. Instantly, it was as if they stood rooted in place, struggling against invisible bonds.

The big man grabbed my hands. "That won't hold them long." His words tumbled out fast, but polite. "Valentine Shapiro, I beg your assistance and that of your friend to send these two felons back through the portal and rid the world of them for good."

Now that's what *I'm* talkin' about. "Hold on, Shade, a little longer," I called out, then turned to the man who held my hands. "You got it," I said with a grin. "What do you need?"

"Just trust me . . . and give me everything you got."

Lola was waking up with my proximity to such a large, handsome specimen of the male species, but I didn't think he was talking about that . . . or my paltry material possessions. "How?"

He didn't answer. Instead, he threw his head back and muttered some words that sounded like Latin.

A thread of magick from inside the man latched on to that tendril of interest from Lola and twined around it, braiding the two strands into a larger, stronger rope of energy. Letting go of my left hand, he thrust his right hand toward the struggling Jacksons. A strong breeze came out of nowhere, blowing from us to them, and the magick pulled on more of Lola's energy. Just as they broke free of their entanglement and tried to rush us, the rope of energy reached them, and I could feel it circling them like a lasso, anchoring them in place.

They hurled insults and curses, but nothing else, thank heavens. All my attention was caught up with noticing that Lola's energy was leaving me in a steady stream. Crap, this guy was draining my chakras . . . just like Lola did to the men she came in contact with. "What are you doing?" Would he drain me dry to stop the man who appeared to be his nemesis?

"I'm sorry," he gritted out, "but I need your strength. I'll try not to harm you."

Try? What was this *try* crap? I struggled for a moment, then realized he was exhausting his own energy just as much as he was mine. If I wanted this to succeed, I had to work with him, not against him. Shade was being a real trooper, holding the portal open, though he was bent over with the strain. Could I do any less?

I sank to my knees and let loose all the restraints, letting the guy take everything he needed. He fell to his knees alongside me, never letting go of my hand, never stopping the braiding of our energies. We faced the gorgeous panoramic view, the villains on our right, the portal on our left, and the sound of *Grandma Got Run Over By a Reindeer* playing next door.

What a strange way to die.

Slowly, we drew the Jacksons, kicking and cursing, closer to the bar and the portal. While we struggled with the bad guys, Shade lowered the books to the floor so the portal flickered in front of the bar. Good. All it would take was one good shove and they'd go through. Though where I could muster up the strength for that, I had no idea. I swayed, barely able to stay on my knees.

They were within a couple of feet of the bar, but had dug their heels into the carpet, their teeth gritted, to slow their forward movement.

"Just a bit more," my partner said. "Now, push!"

Huh? There was no way I could push with my body, so I did the next best thing. I gathered up everything I had within me . . . Lola's energy, my energy . . . hell, any bit of energy I could scrape up . . . and threw it at him.

As I fell limply to the floor, the man shoved both Jacksons through the portal, yelling, "Close it!"

The pulsating green portal irised shut, cutting off the braided cord and sending all that energy barreling back along our connection. Oh, crap. I tried to ward off the backlash, but no luck. It slammed back into both of us like Thor's warhammer, and I knew no more.

Sometime later, I came slowly awake, expecting the worst. But I felt remarkably . . . fine. Opening my eyes and switching on the light, I found myself back in my bedroom again, this time with a strange man lying beside me. But it wasn't some random stranger—it was the man who'd gotten rid of Trevor and his father for good. What the heck?

SHE'S AWAKE, Fang said from outside the door. OPEN THE DOOR, DEMON BREATH. FIND SOME USE FOR THOSE OPPOSABLE THUMBS.

I smiled. It was good to hear Fang's voice again.

The door opened and Fang flew through it, jumping up to lick my face furiously. YOU ALMOST DIED. DON'T EVER DO THAT TO ME AGAIN.

Hugging him to me, I ruffled his fur. *I'll try not to.*

He snuggled next to me and laid his head on my leg, sighing with pleasure. Shade entered—apparently the "demon breath" Fang had addressed—followed by Micah. "What happened?" I asked.

"You don't remember?" Micah asked, raising his eyebrows.

"Uh, let me see. Bad guy waves gun around, green cloud vomits demons, good guys kick butt, then nothing."

He chuckled. "The backlash from the power rebound knocked the two of you out, but Shade had the presence of mind to call for help."

I winced. Yeah, like I should have done *before* it happened.

"How did you get us down from the tower?" I couldn't imagine.

Shade started to explain, but Micah held up a hand. "Let's just say it taxed our ingenuity, but we had assistance from the SCU and the Movement." He smiled. "Everyone wanted to help, and they fought over who would act as the templates to heal the two of you."

No wonder I felt so good. I shook my head at Shade. "You shouldn't have."

"It was necessary," Shade said. "I *am* careful, you know. Micah and some others monitored me to ensure I was in no danger."

Well, that was all in the past. But I wondered . . . "Who won the fight to heal us?"

"Josh was your template and Andrew helped with the other guy," Micah said. "They wanted to atone for causing the books to go missing in the first place."

Oh, the books. Where were they?

CHILL, Fang said. THEY'RE ON YOUR DRESSER. YOU GUYS GOT RESTLESS WHENEVER WE TOOK THEM AWAY SO WE LEFT THEM NEAR YOU.

Good. He was right—I could feel them there.

Then I realized what Micah had said. Josh and Andrew? Eww. "Does that mean we'll be living with their memories the rest of our lives?" I searched my mind for any lingering adolescent male idiocy, but couldn't find it.

"No," Shade assured me. "You were unconscious so it didn't transfer. It took a lot longer to heal you that way, but he didn't get any of your memories and you won't have his."

THANK HEAVENS, Fang said with a sigh. I DON'T KNOW IF I COULD LIVE WITH YOU IF YOU HAD JOSH IN YOUR BRAIN.

Me either. Feeling the man stir behind me, I stood up and looked down at him.

He opened his eyes and smiled. "Valentine Shapiro. We did it."

"Yep, but . . . who *are* you?"

He swung his legs to the floor, then rose unsteadily and came around the bed with his hand outstretched. "Jack Grady, the real keeper."

Exactly as I'd suspected, but Trevor had claimed the same thing.

NO LIE, Fang said. HE'S TELLING THE TRUTH. BUT IT'S HIS STORY TO TELL.

"How'd you get trapped in there with Trevor's father?" I asked.

"It's a long story," Jack said.

Micah held up his hand. "Why don't we do this in the other room so you two can get something to eat and drink first?"

"Now you're talking," Jack said with approval. He gathered up the books and brought them with him, as if he couldn't bear to let them out of his sight. As he set them on the dining room table, I poured us each some juice and Shade started breakfast on the stove.

"Go ahead," Shade said. "I can cook and listen at the same time."

Jack nodded. "You see, when the folks in Ireland burned my mother as a witch, my father brought me and my sisters to California."

Shade stopped what he was doing at the stove. "They *burned* her?"

Jack shrugged. "I was just a boy at the time."

"Go on," I urged him, not wanting to go off on tangents.

He nodded. "I'll make this short. My father had heard about the gold, so he hoped to make his fortune there, though we were too late for the rush. My sisters and I joined the Demon Underground, of course, and the Underground had taken the encyclopedia away years before from a full mage demon . . . at great cost, you might imagine."

We nodded, and I made hurry-up motions.

He shrugged. "The books chose me as keeper—"

"How?" I said, then shook my head. I wanted to know, but I wanted to hear the end of this story first. "Never mind. Go on."

"So when the mage demon's son—that would be Garrett Jackson—stole one of the books and caused an earthquake that nearly tore California off the map, it was my duty to hunt him down and stop him."

Shade placed some toast and jelly in front of us and Jack grabbed a slice. He took a huge bite and closed his eyes in ecstasy, as if he'd just had a taste of heaven from a five-star chef. "Do you have any idea how long it's been since I had anything to eat?"

"Yeah, pretty much," I said impatiently. "Eat all you want later, but continue your story. How did you stop Garrett Jackson?"

After he swallowed another bite, Jack said, "Being keeper grants you the power of the books to draw on, providing your intentions are pure and you know what you're doing. He was too powerful, so I used the magick in the books to create a doorway to another world, then tricked him into going through it." He paused for another bite.

"And?" Micah prompted.

He looked rueful. "Unfortunately, the only way my ruse would work was to go through it with him and close the door behind me."

I stared at him in awe. Now here was a real hero.

He grimaced at my expression. "Don't look like that. Time passes faster there, and we didn't age. I kept him from contacting his son, and we got along all right until I learned he'd found a way to whisper to folks on this side."

The light dawned. "Oh, so that's who was talking to Josh and Andrew. Trevor's father—he was the dark magick everyone sensed?"

"That's right."

"So the books *aren't* bad as Trevor said?" Shade asked.

Jack swallowed, then answered, "Well, they can be dangerous in the wrong hands."

"Like a mage demon's, I take it?" Micah said.

"Yes, but the books themselves aren't dangerous. It's the intentions of the person reading the spells that matters."

"Okay, go on," I urged him.

"Once I learned what Garrett was doing, I knew his son would sense the awakening. I blocked that link and had Andrew hide the books in the best spot I could think of." He glanced at me. "I tried to get *you* to find me, but Garrett kept fighting me, blocking me."

Well, that explained the intermittent nature of Jack's communication. And, speaking of that . . . "Can you still speak to me in my mind?" I asked, not sure I liked the idea.

Jack shook his head. "No, I'm no longer the keeper of the books. Once I got back into this world, they chose someone else."

Uh-oh. What kind of person could handle that kind of power? "Who?"

"Why, you, of course," he said. "That's why the books made their way to you when you were a child."

Micah frowned. "What about my father? He had the books before Val."

"He could have been a keeper if he'd had the training, but when the books became aware of Valentine, they chose her as the next keeper."

Me? "But . . . but . . . "

"And that's why I was able to use your magick to send them back. Together, two keepers and a shadow demon were stronger than two mage demons. Once you gave up every last iota of your power to save the world, you became the keeper."

No, no, I couldn't take this responsibility. "I can't do that. I won't be able to protect the books." I glanced guiltily at Micah, wondering if Shade had filled them in on the no-longer-a-virgin newsflash.

Micah nodded. "When you didn't heal as fast as we expected, Shade explained what happened."

Jack raised an eyebrow. "You mean now that you are no longer as pure as the driven snow, you lost your powers?"

Oh, crap. I forgot he'd been in and out of my mind. I winced. "Yeah, that. I'm no longer the Slayer. I won't be able to safeguard the books the way they should be."

"No problem," Jack said. "Didn't you hear me earlier? Being the keeper comes with a great deal of power."

As I gaped at him, Fang broadcast the question in my mind to everyone at the table. YOU MEAN SHE WON'T BE A WUSS ANYMORE?

"I don't understand what a wuss is," Jack said, "but I'm certain the new keeper is no such thing. In fact, she'll be very powerful."

I gulped. "But I don't know how to use that kind of power."

Jack waved that away as if it were nothing. "I'll teach you."

"You don't mind giving it up?" Shade asked.

"Nope," Jack said. "Being keeper can be quite a burden, too. I'm glad to retire."

I had just about resigned myself to being normal and now he wanted me to be some kind of super demon? I gulped. How could I possibly handle this?

AS YOU ALWAYS DO, Fang said, jumping up to put his paws in my lap. WITH PANACHE, A QUIP AND YOUR FAITHFUL HELLHOUND BY YOUR SIDE.

Somehow, that wasn't very reassuring.

As I stroked his fuzzy ears, Fang added, REMEMBER MARINA'S PROPHECY?

I thought for a moment, then murmured, "Seek not, lest you find more than you bargained for. Keep not, lest you are prepared to meet your destiny." Well, I had definitely found more than I bargained for.

Jack smiled. "Are you ready to meet your destiny, Val?"

It would help if I knew what that was . . . .

Wondering, I placed a hand on the books. Something seemed to snick into place, as if reestablishing a bond I hadn't known was there, making me whole once more and opening up a vista of possibilities for the future. The books couldn't speak, but they did have an awareness, a sentience, unlike any inanimate object I'd ever seen. They seemed to promise me joy along with an important purpose in life, but not without hard work, sorrow and pain.

Should I accept this destiny? I took a deep breath, knowing that no matter what decision I made, it would change my life forever.

"I'm ready."

Reader Letter

Thanks to all of the fabulous fans who took the time to read my books and leave me such wonderful feedback on Facebook—you're awesome! Not to mention incredibly wise and discerning. :-)

Val and Fang (and Shade!) have received such a positive response that BelleBooks and I decided to publish this third book and at least one more. It's such fun to write about their adventures that it's not a hardship at all. So, to whet your appetite for the next one, an excerpt of chapter one follows.

Enjoy—and let me know what you think on my Facebook page!

Parker Blue
Colorado Springs, CO

MAKE ME

Book Four
The Demon Underground Series
Coming Spring 2012

EXCERPT

CHAPTER ONE

I crouched in the darkness of an ancient live oak, armed with only my wits, listening for any sign of the vampire. Nothing but the rattling of branches and the soughing of the wind through the leaves here on the longest night of the year.

Creepy.

I wasn't hiding out of fear. I just wanted to get a bead on him before he found me first. Now that I'd lost my strength, speed, and healing ability, and I hadn't learned how to use my supposed new powers as keeper of the *Encyclopedia Magicka,* I needed any advantage I could get. And the live oak, with its leaves and gnarled branches as big around as my waist, shaded me from the revealing gaze of the moonlight.

"Val Shapiiiiiro," he crooned, the eerie mocking sound seeming one with the breeze. "Come out, come out wherever you are . . . . "

Too close! He'd found me.

Lust for the hunt sizzled through my blood and I whirled toward the sound. "Make me," I growled.

He rushed me, inhumanly fast. I leapt up to one of the low branches and lashed out with a *savate* kick, hoping to score a field goal with his head. He ducked.

Too slow, dammit. I stumbled for a nanosecond on the uneven surface then regained my balance as he appeared on the bough beside me. His infuriating grin flashed in a sliver of moonlight. I struck out with my fist, hoping to smash the fangs off his face. Blocked.

I couldn't let him take the offensive. And though I might have lost my speed and strength, I still had my martial arts training. I battered him with a series of blows, but he was so fast, none of them connected where I wanted. I tried a low blow—a kick to the 'nads, but he stopped that, too.

Frustrated, I leapt up to grab the branch above me, planning to swing up and over it and use the momentum to knock him off his perch. Instead, he tackled me. I lost my grip and we both hit the hard-packed earth, knocking the wind out of me.

Taking advantage of my momentary pause and gasp for air, he straddled my waist and hooked his legs over mine so I couldn't move, then grabbed my wrists and pinned them above my head.

Crap. He was too strong—I couldn't get free, no matter how hard I struggled.

He grinned, looking way too happy with the situation. "Yield, darlin'?"

Never. I still had one weapon left. I hated to use it, but I hated to lose even more. I called on the succubus inside me and she leapt to the fore, eager for action. The purple eye flash that came with the use of my demonic powers reflected in his eyes as my succubus Lola surged forth and slammed into his chakras, instantly making him my slave.

His lust for Lola made it impossible to disobey me. I paused for a moment, trying to catch my breath enough to tell him to shove off.

His smile turned wicked as he released my wrists and his hands started to wander where only one man's hands had gone before.

This was *so* wrong. "Get off me," I yelled, shoving against his shoulders.

He took his time rolling off, his lascivious gaze and knowing smile never leaving my face as he hooked his thumbs in the belt loops of his jeans.

I scrambled to my feet, releasing him from Lola's clutches so fast it made us both stagger. "*Seriously*, Austin?" He looked different without his Stetson . . . edgier, more dangerous.

Alejandro's cowboy lieutenant ran a hand over his face and chuckled softly. "Hey, you were the one who played your ace in the hole . . . darlin'."

My face heated. Crap. He always made me feel young and foolish. No matter that at eighteen, I'd been slaying vampires for years. No matter that I could make any man alive do whatever I wanted. No matter that brave cops, vampires, and demons feared me as the Slayer. None of it mattered when Austin gave me his knowing look. It was as if he gazed deep into the insecurities of my soul and laid them bare.

I averted my gaze and pretended I was absorbed in brushing twigs and leaves from my T-shirt and jeans. "I had to," I muttered. "It was the only way I could win." He'd already beaten me once. I couldn't let him win two out of three.

"I know," he said softly. "Took you long enough."

I shrugged. "I don't like to use my powers unless it's absolutely necessary."

"And that's why you lost the first time. If I'd really been out to get you . . . " He shrugged.

"I know, I know." I'd be dead. Thank goodness, this was only practice. I didn't want the word to get out to the general vamp population that the Slayer had lost her powers, or I'd be challenged by every one of them not affiliated with the New Blood Movement . . . and maybe even some *in* the Movement.

"Best two out of three?" I asked. This time, I'd be faster on the draw with my secret weapon.

"I'll pass," he drawled. "Now that you've figured out when to play your hole card . . . well, let's just say I don't think either of us would be comfortable doing that again."

Boy, make me squirm, willya?

Someone slammed into me from the side, taking me down again. Another vamp—Luis. I shoved Lola into him so fast, he didn't get a chance to try anything. "Stop! Don't move." I scrambled to my feet and, just in case Austin tried anything more, I hooked him with one of Lola's energy tendrils as well. "You, too."

I'd learned my lesson and wasn't about to—

Wham! I was down on the ground again. A third vamp? *You're kidding me.*

I shook my head. No problem. I could handle three without even breaking a sweat. I lunged out with Lola to take care of *numero tres,* and got nothing but a hard slap across the face.

Crap. It was Rosa. Lola wouldn't work on her. "Stop her," I gritted out, sending a surge of power along Lola's energy strands.

My two marionettes obeyed instantly, grabbing her and pulling her off me. They looked murderous, so I added, "Hold her—don't hurt her." Alejandro wouldn't be pleased if he found out I'd let two of his lieutenants tear the third limb from limb.

Rosa—smart girl—didn't fight them. She just smirked at me.

"Lucky hit," I said, raising up on one elbow to feel my jaw. She packed quite a wallop.

"Not lucky," she spat. "You, you call yourself the Slayer? If I used my knife, you'd be dead right now. *Muerto.*"

I could have pointed out that she'd be one dead undead bloodsucker with a single word from me, but kept my trap shut. After all, they were helping me regain some skill and confidence by sparring with me in private. It was my own damned fault that I'd assumed they'd come at me one at a time. The least I could do was act grateful.

And I was, I really was. I hadn't known until tonight that the Movement used the clearing in the center of the woods around the mansion as their private training grounds. But I'd ignored their suggestion and avoided the open space. Instead, I'd taken to the trees, hoping it would give me some advantage. Not so much.

I cast around with my senses but didn't detect any more bloodsuckers. "Any others waiting in the wings to take a swing at the Slayer?" I asked before I got up again. I didn't want to meet the ground up close and personal for a fourth time.

"No," Austin and Luis answered in unison.

Good. I got slowly to my feet. The adrenaline was gone, so I was starting to experience the pain of tonight's punishment. Dang, it sucked to feel human. It was times like these that I regretted giving up my powers. "Why do you care anyway?" I asked Rosa. She'd sounded so pissed.

Still held captive by the other two vamps, she rolled her eyes. "Because you need to protect Alejandro's back."

"Why? I'm not his bodyguard. Doesn't he have, like, a whole *vein* of bloodsuckers to do that for him?" I knew Tessa's prophecy made him think of me as his personal talisman, but sheesh, that was taking it too far.

"For when he goes to Austin," she clarified.

I glanced at the cowboy vamp, confused. "Goes to Austin for what?" And, realizing she'd calmed down and the two guys were both still in Lola's thrall, I let them go, despite Lola's protest.

Rosa rubbed her arms and sulked. "Stupid *chica.* Not him, the city. Maybe you've heard of it? The capitol of Texas?"

Oh.

But . . . "Since when are we going to Austin?" I asked.

Luis folded his arms. "Alejandro hasn't told her yet."

He and the cowboy vamp exchanged an unreadable glance. "Let's take her to him," Austin said.

I heaved a sigh. Secrets. I hated secrets.

Luis nodded briefly, and the three of them headed back to the house. They didn't even look back, just assumed I'd follow them like a good little girl. Hell with that. They could keep their secrets.

Fang trotted up from his place on the sidelines. Part scruffy terrier, part telepathic hellhound, part smart-aleck-bane-of-my-existence, he sat on his haunches and grinned up at me. POUT MUCH?

We'd decided to have him sit this one out to see what I could do without him. I thought he'd be upset that he couldn't mix it up with me, but with that snarky comment, I wondered . . . "Did you enjoy watching them beat the crap out of me?" I asked.

He snorted. NOT SO MUCH. BUT IT WAS NECESSARY.

"Maybe," I muttered. "But is this meeting necessary? Not so much," I mocked.

YOU DID AGREE TO WORK FOR HIM UNTIL THE BOOKS WERE FOUND AND HE COMES OUT OF THE CLOSET.

I know. I'd found the books, but he hadn't done the second part yet.

SO, THIS IS PART OF YOUR JOB. WHAT'S THE MATTER? YOU'VE ALWAYS WANTED TO TRAVEL MORE.

Yeah, but not this way. Okay, yes, I was pouting. So sue me.

Fang didn't say a word, just looked at me with reproachful brown eyes framed in his adorably fuzzy face. Dang. He'd pulled out the big guns. I gave up. "Okay, okay. I'm coming."

I hobbled toward the house, feeling every ache and pain the vamps had hammered into me. More like eighty than eighteen.

NEXT TIME, WEAR SILVER, my unfeeling hellhound advised me.

I'd thought of that, but it seemed like cheating when the vamps were supposed to be helping me. Then again, being a vampire was kind of cheating, too, wasn't it?

Fang just snorted, which I took to mean he agreed with me.

Alejandro's people had been careful not to create any paths into the woods, but it was easy to follow the lights to the house. I trudged up to their back door and saw that Austin was waiting there for me, holding the door open. He'd put his hat back on, too, so he looked more like himself. "I'm coming," I muttered.

"I know."

He grinned again, but didn't move when I passed him. Our energy fields intersected in the close confines of the doorway and Lola licked into him. I didn't pull back—he deserved a good licking.

The tall, lean cowboy didn't react, though. He just raised an eyebrow as if to say, "You really want to go there?"

POINT TO AUSTIN, Fang said with a laugh.

Shut up. I shoved past him into the kitchen, disappointing Lola once more. "In his study?" I asked without looking back at him.

"Yes, ma'am." Austin didn't bother to hide the amusement in his voice.

I tried not to stomp out my frustration as we headed to find Alejandro. Luis gestured me into the room I'd visited far too often. Very masculine, very Mediterranean, very dark . . . except for the sun-drenched mural of a beach scene covering the wall across from Alejandro's desk. Then again, if I'd been unable to see the sun as long as he had, I'd probably want a view like that, too.

I flopped into a chair across from Alejandro and his massive wooden desk and said, "So, boss, what's this I hear about us going to Austin?"

Luis scowled. He hated it when I treated Alejandro so informally. That's why I did it, of course, and Alejandro didn't mind. Luis and Austin took up positions behind their boss and I wondered where Rosa was.

MAYBE SHE WAS PUT IN A CORNER FOR SPILLING THE BEANS, Fang suggested.

"I am afraid the trip to Austin is necessary," Alejandro said.

"Why?"

The vamp leader absently rubbed the bust of Cortes he kept on his desk. "The situation in the state capitol has changed. The legislation we were counting on to protect us when we come out and keep the unaffiliated ones in their place is . . . stalled."

I grimaced. I hated politics as much as I hated secrets.

MAYBE BECAUSE THEY GO HAND IN HAND.

Probably. "What does that mean, stalled?"

Alejandro shook his head, a puzzled expression on his face. "I wish I knew. My calls are not being returned, and there has been no communication from my supporters. We shall have to go there to see what is happening."

I was all for getting those laws in place so the Movement could come out and I could satisfy my contract with Alejandro, but . . . "Why do you need me?"

"Because you can go where I cannot," Alejandro said with a smile.

Who was going to keep a vampire out of anywhere he wanted to go? "Like where?"

Austin's mouth quirked up. "Like daylight."

Oh.

"Indeed," Alejandro agreed. "You are the only one I can trust to protect my interests while I'm there, to live in my world and not reveal what you discover, to act for me during the daytime."

Fang huffed with amusement. HE WANTS YOU TO BE HIS RENFIELD.

I didn't find that at all funny. It was a pretty tall order. But, unfortunately, I couldn't argue with the vamp leader's logic. "Rosa seemed to think you wanted me to be some kind of bodyguard."

Alejandro waved away my objection. "Rosa is overly protective. We cannot invade another vampire's territory without permission. Without it, we risk . . . much. I have gained that permission, but have agreed to bring only four with me. I shall take Austin and Vincent, and leave Luis and Rosa in charge here."

No wonder Rosa was peeved, with only two vamps to guard her boss's back. "If I'm the third, who's the fourth? Fang? Does Fang count?"

FANG ALWAYS COUNTS.

"No, Fang does not count as the fourth," Alejandro said with a smile, "though I see no reason why he cannot come. The fourth will be Jack Grady."

Grady? The former keeper who was supposed to be training me on how to tap the magick potential in the *Encyclopedia Magicka?* Ha. The only thing he'd done the past few days was pig out on Gwen's food and hog Shade's bed. "Why him?"

"The encyclopedia can be a powerful weapon in our favor. He knows how to wield it, and you do not. We need him to get you up to speed as fast as possible."

Good luck with that. I'd tried with no luck.

"I have already spoken with Mr. Blackburn and the Demon Underground has agreed to let me take both of you," Alejandro said. "I have made arrangements for a place to stay so we can leave tomorrow night when the sun goes down."

Why not? I'd only been to Austin a few times before, and it would be something different than the same old, same old. "Do you have any idea how long we'll be gone? Mom will kill me if I miss Christmas." And since Mom and I had kind of a truce going on, I didn't want to screw that up.

"It's little more than an hour away," Austin drawled. "I think you'll be able to come home to mommy when you need to."

I clamped my lips on an unwise comeback and resolved not to let him get to me. "Okay. Should I pack?"

"Yes," Alejandro said. "Pack for a couple of weeks. It'll make it easier than returning here for a change of clothing or necessities. You may go now if you wish."

I wished. Glancing down at Fang, I asked, *You ready?*

In answer, he got up and trotted away, pausing in front of the study door to glance expectantly over his shoulder at Austin.

The cowboy rolled his eyes, but followed Fang's unspoken bidding and opened the door for him.

How do you do that?

CHARISMA, BABE, SHEER CHARISMA.

Shaking my head, I followed him down the hallway and out the front door. I straddled my Valkyrie motorcycle and waited for him to jump up into his own leather and sheepskin seat, then put on his goggles.

I sped home on the dark, silent streets of San Antonio. There weren't many people out in the early hours of the morning, so I was able to drive on autopilot and make plans for the unexpected free time. I could take a hot bath to soak out my aches and pains, maybe even get some extra sleep before I had to show up at Alejandro's tomorrow. After all, who knew what awaited us in the state's capitol?

When we arrived home, I took off Fang's goggles and he jumped down.

"Hungry?" I asked. Usually, he'd be pestering me for food right about now.

SORRY, BABE, BUT IT'S THE WINTER SOLSTICE.

"So?" What did that have to do with anything?

A dark cloth fell over my head and someone grabbed me, trying to pin my arms. What the . . . ? I struck out with my foot, connecting with someone who let out an "oof."

YOU'LL HAVE TO SEDATE HER, Fang said, and I felt the sudden prick of a needle in my arm.

My mind grew fuzzy. *Fang? What's happening?* No response. "Thanks, Fang," another man said. "We owe you one." I had only one thought as I lost consciousness. *Traitor.*

CPSIA information can be obtained at www.ICGtesting.com
Printed in the USA
LVOW101728130412

277540LV00004B/51/P